SNOWBOUND
Wedding
WISHES

LOUISE ALLEN

✳

LUCY ASHFORD

✳

JOANNA FULFORD

H HARLEQUIN®
entertain, enrich, inspire™

ISBN-13: 978-0-373-29711-5

SNOWBOUND WEDDING WISHES
Copyright © 2012 by Harlequin Books S.A.

The publisher acknowledges the copyright holders of the individual works as follows:

AN EARL BENEATH THE MISTLETOE
Copyright © 2012 by Melanie Hilton

TWELFTH NIGHT PROPOSAL
Copyright © 2012 by Lucy Ashford

CHRISTMAS AT OAKHURST MANOR
Copyright © 2012 by Joanna Fulford

Recycling programs for this product may not exist in your area.

www.Harlequin.com

Printed in U.S.A.

Louise Allen has been immersing herself in history, real and fictional, for as long as she can remember, and finds landscapes and places evoke powerful images of the past. Louise lives in Bedfordshire, England, and works as a property manager, but spends as much time as possible with her husband at the cottage they are renovating on the north Norfolk coast, or traveling abroad. Venice, Burgundy and the Greek islands are favorite atmospheric destinations. Please visit Louise's website—www.louiseallenregency.co.uk— for the latest news!

Lucy Ashford, an English studies lecturer, has always loved literature and history, and from childhood one of her favorite occupations has been to immerse herself in historical romances. She studied English with history at Nottingham University, and the Regency is her favorite period.

Lucy has written several historical novels. She lives with her husband in an old stone cottage in the Peak District, near beautiful Chatsworth House and Haddon Hall, all of which give her a taste of the magic of life in a bygone age. Her garden enjoys spectacular views over the Derbyshire hills, where she loves to roam and let her imagination go to work on her latest story.

You can contact Lucy via her website—www.lucyashford.com.

Joanna Fulford is a compulsive scribbler, with a passion for literature and history, both of which she has studied to postgraduate level. Other countries and cultures have always exerted a fascination, and she has traveled widely, living and working abroad for many years. However, her roots are in England, and are now firmly established in the Peak District, where she lives with her husband, Brian. When not pressing a hot keyboard she likes to be out on the hills, either walking or on horseback. However, these days equestrian activity is confined to sedate hacking rather than riding at high speed toward solid obstacles. You are invited to visit Joanna's website at www.joannafulford.co.uk.

CONTENTS

AN EARL BENEATH
THE MISTLETOE

Louise Allen

Dear Reader,

When I was writing this story I had a real valley in mind, one of the lovely chalk streams that cut through the Chiltern Hills with beech woods on the slopes and tiny hamlets and villages tucked away. These valleys are lovely in the summer, but in the winter, under snow, they have a special charm and remoteness, and I especially love the area because my ancestors came from there. Many of the characters in this story share their names— and doubtless their liking for the local home-brewed ale!

I wish you a very happy festive season,

Louise

Look for Louise Allen's next Regency
FORBIDDEN JEWEL OF INDIA
Coming soon.

Chapter One

18th December 1814—the Chiltern Hills, Hertfordshire

'You have to agree, Ajax, that it would be unpleasantly ironic to survive five years of being shot at, blown up and starved in the Peninsula to die of exposure in some Hertfordshire valley.'

The big grey flicked one ear back and carried on plodding through the driving rain. An intelligent animal, he probably thought it was not so much ironic as foolish.

'Rodgerson's directions were clear enough.' Hugo kept talking as he scanned the sides of the valley for any glimmer of light. He was beginning to shiver and feel sleepy and neither was good, not when he'd been riding since daybreak. He was soaked through to the skin despite the oiled wool cloak that had seen him over the Pyrenees in winter on one occasion. 'That cross-country cut to get us on to the Northampton road without having to go out to Aylesbury would have saved hours.'

But a bridge had been down and then a road flooded and he had turned north in the fading twilight, using his pocket compass and a sodden and tattered route map. They must have gone clear between Berkhamsted and Hemel Hempstead, either of which would have provided a comfortable inn for the night. Instinct told him he was heading north-west now, which should be correct, but it was pitch-dark, his tinderbox was damp and the low cloud obscured the stars. Every yokel for miles around seemed to have vanished into their dwellings—wherever those were hidden. He couldn't blame them, he'd settle for a flea-infested hovel himself, if one presented itself.

'First cover, we're taking it.' Ajax did not bother to flick an ear that time. The horse was big and tough, but both of them were out of practice at being quite this cold and wet. 'This will teach me to underestimate the terrain,' Hugo muttered. And it would teach him to be antisocial and avoid invitations as well. He could be putting on a cheerful face in the midst of some jolly family gathering preparing for Christmas, right this minute.

Hunching his shoulders sent a fresh trickle of icy water down his neck from the brim of his hat as he narrowed his eyes against the rain. Hordes of children, irascible great-aunts, flirtatious young ladies, too much rich food, charades...possibly dying of exposure was preferable after all.

They were in a shallow valley. To his right was a river and what he assumed were water meadows, now impersonating a lake. To his left rough grazing sloped up into scattered trees and scrub. Someone, surely, must live in this landscape? Would the trees thicken up and offer any more shelter?

There. Ahead and to the left, a flicker of brilliance like a star, only too low and too yellow to be anything but a man-made light. He turned Ajax's head towards it and almost immediately the squelch of hooves into waterlogged earth became the splash and crunch of metal shoes hitting the stones of a rough, potholed track.

As they came closer he could see the shapes of huddled hovels and small cottages higher up the slope. They seemed to be in darkness, but the light shone steadily from an unshuttered window in the slightly bigger building nearest the track, a beacon to guide him in. Against the sky he could just make out the jut of a pole above the door with a battered tangle of twigs thrashing in the wind at the end of it. 'An ale pole, Ajax. There will be something for me to drink, at least.'

The ground came up to meet him with a force that jarred his tired legs as he slid out of the saddle in front of the entrance and he steadied himself with a hand on the pommel while he thudded on the panels with his other fist.

No reply. Damn it, he would break in if he had to and pay for the damage afterwards…

The door swung open spilling light and heat into the rain. Hugo blinked against it, looked down to meet the concerned gaze of the woman holding the door open and said the first thing that came into his head. 'You are as wet as I am.'

Hell, she'll think she's facing a lunatic. But it was true. Wide hazel eyes smiled up at him out of a freckled face that was rosy with damp heat. Brown curls stuck to her forehead and cheeks, her sleeves were rolled up to reveal hands and forearms that dripped water and her wide white apron was soaked and glued to her skirts.

'But not as cold, I will wager,' she said with a laugh in her voice, turning to call over her shoulder, 'Boys! Quickly. Come in,' she added, 'Before you drown. You will not be going any further tonight, that is for certain.'

'My horse, ma'am. Can I get him under cover?' Ajax stuck a wet muzzle forwards as though to emphasise the point as two boys erupted out of the inner doorway.

'Mama?' They skidded to a halt at her side and regarded him with avid curiosity, revealing themselves to be virtually identical twins.

'Nathan, Joseph, where are your manners? Help this gentleman stable his horse and then bring him inside. You will excuse me,' she added with a dazzling smile that made him blink even as it sent a surge of hot blood through his chilled body. 'I am sparging the mash and one just cannot leave it. I will be back presently.'

'Sparging? Of course you are. Yes.' Bemused, Hugo regarded her retreating back. She had delivered that airy speech with the same tone—and accent—as any lady explaining to a guest why she must leave him for a short while. What sort of ale house was this? Her hair was coming down, but the exposed skin of her nape was white and soft and her hips swayed enticingly as she walked away from him. Soft, warm, delicious.

'Good evening, sir.' He yanked his wandering attention back. 'If you go to that door, we'll bring a lantern the inside way.' The boy with the fewer freckles on his cheeks pointed to a stable door.

Nathan, that one, Hugo thought, recalling the quick glances each had thrown their mother when she had said their names. And Joseph's ears stuck out rather more and his eyes were a darker hazel. Hugo walked into the warmth and smell of stabled beasts and the blissful relief of getting out of the insistent rain.

There was a stall in front of them, empty except for Joseph scattering straw on the stone. Nathan ducked out of the next stall with a stuffed hay net bouncing behind him. 'I've stolen Sorrowful's,' he said, 'but I've left him a pile on the floor. He won't mind.'

'Are you certain?' Hugo looked at the smallest, gloomiest donkey he had ever seen. It gazed mournfully back.

'He always looks like that, sir.' Nathan climbed on a bucket to hook up the net. 'That's a big horse. Are you in the army?'

How old were they? Six, seven? He wasn't used to children younger than the wet-behind-the ears subalterns they'd send him to make his life hell, but these looked as bright as buttons, the pair of them. 'I was. Cavalry. I'm selling out now.'

He heaved off the saddle and the saddle bags and slung them over the stall divider. The boys stared wide-eyed at the big sabre and the holsters. 'And those are not, under any circumstances, to be touched,' he added as he took off the bridle. How do you talk to children this age? He decided the tone he used to the subalterns would have to do.

'No, sir.' They took a step back in unison.

'Are you a general, sir?' the least-freckled one asked.

'Major, Nathan. Can you fill that bucket with water, please?'

The boy's eyes opened in awe at this magic knowledge of his name. 'Yes, Major.' He picked up the bucket and ran, colliding with his brother who staggered up with a bucket full of what looked like lumpy brown-and-white porridge.

'Culm and used mash, Major. That'll perk him up.'

'His name's Ajax. Thank you.' He took the bucket from Joseph and tipped it into the manger. From the smell of it the mixture was something to do with brewing. He just hoped he wouldn't end up with a drunk horse. Ajax put his head in and began munching. On the other side a brown cow stuck her head over the barrier.

'That's Eugenia,' Joseph confided. He copied Hugo, who had twisted a handful of straw tight into a knot and was rubbing the horse down. The lad dived confidently under the stallion's belly and began to scrub at his muddy legs. A couple of hens fluttered up to the manger and began to peck at the feed.

'This is a veritable Noah's Ark. What else have you got in here?'

Nathan clanked back with the water, only a third of which had been spilled. 'Four rabbits, a dozen chickens, Sorrowful and Eugenia. Maud and her litter are in the pigsty. We haven't got a horse. Mama sold Papa's horse, but she had to, to get the animals we needed.' The boy spoke briskly, but his voice was tight.

Ajax's skin felt warm now. He'd do for now if Hugo could find some sort of rug for him. 'Is your father dead?' There was a subdued *yes* from knee level where both boys were hard at work.

Hugo frowned. Perhaps he shouldn't have put it so bluntly. The realisation that the man of the house wouldn't be arriving at any moment made the whole situation awkward. Normally he would not have thought twice about spending the night under the roof of some lusty country alewife, but that warm, wet, laughing lady was something else altogether.

'Got an old rug for Ajax's back?'

'Sacks,' Nathan offered. 'We've got heaps of them.' He dived into a dusty corner and dragged some out, then both of them regarded the knife Hugo pulled out of his boot with close attention.

'And that is not for touching, either.' Hugo slit a dozen sacks and covered Ajax's back, two deep.

'No, Major,' they chorused, then took the lantern and led the way to an inner door that opened on to the room Hugo had first glimpsed.

He followed with his gear and realised he was in the public taproom of the ale house. Benches and tables lined the walls, barrels rested on stands along the back next to a rack of tankards and there was a fire in a wide hearth. The twins went to throw on more logs and Hugo laid his sabre and the holsters on the high mantelshelf, out of sight from boy-height.

'Is your horse settled, sir?' The alewife came up steps in the corner from what must be the cellar. Her face was dry, her hair twisted up into a white towel which, with the vast, fresh white apron she had put on, and her sleeves rolled down again, gave her a curiously nun-like appearance.

And then she came fully into the room and smiled at him and all thoughts about nuns vanished. As did cold, hunger and the discomfort of wet clothing. 'Excellently, thank you, ma'am.' She was not a beauty, but with her smile the sun came out and a heat, nothing to do with sunlight, flowed through his blood again. 'Your sons have been most helpful.'

'The gentleman's a major, Mama,' Joseph reported.

'Indeed? And does the major have any dry clothing?'

Hugo laid the saddlebags on the table and investigated. 'One slightly damp shirt.' There were clean drawers as well and, wrapped in the shirt, they had stayed dry. 'Dry, er, underthings.' Hugo draped his dripping cloak over a couple of chairs where it started to create a small pond on her well-brushed flagged floor. Under it he still wore his uniform, sodden, glued to his body by water.

'Goodness, you *are* wet.' She appraised him quite openly with as little self-consciousness as she might one of her boys. His body responded predictably. 'And large. None of my late husband's things will do, but luckily Peter Bavin who helps out here leaves a set of clothes in case he gets drenched when we're working. Those will fit, I imagine, if you have no objection to homespun?'

'No, ma'am, thank you.' Anything other than being draped Roman-style in a blanket in her presence would be acceptable. He catalogued brown hair escaping already from the turban, freckles across a slightly tip-tilted nose, a determined little chin and wide hazel eyes that seemed to reflect every thought and emotion. And surely she was too young to be the mother of these boys? What was she? Twenty-five, six?

'There is still hot water in the copper downstairs and a tub, Major. I have put soap and some towels beside it. Supper will be almost ready when you are done. We can make a bed up for you here in front of the fire.'

'I am being an unconscionable trouble to you, ma'am. I can dry off in the stable and eat out there. Spend the night there, too.' The atmosphere of this little family felt so warm and close, so alien to his own experience of home life, that he felt awkwardly like an intruder, which was unsettling. As though his hostess was not unsettling enough.

'Indeed, you could sleep in the stable,' she agreed cheerfully. 'And you will probably catch pneumonia and die on me and that would really be a nuisance.' When he opened his mouth to protest that he had no intention of doing any such thing, she just laughed. 'I am teasing you, Major. We would be glad of your company, would we not, boys?'

Women did not tease Major Hugo Travers, Earl of Burnham. They made eyes at him on a regular basis, and he could deal with that tactfully when he did not want what the fluttering eyelashes and bold suggestions offered. This one had obviously not thought through the implications of his presence and it was his duty to point it out to her. It would be helpful if his thawing, dripping, body was not expressing an interest in making those hazel eyes sparkle even more or wondering what that generous mouth would feel like pressed against his.

'Ma'am, I gather that you are alone here, with the exception of your sons. Under the circumstances...' It was difficult to find the right way to put it with two lads listening to every word.

'Are you afraid that your rest will be disturbed by these two hellions?' The concern in her voice was at odds with the quizzical smile on her lips. She obviously understood exactly what his scruples were about and chose to ignore them. Those candid eyes challenged him to argue. 'I can turn the key in the lock if that will set your mind at rest?'

'Of course, thank you.' He could hardly pursue the subject, not with the boys watching him wide-eyed. 'My name is Hugo Travers. Major.' No need for the title.

'Emilia Weston. Mrs,' she said, equally formally, then switched back to practical housewife in a blink. 'Now, that water is not getting any warmer. Leave the damp shirt,' she added as Hugo bundled his dry underwear into the saddlebag and carried it towards the stairs, feeling that he had somehow come out the worst from that encounter. He was not, he realised, used to dealing with women in a domestic setting, not unless they were servants.

He found himself in a cellar running back into the hillside. A copper stood on its brick base, the glow of the fire beneath reddening the brick floor. Stone troughs stood around, pipework and spouts jutted from the walls and a row of barrels lined the walls. The floor was still wet around the biggest trough and a sodden mass of malt grains filled it halfway, steaming gently.

There was at least one more room at a higher level behind the wall, he realised as he dredged up the faint memories of the brew house at Long Burnham Hall. The trough was a mash tun, the mass of wet grains was the mash, and sparging must have involved soaking it in hot water. Not an easy job for a slight woman on her own. He stood frowning at the signs of activity: buckets and poles and sacks. Where was this Bavin fellow who was supposed to be helping her?

Mrs Weston had dragged a tub close to the fire and set a bucket beside it, alongside a stool with a piece of soap, towels and a small mirror. Hugo began to bail water out of the copper and into the tub, uncomfortably aware that she had set the things out for him as a wife might prepare a bath for a returning husband. There was an unsettling intimacy about this, which did not help him suppress his instinctive reaction to Mrs Weston in the slightest. Whomever her occupation made her now, his involuntary hostess was also a lady and should not be waiting on a strange man.

He tugged off his boots with difficulty, struggled out of his uniform jacket and hauled his shirt over his head. The heat of the fire on his damp, cold skin made him close his eyes in blessed relief.

'Major?' It was Joseph, peering over an armful of clothes. He dumped them on a barrel and scooped up what Hugo had discarded. 'Mama says these should fit. She says, will you give me your breeches as well.'

Jaw set, Hugo clambered out of the sodden leathers and handed them over, waited until the boy had scampered back upstairs and clambered into the tub, still in his drawers. He wouldn't put it past the unconventional Mrs Weston to come down to check he had washed behind his ears.

'He's got a great big scar right across here!' Joseph gestured across his chest. 'And he's all brown!'

And I really do not *need a mental image of that man without his clothes, thank you, Joseph.* 'Who is *he*? The cat's uncle?' Emilia enquired repressively as she wrung out a pair of socks.

How did boys create holes in their hose without any apparent effort at all? Her back was aching, but if she just finished the day's washing now she could concentrate on making up a bed for their visitor and finishing supper.

'The major, Mama.' Joseph dropped the shirt and stockings into the wash pail and hung the buckskin breeches over a chair.

'The major's got an enormous sword and pistols and a great big knife in his boot. Where do you think he is going, Mama?' Nathan hung over the stew pot, stirring while he counted dumplings with a covetous eye. She had made six more and added some carrots and turnips to the pot. Hopefully that would be enough to assuage the major's hunger.

'Home, I suppose. The war has been over for eight months now.' *Home to his wife and family who will be thankful that their man escaped with nothing worse than a scar. What a blessing for them.* 'Goodness, it is getting cold. Throw some more wood on the fire please, Joseph.'

Would Major Travers be all right on the floor of the taproom? He was starchy enough to refuse the offer of the attic room with the boys, just next to her own, she was certain. Oh, well, he would have experienced considerably worse at war. Once he was dry and warm and fed, he would be all right.

'Is there anything I can do for you, Mrs Weston?' a deep voice behind her enquired as she shook out a chemise. Emilia turned and there he was in the doorway, the colour back in his tanned cheeks, shaved to within a painful inch of perfection, thick black hair combed. He managed to look the English gentleman even while filling out Peter's homespun shirt and leather waistcoat with his wide shoulders. His long legs were encased in battered old breeches and well-darned stockings, his feet in borrowed shoes were set wide apart on the flags.

Do for me? Emilia blinked and tried to rescue some trace of common sense, some ghost of the practical mother and alewife. *Oh, my goodness. Stop looking at me with those dark blue eyes, for a start. That would help.*

Even cold, soaked and grumpy he had been a large, attractive male. Now, for an overworked, lonely widow, this dark, frowning, punctilious major was temptation personified and she must be all about in her wits to even think about it. She swallowed. His eyes narrowed.

Giles always said she wore her thoughts on her face. Emilia dropped her gaze to the embarrassingly intimate garment that was dripping in her hands and wrung it out with a savage twist while she dragged her treacherous thoughts back to practicality.

Chapter Two

'Shall I bring in some more logs?' Hugo offered into the brief silence. No wonder Mrs Weston was blushing—he had seen what she was washing all too plainly. Not that it wasn't a perfectly plain and workaday chemise, but even so…

'And get soaked and cold again? I have only so much dry clothing for you.' She was teasing, rather than irritated, he hoped. The quick blush had vanished and she was composed and smiling again. 'Thank you, but we brought in a good supply of fuel this morning when the rain threatened. You might want to make up your bed now and let it get warm by the fire, though. There are some straw palliasses and blankets and so forth under the stairs.' She pointed to a cupboard. 'When we have the big brew for the midsummer festivities I have helpers here all night and eventually they talk and drink themselves to sleep.'

He found the things as she said, neatly stacked and rolled, blankets and linen folded around sprigs of lavender, all orderly and fresh like everything he had seen of her home and business. How much work did it take for one slightly built woman to maintain this, even with two willing boys to help her? Even as he worried about that, the image of her, strong and slender beneath his body on these palliasses in front of the fire came from nowhere to stop him in his tracks.

'Are your servants keeping to their own cottages in this rain?' he asked as he closed the cupboard door firmly on his fantasies.

That provoked a snort of laughter. 'Servants? This is not a coaching inn, Major! Mrs Trigg comes in once a week to help me scrub, Peter Bavin does a couple of days a week for the heavy lifting—when he isn't trapped on the other side of the river with the bridge down and the meadows flooded.'

She shook out some more garments and Hugo recognised his own shirt and stockings. He should never have let the boy take them, she had far too much to do without his washing as well. 'There,' she said. 'All done.' Everything was draped over airing stands on the far side of the fire, his shirts effectively providing a screen for more intimate items at the back.

'If you will just bring that pot to the table, Major.' The boys scurried around, finding plates and knives and producing bread from a big stoneware crock. There was stew, simple and savoury with fluffy herbed dumplings floating in it, bread and butter, cheese, stewed dried apples and ale to wash it all down with. Hugo tried not to eat like a wolf, despite second and then third helpings being offered.

'Thank you, ma'am. It is delicious, but I'll not eat you out of house and home—you will not have been expecting to cater for a visitor tonight.'

Mrs Weston sent him one of her flashing smiles. 'It is a pleasure to feed anyone who appreciates my food. And we will not go short, believe me. I have ample in stock for the winter and once we can communicate with the outside world, fresh supplies are not so very far away.'

'Where are we? I must have passed between Berkhamsted and Hemel Hempstead in the dark—my map had turned to mush and I couldn't read the compass with no light. I was heading, I hoped, for the road towards Northampton.'

'This is the hamlet of Little Gatherborne. On the other side of the River Gather is Greater Gatherborne and we are about six miles from Berkhamsted that way—' she pointed '—and about eight in *that* direction from Watling Street, which is the road you want.'

'That's a Roman road,' Nathan piped up. 'Joseph and I speak Latin so if there are any Romans left we can talk to them.'

Latin? Boys from a common ale house? He was beginning to suspect that it was a most uncommon one. 'I think they have all gone, Nathan.'

'How do you know my name, Major? No one else can tell us apart.'

'Except your mama, I assume. I am used to having to learn the names of dozens of men at a time. You learn to spot the little differences.'

'Your ears!' Nathan jeered at his brother.

'Nathan! The pair of you, clear the table and then off to bed with you. The major doesn't want to hear boys squabbling.'

Actually, to his surprise, he didn't mind it as much as he thought he would. They were lively and sharp, and even on their best behaviour seemed to fill the room, but he liked their honest reactions to everything and their obvious devotion to their mother. It was not how he had been brought up, but then he had been raised as an orphaned earl from younger than these two were now, and in a very different setting. The mother of these boys seemed to encourage them to express opinions and emotions.

He tried to imagine his elderly guardians confronted by these two and had to suppress a grin. *A gentleman is in control of his emotions at all times. Loss of control is a sign of weakness in a gentleman. The so-called tender emotions are for women and, in men, lead to weakness of resolve, vulnerability and effeminacy.* The old boys had a complete certainty that he had imbibed very thoroughly. It had made him a good officer and landowner, but listening to the enthusiastic chatter now he felt an unfamiliar twinge of envy at their freedom.

Hugo got up. 'Shall I check on the animals?' He had to

make sure Ajax was settling down with no ill effects from his drenching and it would get him out of the house and away from the disconcerting feeling that he was being absorbed into the family when he could not speak the language. That and the decidedly disturbing effect of Mrs Weston's smiling hazel eyes on his equilibrium.

'Oh, thank you.' She looked up from a brisk discussion of how much washing was necessary for boys on a cold winter evening. 'I *would* appreciate it.'

Either Emilia Weston was a very nice woman, Hugo thought, taking the lantern off its hook and lighting it before going into the stable, or she was not used to getting much help. Or perhaps both, which worried him. But there was not a great deal he could do to help; tomorrow he would be on his way. He would pay her well for his bed and board, of course, but still it left him feeling uncomfortable, as though he was watching a delicate thoroughbred mare being put into harness and made to pull a burden too great for her strength, however strong her spirit.

Ajax was dozing, one hoof cocked up, his jaw resting on the edge of the virtually empty manger. The horse opened his eyes and regarded Hugo lazily as he checked on the water buckets, ducked outside to make sure the pigsty was secure, then bolted the outer door. Hugo leaned on the horse's rump for a minute or two, relaxing against the familiar bulk, his mind running round in circles. He was tired. Beyond tired, but not sleepy.

He went back into the house, bolting the door behind him. The taproom was empty, his pallet lying close to the fire promising rest if not sleep. Hugo began to check the shutters and front door locks methodically. His hand was on the open shutter when she spoke behind him.

'Leave that one, please. Just turn down the wick on the lantern, but leave it alight.'

'You are expecting someone?' He did as she asked and turned back, steadying his breathing when he found himself face to face with her. 'The rain has almost stopped.'

'Expecting? No.' Emilia Weston stood untying the strings of her apron, not a brisk mother or a damp, smiling temptress any longer, simply a tired young woman. All the more reason not to reach out and pull her into an embrace that would be anything but comforting, he told himself. 'But then I was not expecting you either, and I assume it was the light from that window that brought you here. There may be other travellers out in this. I have made tea—would you like some?'

She turned before he could answer and went back into the other room. Hugo followed and took the battered old armchair opposite hers, flanking the wide range. 'Thank you, I would appreciate that. Are stray travellers commonplace here, then?' He guessed the tea was her night-time indulgence, an expensive treat. He would send some from the nearest town as a present.

She passed him a cup and leaned back with a sigh, her whole body relaxing with cat-like sensuality. 'Ah. Peace at last. No, you are the first lost soul. But I would always leave a light in the window when Giles went out in the evening and I have never got out of the habit, I suppose.'

'Giles was your husband, Mrs Weston?'

'Call me Emilia, won't you? No one calls me by my proper name any more. Yes, Giles was my husband. He died three years ago.' She sipped her tea and stretched out her toes to the blaze.

Just how old is she? Hugo wondered.

'Giles worked at night. He was a gambler, a card player.' His expression must have betrayed his thoughts, for she added hastily, 'Not a sharp, you understand. He never cheated, he was just a very, very good gambler. We eloped, I'm afraid. I was supposed to marry his elder brother—not that we were in love or anything, just one of those family things. You know?'

Hugo nodded. He knew how these things worked, although there was no one to arrange a suitable marriage for him, that was down to his own efforts. And he had better be getting on with it.

'But Giles and I fell in love,' Emilia said, gazing into the fire. 'And Mama and Papa would not approve because he was the younger son and wild and I was only just eighteen. So we ran away. We were very young and very thoughtless. It did not occur to me how much shame I was bringing on my family.'

Her voice wavered and she glanced up, her face blurred by the rising, fragrant steam. 'I am talking too much and shocking you, Major. I am sorry, but you will be on your way tomorrow and we will never meet again and it is so…soothing to talk to someone like this. But I will stop embarrassing you.'

'No. You aren't embarrassing me.' Normally he would have recoiled from confidences like this, but he was intrigued and to talk to a woman in this way was a novelty. Besides, it was all about *her* feelings and he doubted she would expect him to reciprocate.

'We are like ships that pass in the night. Or, no, that is too well worn a cliché. Perhaps we are two birds sheltering from the storm in a bush and we will fly away on our own courses in the morning. What happened, Emilia? And my name is Hugo.'

'I remember.' It was not as though she would forget anything about this dark, serious man who had arrived so dramatically and who seemed so very alien. He was closed, as though a door was shut firmly on his emotions, and what she saw on the surface, although undoubtedly the real man, was no more an indication of what was happening under the surface than a view of a shuttered house revealed the life of its inhabitants. She liked his bird analogy, even though she was a sparrow and he was, she guessed, an eagle.

It was a novelty, that reserve of his. Her neighbours were unsophisticated people whose lives were unprivileged and whose reactions mirrored that. They worked hard, played hard when they had the opportunity and both loved and hated without concealment. Emilia liked that honesty, responded to it. She and Giles had lived in the open, too, enjoying every happy moment, storing up joy against the black times, pushing away the memories of the families they had left behind.

Perhaps, she thought as she watched those big, capable hands enveloping the china cup, her reserves of joy were running low and needed replenishing, although why that would draw her towards someone full of shadows and detachment, she did not understand.

He was aware of her as a woman, she could sense it. But the boys liked him and she trusted their instincts, as she trusted her own. Whatever Hugo Travers was concealing behind that unsmiling face, it was not villainy.

'What happened?' She made herself go back in time to that dreadful night. 'We were in Aylesbury, west of here. Giles was deep in a game and winning, so they told me, although the money miraculously vanished afterwards. His opponent accused him of cheating, drew a knife. The man said it was in self-defence, but of course, all the witnesses at the inquest were his friends and neighbours.'

The cold swept through her as it had when she had heard the shouting in the inn parlour below, had left the children to run downstairs. No, she would not think about what she had found, only of Giles alive and laughing.

'I had little money and two three-year-old boys to feed,' Emilia went on briskly. 'I went into the market to look for work and helped an elderly man who tripped and fell on the cobbles. He had broken his wrist, so I drove his cart home for him, all the way here with the children tucked into the malt sacks behind. He was the brewer and this was his alehouse. I worked for him for two years and then, when he died, he left it to me, bless him.'

'So you are now the alewife. A hard life.'

That worried him, she could tell. 'It is not restful, that is certain. But would you comment on it if I was not, as you suspect, gentry-born?' she wondered out loud.

She judged from the frown that he did not like the implication that it was snobbery that made him feel that way.

'It would be hard for any woman, alone and with children to rear, and I suspect that things will become harder in the countryside now the war is over. The price of grain will fall, men will be flooding back from the army with no occupation to go to. Victory always has a cost.'

Emilia shrugged away the cold worry that breathed spitefully down her neck, as she did whenever it crept past her defences. 'All one can do is work and hope and plan.'

'What do you plan for those boys? The church?'

She picked up his meaning at once and laughed. 'The Latin? I do not think so, somehow, do you? The law, I hope. I teach them at home and then they go to the vicar in Great Gatherborne for Latin and Greek twice a week. He likes them and finds them intelligent to instruct, so he takes them in return for his household's ale.'

'And one day they will be leading lawyers and maintain their mama in the manner befitting her?'

He grinned; it was the first time she had seen a smile crack that lean face and Emilia blinked at the impact. Enough of her problems—she had allowed this to become too personal and, along with the fear of revealing too much and making him uncomfortable, speaking of the past was like rubbing salt into half-healed wounds.

'And have you far to go tomorrow?' she asked. 'Your family will be worrying that you have been delayed.'

'If the roads are clear, I should be home in two days, easily.' He held out his cup to be refilled when she lifted the teapot from the trivet. 'But no one will be worrying about me, I have no family and the servants just know that I will be back in time for Christmas.'

'None at all?' *What an appalling thought.* She almost said it out loud. What would she do without the boys? And he had no one. 'You will pass Christmas with your friends, no doubt.'

He did laugh then, a deep chuckle. 'With so many of my fellow-officers all back in England together I had invitations aplenty, believe me. I had the choice of family gatherings with, I was promised, a dozen charming little infants all overexcited by the thought of presents, or two house parties well supplied with eligible young ladies on the look-out for husbands. Then there was the lure of a cosy gathering with not one, but three great aunts in attendance. My friends, who I had believed were carefree, sociable bachelors, all turned into devoted family men on arriving back in England and, I confess, I do not understand families.'

'You do not?' Her tiredness vanished as she stared at him.

'I was an orphan from the age of three, brought up by four elderly trustees and a houseful of devoted staff,' Hugo explained without, to her amazement, the slightest sign of self-pity.

'But…were you not lonely?'

'Not at all. Mrs Weston…Emilia, do not look like that! I had tutors and then I went to school and university and later into the army. I made good friends in all of those and when I was at home there was the estate to learn to manage. But I have to confess to not understanding how families work, the intimacy of them. And, frankly, faced with the thought of two weeks of someone else's family *en fête*, it was no hardship to travel home,' he added wryly. 'Besides, I have much to catch up with and plans to make for the new year.'

She must have made an interrogative noise, for Hugo broke off and the shutters were over his eyes again. 'It is time I settled down,' he said abruptly and got to his feet. 'I have been running the estate at arm's length for five years while I have been in the army. And I must stop talking and keeping you from your rest.'

Emilia stayed curled in her chair as he took his cup to the stone sink and rinsed it out with, she guessed, the tidy habits of the soldier. Even as weary as he must be, he still moved beautifully with the unthinking grace of a very fit man. She fixed her gaze on the tea leaves in her cup, but there was nothing to be read there. 'Goodnight, Major. Sleep well.' She wondered if she would.

'Goodnight, Mrs Weston. And thank you.' He paused between the two rooms. 'You should lock this door, you know.'

'Oh, don't be ridiculous,' she muttered as it closed and she stood up and stretched the stiffness out of her back. Major Hugo Travers was certainly dangerous to women, especially one who had been on her own far too long, but it would be the loss of his company she would feel when he went on his way in the morning that would do the damage, not any improbable assault on her virtue.

Her occupation and humble status cut her off from anything other than the polite exchange of greetings with the vicar, the squire and their families, even though they tacitly recognised that she had been *one of them*. The villagers treated her amiably, but also with the reserve that showed they thought of her as *Quality*. She sometimes concluded she was like the governess in a big house, neither family nor servant, stranded somewhere in the middle and lonely as a result of it.

'On which self-pitying note you can take yourself to bed, Emilia Weston,' she scolded herself as she bent to bank up the fire safely. The rain had stopped, the night was still. The major would have a muddy ride tomorrow, back to his waiting servants and his big house and his plans to settle down into the peace of an England no longer at war.

Chapter Three

The silence woke Emilia into a muffled world and the cold blue light brought her out of bed to stand shivering at the tiny window in the eaves. Snow glowed in the moonlight, heaped up in great drifts and banks, whirling through the air as if some celestial hand was plucking the largest flock of geese in the universe. Silent, deadly beauty.

The light from the lantern in the taproom below cut a golden track into the whiteness and she offered up a quick prayer for any traveller caught out in this. Eerily, the beam of light widened. For a moment she did not understand, then she realised that Hugo must be standing at the window and had pushed back the shutter. The guilty flicker of pleasure took her unawares as she pulled on the heavy robe she had made from a cut-up blanket, found her shoes and tiptoed out to the head of the stairs.

The twins were fast asleep with the utter relaxation that only cats and children seemed to be blessed with. Emilia tucked the covers higher over their shoulders and went downstairs. *Why?* she asked herself as she crossed the kitchen and lifted the latch on the taproom door. *What am I doing down here?*

Hugo must have heard the latch. He had already turned, and she saw in the lantern light that he was fully dressed with a blanket slung around his shoulders. 'What's wrong?' His voice was deep and low and sent a shiver of warmth through her.

'Nothing. The silence woke me and then I saw the light spill out on to the snow when you opened the shutter and wondered if everything was all right.' That was a lie and she never lied. What *had* brought her down?

'It is already deep and it is settling.' Hugo pushed the shutter almost closed. 'How close are we to a turnpike road?'

'Too far and when you get there it will be no better than this. Even the mail will be stopped if it is lying so thick.'

'The post boys will get through, even if they have to take a horse from the traces and abandon the mail coach.'

'They will reach the next inn, perhaps. But you are not carrying the mails, so why should you even try?'

Was it really such a prison sentence to be trapped here? But then he had shied away from all his close friends' invitations because he did not want to be with a horde of children—and hers certainly qualified for the description—and he had been uneasy about her lack of a chaperon. Was that what the matter was? Not the interruption to his journey, not the presence of two lively boys, but *her*? Did he expect the poor lonely widow to make a pass at him? The idea brought the colour flaming up under her skin.

'I am an unconscionable nuisance to you and, whatever you say about your supplies, you cannot have expected to be feeding a large man and a considerably larger horse.'

'When the weather is like this the whole hamlet works together and shares food and fuel with everyone, residents and chance-met strangers alike. It is called neighbourliness, Major. Or perhaps on your big estate you are not familiar with the concept of neighbours and mutual dependence.' She was fanning her temper as though she could cover her own embarrassment, and, deep down, her guilty pleasure that he had to stay. 'We will set you to work for your board, Major, never fear. There are several elderly people to dig out and check upon and that will be the first task come morning.'

Even in the poor light she could see him stiffen, presumably with affront at being spoken to like that by an alewife. 'I have helped dig out villages in the Pyrenees, Mrs Weston, you need have no fear that I do not know one end of a shovel from the other. And it is not that I do not understand and appreciate the hospitality of your community, merely that I have no wish to add to its burdens.'

'Excellent. Then we understand each other,' Emilia snapped. He did not like having to explain himself. Presumably majors did not have to very often, let alone ones who were well-bred landowners. 'I will see you at first light, then.' She gathered her inelegant robe around her with as much dignity as she could muster and swept out, remembering in the nick of time to close the door quietly so as not to wake the boys.

Idiot, idiot, idiot, she apostrophised herself all the way back up the stairs. *You go and disturb a man in the early hours, you blush like a rose because you have no sensible excuse for doing so and then you bite his head off quite unfairly because he unsettles you.* Emilia hesitated on the landing at the top of the stairs. Should she go back and apologise? And what, exactly, would be her explanation? No, there was nothing for it but to go back to bed and hope he was still talking to her in the morning.

And what was that about? Dim light struggled through the shutters and Hugo gave up on sleep and sat up in his cocoon of blankets to contemplate his situation. And his hostess.

Another woman and he might have suspected that her visit was an invitation of a most blatant kind and one he would have been sorely tempted by. But no woman bent on seduction, however humble her circumstances, visited a man clad in a frightful garment apparently cobbled together from an old horse blanket and with her hair in plaits, and then picked a quarrel.

He was going to have to get used to the company of respectable women, if he was to find himself a wife this coming Season as he had planned. The idea had seemed reasonable when he had thought of it, months ago in France. It should be easy enough to find a well-bred young lady, a pretty society virgin who would give him an heir and, he had thought vaguely, a few other children to be on the safe side. He was eligible enough not to have too much trouble finding the right bride, he concluded without undue modesty. He had title and lands and wealth and an unblemished reputation.

This theoretical bride had no face in his dreams, no name, no character, now he came to think about it. In fact, he supposed he had not given her much thought at all. But living with a woman like this, in a home, with children, was unsettling. It made him realise that he could not just marry a cipher, he must find a *person*, one he could get on with, one whom he would like and respect.

Finding a bride would not be like buying a horse and he was guiltily aware that he had been thinking in much the same terms—age, bloodlines, temperament, looks... Yes, he was going to have to consider someone he could look upon as a companion.

He shifted uncomfortably on the hard straw mattress. Was this theoretical woman he intended to court going to insist on declarations of love, exchanges of emotion and intense conversations about feelings? He had the suspicion that she would, but how the devil did a man spout this stuff when he did not feel it, or understand it?

A gentleman was self-reliant and kept his feelings to himself, that was how he had been raised. Duty, honour, patriotism, friendship, loyalty—those were the important emotions and gentlemen did not need to speak of them. They took it for granted that their friends felt like that, too.

No true gentleman experienced violent emotions that might burst forth inappropriately—love, despair, fury. Passion. There had been liaisons in the past, of course, but even sexual encounters should not descend into uncontrolled passion and the sort of lady he would be courting would be horrified by those kinds of demonstrations.

No, you did not treat ladies—or respectable ale wives, come to that—as you treated a courtesan.

And that, Hugo concluded, rolling out of his nest of blankets, included removing one's unshaven, unwashed self before she came downstairs to start the day.

Fifteen minutes later Hugo emerged from the cellar, where the copper had yielded enough warm water for a wash and a shave, rolled up his bedding, stowed it in a corner and went out to check on the animals. When he came back the inner door was open and both boys, hair uncombed, were standing in the kitchen, looking confused.

'Mama's still asleep,' Nathan said. This was obviously outside their experience.

'Are you sure she isn't unwell?' Hugo asked. In retrospect she had not seemed quite well last night, standing there shivering in that hideous robe, which was probably why he had wanted to put his arms around her.

Both boys stared at him, wide-eyed with anxiety. 'Don't know,' said Joseph. 'How do we tell?'

'I had better have a look.' Hugo walked softly upstairs. One door stood open on to what was obviously the boys' room, the other was closed. He cracked it open, but the still figure under the heap of blankets did not stir. Now what? Knock and risk disturbing her if she was simply asleep or go in and check she was not running a fever?

He padded across the boards in his stockinged feet until he could see Emilia's face. She looked peaceful enough: there was no sweat on her brow, she was not shivering and her breath stirred a wisp of hair in a steady rhythm. Hugo reached out and brushed it back, his fingers just touching her forehead. Her skin was cool, not feverish. Just tired, then.

It was an effort to lift his hand away. Her skin was smooth, soft, and yet beneath his fingers he could feel the delicate arch of her brow bone, the brush of her eyebrows. He felt himself hardening with desire and cursed his own lack of self-control. He should stop touching her. *Now.* Then Emilia stirred and her lips curved into a slight, tender smile. Something caught in his chest, almost painfully. His hand cupped in an instinctive gesture to caress her face and she opened her eyes.

'Hugo?' she murmured. She had been dreaming about him and here he was bending over her bed, those deep blue eyes intent on her face, his face serious, his hand brushing lightly over her cheek. It was still a dream, of course, a lovely dream. Emilia closed her eyes and drifted away again. Such a real dream…she could feel the cold of the room, the warmth of his breath, smell the soap on his hand.

'Hugo?' Emilia sat bolt upright. 'What is wrong? The boys—'

'Nothing is wrong.' He backed away towards the door as she began to push back the covers. 'They were worried because you were still asleep. Apparently that is unusual. I was concerned in case you were ill.'

'No, I am quite all right. But I *never* oversleep.'

He shrugged, halfway through the door now, in full retreat. She realised what she was doing and left the covers as they were.

'Perhaps you felt more secure with a man sleeping downstairs. More relaxed. We're fine,' she heard him say as the door closed. 'I'll start breakfast.'

Breakfast? Emilia threw back the blankets and almost fell out of bed. The chill of the room was more than enough to banish hazy dreams of tall, blue-eyed men. What on earth did he mean, *relaxed*? That she never slept properly because she always had one ear open for danger, for the boys, for the animals?

Perhaps he was right, she conceded reluctantly, as she splashed cold water on to her shivering body and scrambled into her warmest clothes. But she had never been aware of fear, of being braced for trouble. It was just that it was all her responsibility now, hers alone.

By now there was probably carnage in the kitchen. She bundled her hair into a net as she ran downstairs and then stopped dead, her hands still lifted to tuck in stray locks. The table was laid, the boys were dressed, their hair ruthlessly brushed, and the aroma of frying bacon was wafting appetisingly on the warm air.

'Four eggs,' Joseph said in triumph as he set the basket down on the table. 'One each.'

'Excellent.' Hugo glanced up from the vast skillet he was wielding expertly. The intensity she had seen—imagined?— in his eyes in the bedchamber was replaced by nothing more disturbing than concentration. 'Pass me those slices of stale bread, Nathan, and we'll fry those in the bacon fat. We men will need some solid ballast inside us today. Joseph, pour your mama some tea.'

'You are making breakfast.' Emilia sat down on one end of the bench and smiled rather blankly at her son as he passed her the tea. Order, unburned food, quiet boys. The man was a miracle worker. Or a very good officer.

'Of course. Soldiers cook. It was that or starve half the time when the baggage train got left behind. There, we're ready. Plates, boys.'

Four plates were produced, loaded and conveyed somewhat unsteadily to the table. Tea and milk were poured. Hugo began to slice bread. 'I can't make bread, though,' he said, passing a slice over to her.

'No. I don't expect you have felt the need.'

'I have, frequently. It is just that it always turns out like boot leather.' Perhaps that strange episode last night when she was so irritable with him had been the dream, because he showed no signs of recalling it. Best not to mention it, she would only get bogged down trying to explain something she did not understand herself.

'I have checked the stable and the boys say they'll feed the animals while I dig the pigsty out. Then I had best clear the way to the log pile and we can stock up on fuel inside before you tell me which neighbours I should be digging towards. You said last night there were some elderly ones?'

Oh, dear, it had not been a dream after all. She really had come downstairs in that frightful robe and lectured him on neighbourliness. And then she had slept in and he had felt it necessary to check on her and she had rubbed her cheek against his hand. It was all coming back in blush-making detail. No wonder he had retreated into brisk practicality.

'There's the Widow Cooke and then beyond her, old John Janes. I expect the other villagers will be out digging as well, so you'll all meet up and we can work out if anyone is still cut off.'

'And who would be doing the digging from here if I had not happened by?'

'We would, the boys and I. It would take us a long time, though.' And if she did not have to worry about the old people then she could get on with clearing the waste mash from the tubs. Emilia chewed on a mouthful of bacon, all the more delicious because she had not had to cook it, and gradually became aware that Hugo was frowning again.

He really did not approve of her working with her hands, that was obvious. What had possessed her to confirm his suspicions that she was gentry-born? Although the way she spoke and the fact that the boys were being educated in the classics were clues enough, she supposed. Did he think the labour was beneath her because of her birth or that he simply did not like to see a woman working hard? He was unobservant if he had never noticed just how tough life was for anyone outside the charmed circle of privilege.

'I would warn the boys that the wind might change and they

would be set with their faces in a scowl for ever,' Emilia said lightly and his frown vanished.

'Was I scowling? I am sorry. I think I have the kind of face that always looks serious in repose.' He smiled. 'Is that better?'

Do not do that! Having a large male, in his prime, wandering about the house was bad enough, but even when scowling Hugo was a good-looking man with his strong bones and firm chin and those deep-blue eyes. When he smiled right at her like that he took her breath away.

'Infinitely,' Emilia said and smiled back with determined friendliness. 'Boys, you may leave the dishes this morning. Wrap up warmly and help the major with the wood and the animals.'

Emilia braced herself for the usual tussle of getting the twins into what she considered sufficient warm clothing, finding missing mittens, lost scarves and untangling bootlaces. Hugo simply stood up, said, 'Anyone who is not ready in five minutes will stay and do housework', and a miracle happened. He had no sooner pulled on his boots and put on his scarlet uniform jacket under the battered leather jerkin than both boys were standing to attention, every button done up, boots laced, scarves tied.

'Right, forward march.' He ushered them towards the door and turned at the last moment. 'Let us know when you want us back, General.' And he winked, reducing himself to the same age as the twins with one cheeky gesture.

'Oh, for goodness' sake!' Emilia grumbled at herself as she dumped dishes in the stone sink and lifted the kettle from its hook over the fire. Hugo Travers was not a boy, he was a hardened soldier, probably with a woman in every town across three countries. She was certainly not going to feel maternal about him and she definitely could not afford to feel anything else, except possibly sisterly.

It was foolish to feel sorry for him, just because his childhood had been devoid of family love. Hers had been full of it—and look what happened the moment she strayed from what was expected of her: rejection. She had thought the well of love was bottomless, that she could give her heart to a man and her parents would forgive her, but she had been wrong, or, perhaps, simply unworthy. Hugo obviously had no parents or siblings to disappoint, but he seemed to have acquired incredibly high expectations of himself from somewhere.

Emilia realised she was standing with a kettle of cooling water in her hand and poured it over the dishes. Life had to go on, even when it consisted of dealing with every dish in the kitchen. Hugo might be a good cook, but he seemed to have no idea about the washing up he produced. Servants, of course, on the battlefield or in the home, would whisk away the debris that the master created. She rolled up her sleeves and attacked the washing-up, planning her day in her head as she worked.

The bite of the shovel into the snow, the contraction of his shoulder muscles as he lifted and swung the load to one side, the neatness of the path he was cutting through thigh-high snow were all a simple, satisfying physical effort which most effectively stilled any restlessness his unruly body was feeling. The trouble was, it left his brain free to run in circles like a dog in a turnspit wheel, analysing and speculating. Wanting.

Behind him the boys scurried to and fro with armloads of wood and buckets for the animals. The pig was complaining loudly that it wanted more food, across the frozen valley the sound from the church bells of the main village came clear on the cold air and close to hand Emilia's neighbours called to each other as they negotiated the drifts. He had waved, called that Mrs Weston had directed him to the Cooke and Janes cottages and the other men had stared, but waved back in acknowledgement.

They would all come and investigate once pathways were open, he could tell. The glances in his direction fell short of being offensive, but left him in no doubt that they were watching him and it was out of concern for the alewife and her children, not simply country curiosity. That was good. He approved of that.

He reached the low-roofed cottage and banged on the door. 'Mrs Cooke? Mrs Weston sent me to make sure you were all right. Can I bring your wood in?' There was a tidy stack all along the front wall.

The door opened a crack and a wrinkled face peered out. 'Who be you, then?'

Hugo explained, carried in wood, fetched a pail of water and checked the old lady had enough food in stock before digging on towards the next home, a mere hump in the snow with a trickle of smoke marking the chimney. The boys were on his heels now and set to work clearing old Mr Janes's front step while Hugo made up his fire, brought in wood and promised to send bread and potatoes.

'And who might you be, stranger?' Hugo turned from closing the door to find himself face to face with a red-faced, brawny man. The smith, he guessed, from the size of the man's shoulders. He carried a shovel in both hands and looked ready and willing to use it on more than snow.

'Major Hugo Travers, snowbound here last night. And who are you?'

'Will Cartwright, smith.' He glanced over at the twins. 'Morning, boys. How's your ma?'

'Fine, thank you, Mr Cartwright. The major cooked breakfast this morning and he's got a huge horse!' Nathan confided.

'Has he now? Friend of Widow Weston, are you, Major?'

'Never met her before in my life. I found her house in the middle of the storm and she gave me a bed on the taproom floor.' He wasn't used to explaining himself to villagers, but the man was genuinely concerned and he could not fault him for that.

'Happen you'll have some company this evening, then, because you'll not be going anywhere for a day or so and that's a fact. We tried the lane towards the pike road and it's drifted deep.'

'Then I'll have to stay put and do what I can to help out,' Hugo said amiably. He didn't miss the reference to company. Every man in the hamlet was going to be in the taproom that evening, sizing him up. It should do Emilia's income some good, if nothing else. 'Anyone else need digging out?'

'No. I reckon we've got the old folks and Willie Piggott, who's a bit simple, all safe and sound. Old Janes all right?'

'He needs bread and potatoes.'

'I'll see to that.' The smith nodded, but spared the boys a smile. 'You look after your ma now!'

Hugo trudged back along the deep-cut path. 'What are your chores now?'

'We'd be going to Mr Hoskins, the vicar, for our lessons today,' Nathan explained. 'But we can't because of the snow and the flood and the bridge,' he added smugly.

'And you have no lessons to finish?' Two broad grins were enough answer. 'Well, fetch your books out and I'll set you some.' It was starting to snow again and their mother wouldn't want them racketing about the house, bored with confinement all day.

Hugo bundled them inside, ordered boots and coats off and, when he had them settled in front of the range, chewing their pencils over Caesar's Gallic wars, he went in search of Emilia.

He had hoped she might have taken the opportunity to rest, but noises from the cellar told him otherwise. When he came down the stairs she was standing in the mash tun, her skirts kirtled up around her knees, scooping wet mash out into buckets.

Hugo went down the rest of the stairs two at a time, strode across the floor and lifted her bodily out of the tun. 'What the blazes do you think you are doing?'

She turned, a small, damp virago, pink in the face from indignation and bending over. 'What am *I* doing? What are you thinking of, Major?' Her hair was coming out of its net, her bare feet and legs were shedding wet grains all over his shoes and her hands were fisted at her waist. Her small, vulnerable feet. Her shapely calves and ankles, the slim waist and the womanly curves.

'Thinking?' Hugo realised that he had not been thinking at all. But he was now. She looked edible, vital, alive. Infinitely desirable. He took her by the waist again, drew her close and buried his face in the luxurious mass of her hair.

Chapter Four

Her mouth had been open to protest, but she was pressed against Hugo's front, inhaling warm man as his hands shifted and he settled her more securely against himself. One hand pushed into her hair, sending pins falling free as he cradled her head, the other hand pressed open against her shoulder blades, moving in slow, devastating circles. Her hands were trapped between her breasts and his chest and his heart was thudding against her palms

All the air in her lungs and the blood in her head had vanished. It was wonderful and terrifying and she felt alive as she had not been for years. And it was wrong to be held like this, it had to be if it was this good. Emilia pulled a hand free, fetching Hugo a blow on the ear by mistake.

He set her back a little, just enough that their bodies were no longer touching. 'Ouch! I am sorry—'

'So am I. I didn't mean to hit you.' They stared into each other's faces, their noses almost touching, their breath wreathing white in the cold air. 'I didn't mean for you to stop,' Emilia blurted. She curled her hands around his waist and pulled and Hugo, with a groan that was either desire or despair and was, she thought wildly, possibly both, pulled her to him again.

Kiss me. Somehow she managed to keep the words in her head.

'Major?' called a treble voice from upstairs.

'Hell!' Hugo set her free so abruptly that she sat down on the edge of the tun. He was across the cellar and standing at the foot of the steps before she could gather her wits and realise where she was, what she was doing. What she had almost done.

'Yes? I am down here. Are you stuck with that exercise?' he called up, as calm as though they had been discussing hops and ale recipes.

Both boys came down the steps. 'No, we've finished. Look.' Joseph was waving a sheet of paper under Hugo's nose. 'See, Mama, we've translated a whole page! What are you doing?'

Goodness knows! Embracing a totally inappropriate man in the cellar. He is either sorry for me or he thinks I am pitiful and grateful for his attentions. 'Emptying the used mash,' Emilia said briskly. She pulled herself together and studied her sons. 'Has Major Travers been setting you Latin lessons?' They seemed unusually cheerful about the fact.

'Yes, and they are all about wars and battles!'

'How interesting. I just hope you aren't both going to rush off to the next recruiting sergeant who comes around.' They grinned back at her, knowing teasing when they heard it. Her feet were freezing now she was out of the slightly warm mash. Emilia slid her feet into her wooden pattens and tried to ignore Hugo, who shot her an unreadable glance, although whether it signified remorse at having embraced her or the strains of teaching small boys their Latin, she could not tell.

Hugo sat beside her on the edge of the tun and heeled off his shoes. 'Where does this used mash go?' He rolled off his stockings. Emilia averted her eyes from well-muscled, hairy calves.

'We'll show you.' Nathan seized one of the filled buckets. 'It all gets dumped over here and then when it is dried we use it for the animals.'

Hugo shed coat and waistcoat and rolled up his sleeves. Emilia kicked off the pattens and swung her legs over to get back into the tun.

'No. I'll finish here.' He put one hand on her arm.

She still could not look at him, or think of anything to say with the boys so close. She was acutely aware of her wet skirts and bare calves, of the blood pounding around her veins, of the closeness of him and the warm weight of his hand against the skin of her forearm. From somewhere Emilia found her voice and something coherent to say. 'Of course. I must get some food together. You will all be starving.'

She scrambled back out, jammed her feet into the pattens, let down her skirts and hurried upstairs without stopping to look back at Hugo or brush off the grains that clung to her legs. She heard the scrape of the wooden shovel on the stone base of the tun, the laughter of the boys as they fought over who was carrying the next bucket, then she was in the kitchen with the door safely closed behind her.

This was a disaster. What had she done? What had she risked, simply because of the aching need for strong arms around her, for the respite from being continuously in charge? And, yes, she thought, if she was going to be honest, she had wanted that fire in the blood, that sensual tingle between a man and a woman.

Emilia pulled onions and carrots out of their sacks and began scrubbing them to add to the soup that simmered on the hob. She worked as though she could rub away the feel of Hugo's arms around her, the scent of him. She had made her decision when she had slipped away from that ball and fallen, laughing, into Giles's arms. She had chosen love and laughter and joy for however long it lasted. And she had been blessed with four years of happiness and two wonderful sons.

But you paid the price of whatever your choices brought you. The boys had her total love and every moment she could devote to them, to building their futures. And the price for that was hard work and maintaining her reputation, not dallying with big strong soldiers. They were such good boys, so bright, so loving. She chopped the roots with savage swipes of the knife. They deserved the lives of opportunity their grand-parents could give them.

But that was part of the price, too. And she had written three times and been rejected. So, no more false hope. One large tear plopped into the stock. 'Stop it,' Emilia said out loud.

'Stop what?' asked Hugo's deep, concerned voice.

'Stop being foolish,' she snapped back as she peered into the jar of peppercorns and estimated how many she could afford to grind up for the soup. It kept her face turned from him, too. 'Where are Joseph and Nathan?'

'Checking on the animals and taking Ajax a bucket of mash. They offered,' he added, coming fully into the room and leaning his broad shoulders back against the door. 'I was not trying to get them out of the way, although it is convenient, I have to admit, for we need to talk. I should not have touched you. I do not know what came over me, which is hardly original or convincing, or even an excuse.'

'I am not a loose woman,' Emilia said with painful clarity, her eyes focused on a jar of pickled mushrooms. 'I have only ever slept with my husband. I wanted to be held and I suppose you could tell that. I apologise for not making it clear that no such thing must happen.'

'Damn it.' Hugo was at her side in two long strides. He took the jar from her hands and banged it down on the table. 'I do not need telling that you are virtuous. Nor do I need telling that your reputation in this hamlet is precious. I am on my way home, intending to seek and woo a wife.'

There was only the corner of the table and a large jar of pickles between them. Somehow she had to fight. 'It seems to be something other than your good intentions in control,' she said drily.

He gave a painful snort of laughter and pulled her round the table, setting the pickle jar rocking, and held her tight against him. 'You think that desire drives me? You are an attractive woman, you feel good in my arms and my body sends me messages about more than holding you. I can ignore that. What I find it hard to ignore is the ache in my chest and the need for my arms to be around you.'

His cheek was pressed against her hair again. They were just the right height for that, Emilia thought hazily as she hung on to as much solid man as she could get her arms around. 'You are sorry for me, that's all,' she muttered into the rough home-spun shirt that smelled of her soap and his skin.

'I am sorry for a lot of people, from the Prime Minister to beggars in the gutter,' Hugo growled. 'I do not have the urge to cuddle any of them.'

For a second, a blissful second, she relaxed against him, her soft curves fitting with erotic rightness against his hard angles. Then she felt his body harden into arousal, unmistakable against her stomach, and she pushed him, hard in the centre of his chest. For a second she thought he would not release her, she could almost feel decency and desire warring in him, and then he opened his arms and stepped back.

'It seems you cannot control your desires as well as you boast, Major,' she said, her voice unsteady.

'Emilia… Hell, the boys are coming.'

'You have ears like a cat,' Emilia said as her sons burst into the kitchen. She pulled the greased paper off the jar of pickled mushrooms and delved in with a spoon to find enough to go in the soup. 'Quietly, boys. Go and wash and clear your work off the table.'

It was like being two people. One was the sensible, hard-working mother and alewife who was capable of carrying on calmly despite chance-met travellers, snowdrifts or anything else life threw at her. The other was a yearning, passionate creature who wanted to be loved and held and to share joy and troubles with someone who understood.

But of course Hugo Travers did not understand. He was a gentleman, someone of sufficient standing to take part in the London Season when he searched for a wife. He was also was gallant and sympathetic and grateful for the shelter. And not averse to embracing a woman, a cold whisper of common sense told her. Perhaps he had hoped to see if she responded by lifting her face to be kissed and then he would not have been so gentlemanly. *Or perhaps he needed hugging, too,* the trusting part of her countered. *It might have begun as a hug, but it almost got out of control.*

Emilia ladled out soup and they sat down. Hugo already knew his way around her kitchen, she could see, for he had found the bread and was cutting it. She had the sense that he was used to moving from billet to billet with the army, settling in and making himself at home wherever he found himself. He was acting as though nothing had happened—she must match his control.

'You'll have business tonight,' he said as he passed her a slice. 'Either the result of a strong thirst from shovelling or a wish to check on the stranger under your roof. Your neighbours are protective.'

'Were they hostile?' she asked, anxious that he had been insulted.

'No. They were reserved, but they made it quite obvious that they were watching. Your smith in particular wished to make it clear that he will dismantle me with his bare hands if there is anything amiss.'

'I nursed his wife last year when she was sick,' Emilia explained. 'Joseph, why are you opening and shutting your mouth like a gudgeon?'

'Why would Mr Cartwright hit the major, Mama?'

'In case the major is a dangerous rogue in disguise. He might be here to rob us of all the gold sovereigns under the floorboards and our wonderful silver tableware.' She swept a hand round to illustrate the horn beakers, the pewter plates, the earthenware jugs. The boys collapsed in giggles.

'It is a good thing we will have some company,' she added. 'I want barrels shifting and we need several strong men for that.' And with the taproom full of people there would be no temptation to look at Hugo, much less yearn for the caresses that were so dangerous.

'Will you brew again before Christmas?'

Emilia laughed. 'Of course! This is good weather for it because when it is cold I can control the fermentation better. Besides, we will need plenty for the Christmas celebrations.'

'But not today.'

She suspected that was an order. 'No, not today,' Emilia agreed. 'I have the housework to catch up with and baking to do.'

Hugo took himself off to the stables while she worked. Probably escaping from the reality of being trapped with two small boys, a never-ending list of menial chores and a foolish woman who cast herself into his arms. *He hugged me first*, she told herself, sweeping the hearth with unnecessary vigour.

Hugo strode into the stable, stripped the sacks off Ajax's back and set to with brush and curry comb. The big horse grunted with pleasure at the strength of the strokes and leaned into them.

He had to do something physical. Getting into a fight was the most tempting solution, but there was no one to spar with, only himself to beat up, mentally.

What had he done? He should never have touched her, let alone caressed her, allowed himself to become blatantly aroused. Damn it, he had boasted to her that he could control himself.

Disgusted with himself, Hugo swore, viciously, in Spanish, Portuguese and, for good measure, French. Emilia had pushed him away. Had *needed* to push him away. That fact alone was shocking. He simply did not behave like this. If he took a mistress, then it was a considered act, properly negotiated like everything else in his life.

She had pushed him away. Rejected him. *Of course she*

did, she's a decent woman. That did not help. Hell, he wanted her and he wanted her to want him. He should have had some restraint, he was the one with years of disciplined living and trained self-control behind him, he was not the lonely over-worked one who should have tumbled into his arms with grat-itude.

Coxcomb, he thought and added a few choice epitaphs. *Emilia is not lonely. She has her sons to love and a village full of people who like her and protect her.*

Perhaps *he* was lonely. How could that be with dozens of friends, innumerable acquaintances? *And no one to love,* a small inner voice murmured. Well, that was easy enough to deal with. When he got out of here he would get on with finding a wife, a rational, intelligent, suitable wife who would fill any empty niches in his life. Not love, of course, whatever that was.

He began to talk to Ajax in Spanish. 'She'll be blonde. Blue-eyed, I think, or grey. Quite tall. Very elegant and self-possessed, but quiet. I don't want a chatterer.' *Not someone who makes jokes at mealtimes and who teases me.* 'Responsive in bed, of course. An iceberg would be unpleasant to live with. But not demanding reassurances all the time that I love her or some such nonsense.' *Not melting into my arms as though I am all she desires and then pushing me away.*

'Is that Spanish?'

Hugo dropped the curry comb and Nathan dived to pick it up. 'Yes, Spanish.' *Thank God.* 'Thank you.' He took the metal scrapper and cleaned the dandy brush.

'Why are you talking to Ajax?'

'He's the only thing around here that doesn't answer back,' Hugo said with some feeling. 'Pass me the hoof pick, will you?'

The old long-case clock in the corner of the taproom chimed four. The house was clean, the fires made up, a somewhat muscular chicken was in the pot for dinner and the boys were with Hugo.

Emilia sat down by the hearth and contemplated doing nothing for an entire, blissful, half-hour of self-indulgence. Only her mind refused to relax and every time it did she found herself thinking about that embrace.

But brooding about Hugo made her think of his lack of a family and that led inevitably to her own. The boys were growing up without their grandparents. Her parents would never know her sons. It was Christmas—surely a time for forgiveness and new starts? She would write, try again one last time. Perhaps if she made it clear they did not have to see her again, that she wanted nothing for herself, their ruined daughter, they would relent towards the boys.

Paper was expensive and she could not afford to waste it. She sat at the table, chewing the end of her pen and composing in her head and then wrote, slowly, taking care over every word.

There, done. Emilia scrubbed the back of her hand across her wet eyes. At least she hadn't dripped tears on the page, that really would have looked like a plea for sympathy. She folded the sheet carefully, wrote the direction on the front and went in search of the sealing wax.

Where had she left it? The taproom, she realised after ten minutes of fruitless rummaging in drawers. She had used it to seal that order to the maltster last week.

She was halfway across the room when she heard the sound of footsteps from the direction of the stable. The high mantelshelf over the hearth was out of reach of small boys. She reached up to hide the letter and when they came in with Hugo on their heels she was making up the fire. 'Goodness, this chimney is smoky.' She mopped at her cheeks, smiled and ignored the swift frowning glance that Hugo sent her.

He strode across the room and tucked his roll of bedding more tidily into the corner.

'You could put it back into the cupboard, for the moment,' Emilia suggested.

'I don't think so, do you?'

The level look brought the colour to her cheeks. Of course, he wanted to reinforce the point about where he was sleeping when the villagers came in this evening. *I wish it was upstairs.*

Hugo had been correct in his prediction. Every man in the village, including old Mr Janes, found their way along the narrow paths, some bringing their shovels with them in case they had to dig their way back.

Emilia sent the boys to bed and heated a large pot of mulled ale over the fire. Hugo was sitting at a corner table, apparently engrossed in the pile of tattered news sheets he had found with the kindling. He looked up and exchanged unsmiling nods with the men as they came in.

They crowded into the taproom, blowing out lanterns, filling the space with the smell of tallow, wet wool, tobacco and hard-working man with a rich undertone of cattle.

'Good evening, everyone.' Emilia straightened up from her stirring and smiled at them as they stamped snow off their boots and heaped coats in the corner. 'Would some of you do me a favour and bring two barrels up?'

'Aye, I'll do that for you, Mrs Weston.' Cartwright, the smith, rolled his broad shoulders. 'The major here will give me hand, I've no doubt. The two of us will manage.'

Damn. That was a deliberate challenge. It normally took four of them to roll the barrel on to the carrying cradle and get it up the stairs. Two men *could* do it, if they were strong enough, but Joseph had reported that Hugo had a big scar across his chest. Was it a recent wound? But there was nothing she could do about it, they were on their way downstairs.

There was bumping and a thud or two from the cellar. The other men stood around nudging each other. *Really, they are such boys,* she thought crossly. Then there were heavy footsteps on the stairs and the blacksmith appeared carrying the front handles of the wooden cradle. She held her breath, the weight of the contraption would be tipping down now on the man still on the stairs. If he fell, he would be crushed by the barrel.

But Cartwright kept coming and Hugo emerged, his jaw rather set, but not visibly struggling. They rolled the barrel on to its rest and set down the cradle. 'Game for the other one?' There was grudging respect in the smith's eyes.

'Some of the others will do it, if they will be so good.' Emilia pressed a beaker of mulled ale into his hands and gave another to Hugo. 'On the house for those who carry.'

It had broken the ice, although why Hugo's ability to lift heavy weights should convince the smith that he was a good man eluded her. Some strange male code, no doubt. Emilia set out mugs and began to fill orders.

Two hours later her cash dish was full of coppers, a cut-throat game of dominoes was going on between Billy Watchett, the ploughman, and one of the Dodson brothers, someone was attempting to wager a piglet against a load of hay on a card game and Michael Fowler was telling anyone who would listen that his heart had been broken by that flighty Madge Green from over the river.

Emilia set a fresh jug of ale down on the end of the table and leaned a hip against it for a brief rest. In the corner Lawrence Bond, a smallholder, smiled and moved his head towards the bench beside him as though in invitation. She pretended not to notice. Bond was the son of a yeoman and apt to give himself airs as a result. He would flirt if he had the opportunity and, of all the men in the village, he was the only one she would feel uneasy about being alone with.

Behind her Hugo was deep in conversation with the smith and his cronies and she shrugged off the discomfort the small-holder's scrutiny evoked and listened.

'So what'll you be doing with yourself now you're out of the army?' someone asked.

'I've some land to look after and I was thinking of politics.

I ought to take my... I ought to think what to do about that,'
Hugo replied.

No one else picked up on it. Feeling as though she had lost
the air in her lungs, Emilia made her way back to the fireside
and blindly stuck another slice of bread on the toasting fork.
Take my seat is what he had almost let slip. His seat in the
House of Lords. Hugo was an aristocrat.

Chapter Five

Aristocrat. It was not until she heard the word in her head and felt the sharp pang beneath her breastbone that Emilia understood her own foolishness. Part of her, some part that was utterly out of touch with reality, had been dreaming that her handsome major would want her, kiss her, fall for her. Ridiculous, even if he had merely been a landowning officer, for he was too decent to seduce her and anything else was simply moonshine.

But an aristocrat? Connections, respectability, dowry were all. The only relationship Hugo Travers, Lord Whatever He Was, could have with her was as a kindly passing acquaintance or to take her as a mistress. She almost laughed at the notion of herself as mistress-material as she brushed ashes off her worn skirt and held out one chapped hand to the warmth of the fire.

'You'll have that bread in cinders,' old Mr Janes cackled. 'Looking for your lover in the flames, eh?'

'You're a dreadful old man and you've had too much mulled ale,' she scolded him, pulling back the toasting fork and setting it aside. Years of practice putting on a cheerful face for the boys under all circumstances stood her in good stead with adults, too, she was learning.

He grinned, revealing one remaining tooth and a great deal

of gum. 'I'm old, that's a fact, my pretty. But you gets wisdom with age.'

'And what's your wisdom telling you now, eh, Grandfer Janes?' one of the younger men called.

'It's telling me we're having snow from now until Christmas morn and none of us is getting out of this hamlet for a week, so we'd best be thinking what we're going to do about the Feast.'

'Are you certain?' Hugo's deep voice cut through the buzz of comment.

'Aye, he's certain,' the smith said. 'Best weather prophet in the Chiltern Hills is Old Janes. Best make your mind up to it, Major. You're spending Christmas in Little Gatherborne.'

Hugo's face in the candlelight, through the haze of tobacco smoke, was unreadable to anyone who did not know him as she was beginning to. His lips moved. She thought he murmured, 'Hell', then he asked, 'What feast?'

'The Christmas Feast,' Cartwright explained. 'We hold it every Christmas Eve over at Squire Nicholson's big barn in Great Gatherborne. Everyone comes from both villages and the farms all around, there's dancing, music, games for the little ones, food.'

'So where will you hold it over here?'

'Don't see how we can,' someone complained. 'None of us has a barn and Squire provides the beast for roasting.'

'What's the barn up the hill, then?'

'That belongs to Sir Philip Davenport. He's got a big house down the valley,' Emilia explained. 'I think he's going to sell it to the Squire. It's empty, though. We could use it if it isn't locked.'

'What, without asking? He'd be powerful mad and he's a magistrate.' That was Jimmy Hadfield, who'd had a close scrape over a poached pheasant or two if she wasn't mistaken.

She couldn't ask Sir Philip, that was for certain. She had actually danced with him, just the once, at her very first, and last, ball on the night she and Giles had eloped. If he didn't know who she was, he would not see her, the humble alewife, but if she told him her real identity to gain an interview he would be highly embarrassed. And it would be even more embarrassing for her parents if he let slip to society that Lord Peterscroft's wanton daughter was running a rural alehouse.

'I could have a word with him afterwards,' Hugo said. 'If we don't do any damage—' The rest was lost in a roar of approbation.

'What about food?' Emilia managed to make herself heard above the din. 'The squire gives us a bullock.' She tried to sort out the conflicting emotions in her head. Delight, of course, that the hamlet could have its Feast after all and a grudging resentment that Hugo would stroll into see Sir Philip, exchange a few casual words and it would all be settled. Once she had accepted that kind of privilege without thought. Now she knew she could never be that girl again.

'None of us has got any spare livestock,' someone said from the back of the room. Gloom descended.

'Has anyone got an animal you could spare if you had the money to replace it?' Hugo asked. 'I'll buy it as my contribution to the feast.'

That settled it. Several meaty palms slapped Hugo's shoulders before the men recollected who he was and then, when he showed no sign of taking exception to the treatment, he was offered a quantity of dubious snuff and a tot of Granfer Jane's even more dubious, and decidedly illegal, home-distilled spirits, which rendered him speechless after one mouthful.

Emilia filled another jug with ale. This was going to turn into a planning meeting and that required lubrication. Across the room she met Hugo's eyes. He raised his eyebrows and grinned and she found herself grinning back. He was a good man, she had known it instinctively, and it was pleasant to be proved correct. If only she could hold on to that and not allow those wicked, wistful longings to creep in when she looked at him, thought about him.

'Now then.' She clapped her hands for silence. 'How many people will be coming do we think?'

The boys were muttering at his heels as Hugo dug his way through the fresh snowfall so they could feed the pig. They had been subdued all through breakfast, he realised.

'What's the matter with you two?' The three of them hung over the sty door and scratched Maud on her broad, bristly back as she rooted vigorously in the trough.

'We were going into town to buy a present for Mama for Christmas and now we can't,' Nathan said. 'We left it too late, but we were saving up and…' His voice wavered.

'Then you'll have to make something, won't you?' Hugo said briskly. 'What would she like?' He thought about the craftsmen he had met the night before. The carpenter had seemed an amiable, easy-going man. 'If you can think of something to make from wood, I expect Mr Daventry would take you on as apprentices for a few days.'

'Mama said the other day she didn't have a nice shelf to put the pretty jug we bought her on safely. If we made her one, she could put it in her bedroom with flowers in the jug,' Joseph suggested. They both looked enthusiastic.

'Come on, then, we'll dig our way through to the old folks and then go and find Mr Daventry.'

When they came back, cheerful and hungry after a hard morning digging and negotiating, Emilia was standing in the sunshine on the front step, shaking out a duster. He felt a ridiculous stab of pleasure at seeing her there, as though she was waiting to welcome him home. Warmth spread through him when she saw them and smiled straight into his eyes, her face open and happy. She made him think of fresh-baked bread, wholesome and edible and tempting.

He was forgiven for yesterday's insanity. He wanted to taste her skin, to nibble, very gently, at those sweet curves. *Stop it, she's a decent woman*. But what was that feeling in his chest, that ache that made him want to hold her and protect her and, yes, make love to her?

'What a marvellous morning!' she called when they came into earshot and he wiped his thoughts off his face. 'But Granfer James says we'll have snow again later. I've just been and taken him some chicken broth.' They stamped into the yard, kicked snow off their boots and stacked shovels under the eaves. 'What have you been up to?' Emilia asked. 'I sense mischief. Or secrets.'

'Men's business,' Hugo said. 'I've hired these two out as apprentices to Daventry the carpenter. He needs a hand. That's all right, isn't it? I can set them some Latin exercises for this evening.' He winked at her over the boys' heads and shook his head when she opened her mouth, obviously to demand to know what on earth he was about.

'I see.' Emilia clearly did not, but she was willing to trust him and play along. It provoked the most unexpected sense of partnership. 'I had no idea Mr Daventry had so much on that he needs assistance, but we must be neighbourly. You two are to be back before it starts to get dark, or as soon as it begins to snow, do you understand?'

Goodness knew what Hugo and the boys were plotting, but she guessed it must be something to do with her Christmas present. Emilia had realised they were fretting about it and had been racking her brains for something she could hint that she wanted that they could make her. Their own presents had been bought weeks ago, the last time she had been into Aylesbury.

But what about Hugo? Whatever she thought of, she was going to have to make it right under his nose... Nose! Of course. There was that fine white cotton she had bought for summer underwear. There was a good yard left, more than enough for handkerchiefs with his initials in the corner. She could whip those up without him noticing she was doing anything other than her usual sewing.

She had the fabric spread out on the table when he came back from seeing the boys off after luncheon. 'What are you making?' He hitched a hip on to the corner of the table. Big, relaxed, male. Gorgeous.

Emilia felt the blush rise and turned it to her advantage. 'Female underthings.'

'Ah.' He was off the table and over by the hearth at once, just as she had hoped.

'Thank you for helping the boys.' She took up the scissors and cut along her markings, careful to get the edges straight. For some reason her hand did not seem quite steady.

Hugo sat down on the arm of her armchair. 'My pleasure. They were fretting about not being able to finish their shopping.'

'It seems very quiet without them.' She had ruined that square—oh, well, it would make a smaller handkerchief for her. With an effort of will Emilia completed the six squares, folded them all into her workbasket and cleared up the scraps.

'In the summer they must be out a great deal of the time,' Hugo observed. He did not move as she came and set the basket down by her chair.

'Yes. Of course. It is just that…' Her normally fluent tongue seemed to be in knots.

'That having me in the house when no one else is here is disconcerting?' Hugo asked with devastating directness.

'Yes.' Emilia found she had no idea what to do with her hands, which appeared to want to tie themselves into knots.

'Why? Do you feel unsafe with me?' He stood up and she found they were almost toe to toe. 'Is it because of yesterday?'

'No! It is just that I want…I mean I…'

'You want me to hold you?' he asked softly.

'Yes. No,' she corrected with desperate honesty. 'I want you to kiss me.'

'What an extraordinary coincidence,' he said. She glanced up at him, confused. 'I was just thinking how much I would like to kiss you.'

It was not tentative, or gentle or subtle. Teeth bumped, she trod on his feet, his hands were so tight around her waist that she was breathless. It was wonderful and life-affirming and dangerously exciting.

When they fell apart, Hugo's eyes were dark, deep blue and he looked faintly stunned. 'I am sorry.'

'Why? I am not.' She wasn't. She should be, but she couldn't find a whisper of regret anywhere.

'My technique seem to have become inexcusably clumsy.' His grip on her waist loosened, but he did not let her go.

'Perhaps it is a while since you kissed a woman?' she suggested. The sudden calculation she could see in his eyes was amusing.

'A month or two,' Hugo admitted. 'I am not in the habit of wantonly kissing my way around, you understand.' He cocked an eyebrow quizzically, but Emilia sensed he was concerned with how she replied.

'No, I can tell that.' His hands were still warm on her waist, she was no longer treading on his toes, so she reached up, curled her fingers around the strong column of his neck and drew him down. 'We could try again?'

'I would appreciate a second chance. You disconcert me, Emilia.'

Disconcert him? Me, plain ordinary Emilia Weston? Then his mouth closed firmly over hers and his tongue swept along the fullness of her lower lip and she let herself sink into the sensation. It was strange to know what she was doing, to know what to expect, and yet to be experiencing it with a different man.

And any memories were lost almost immediately. Hugo

tasted different, felt different, kissed differently. She had thought that to make love with any other man would feel like disloyalty to Giles, although she knew he would never want her to be alone after he had gone. But this felt right and wonderful as sensations she had almost forgotten about tingled and throbbed and ached deliciously from her lips to her thighs.

Hugo explored deep into her mouth as though he wanted to drink her in and she responded with as much boldness, learning the taste of him, teasing him with nips and licks, digging her fingers into his broad shoulders.

When he lifted his head finally they stared at each other until he released his grip on her waist and she dropped her hands from his shoulders. Emilia groped her way to the nearest chair and sat down on it with a thump. Her breasts felt heavy, as sensitive as if he had been caressing the naked flesh, and between her thighs the pulse of arousal beat a distracting, insistent rhythm.

'I did not send the boys to the carpenter's so I could do that,' Hugo said abruptly. 'It has just occurred to me that you might believe I had schemed to get them out of the house.' He put one hand on the mantel and stood looking down into the fire, then abruptly swung the kettle over the heat.

'No. It never occurred to me that you would do such a thing.' Was she being hopelessly naïve and trusting? But did men set on selfish seduction raise such concerns? Perhaps they did if they were very subtle. Emilia gave herself a mental shake. Every instinct had told her to trust Hugo from the moment she set eyes on him. 'I asked you to kiss me.' She ought to feel shame at being so bold. She certainly should feel alarm at what she was doing.

'I am honoured. And flattered. And I think we should stop this right now while there are only kisses between us.' He began to spoon tea into the pot as though the banal domesticity of the act would somehow disperse the tensions that thickened the air between them.

What is this? she wondered, but did not ask. Hugo was apparently too decent to seduce her and leave her and she was impossible as a mistress—no man, certainly no aristocrat, offered an alehouse keeper with children a *carte blanche*.

'That would certainly be sensible,' she agreed, dredging up remnants of common sense from wherever they had vanished to. 'It would also be a saving on the housekeeping if you stopped heaping tea into that pot.'

'Oh, Lord!' He peered into it and began to spoon tea out again. Emilia laughed and for a minute or two while she fetched mugs and milk it was as though those kisses had never happened. Then Hugo looked up, straight into her eyes and said, 'I have never met another woman like you, Emilia. I doubt I ever will again.'

What could she say to that? What did it mean? He seemed blurred somehow and then she realised it was not her emotions playing havoc with her eyesight, but the light dimming. 'Oh, no, here comes the snow again.'

'I'll go and get the boys.' Hugo swept his heavy cloak from the peg, clapped his hat on his head and went out, snowflakes swirling into the room in his wake.

They melted in the warm air and all trace of him was gone, only the two mugs standing on the table left to mark that she had not dreamed the last half-hour.

'You are going to break my heart, Hugo Travers,' Emilia said. But hearts had been broken before and no one died of it, not while there were stockings to darn and boys to feed and ale to brew. She swirled her big white apron around her waist and went to survey the larder shelves in search of inspiration for supper.

'Have you done your Latin exercises?' Hugo felt the concerted power of two sets of eyes on his back, but he did not look round from grooming Ajax.

'Yes, Major. And we've done our chores and Mama says

we are under her feet because she is trying to sweep. Is it ever going to be Christmas?'

'Today is the twenty-third. Christmas Eve is tomorrow. How are the shelves coming along?' He sponged Ajax's muzzle and the big horse sighed gustily, spraying him with water. He was bored, standing in this stall. The deep, narrow paths through the snow were unfit for anything but walking, but he would take him out in a minute.

'Really well, they are finished almost. Mr Daventry has carved a star on both ends for us and he is going to help us put our initials on it this afternoon.' There was an anxious pause. 'Do you think we have enough money to pay him for the wood and carving the stars and helping us?'

'How much have you got?'

'Two shillings and four pence halfpenny.'

Hugo had already spoken to the carpenter, agreed a price and promised to make up the difference. 'Well, that should do it. Do you want to come and help me exercise Ajax?' He untied the halter rope, slid the bridle on to a chorus of excited agreement and led the horse out into the front yard. 'Come on, then, up you go.'

He swung Nathan up, then Joseph. They were almost too excited to speak. Hugo put the reins into Nathan's hands and walked away into one of the pathways through the snow. Ajax plodded behind, the boys' feet brushing the tops of the snow banks.

It was a relief to get right away from the house. He had been trying to ever since he had yielded to temptation and kissed Emilia and felt the ache of desire sweep through him, felt the pain under his breastbone that he did not understand intensify. He had dug, visited, joined the other men in planning, helped clear the barn and select the beast for the roast. And every time he had gone back to the house the very lack of contact, the control with which Emilia ignored what he had done, scarified his pride.

That would be sensible, she had said when he had summoned up every ounce of his crumbling will-power and said that they should put a stop to it. Whatever it was. She had spoken calmly, dispassionately, as if she had taken all she needed from him. Certainly she was not hurt or desperate to be back in his arms. He had thought she needed him more than he needed her and it seemed he was wrong.

I do not need her. I need a wife.

The ride had been a wild success. After half an hour Hugo swopped them around so Joseph had the reins, by which time they had their voices back.

'Are you married, Major?' Nathan asked.

What? For an appalled moment he thought he was being asked his intentions towards their mother, then he realised his own conscience was imposing undertones on a perfectly innocent piece of curiosity.

'No.'

'Why not?' Joseph enquired earnestly. 'Aren't you really old not to be married?'

Chapter Six

'I am twenty-eight,' Hugo said. 'Which is a perfectly good age to get married. And besides, I have been away fighting.'

'So who are you going to marry?'

'I haven't met her yet.' It felt important to state that.

'How will you find the right one then?' Nathan asked. 'A wife has to be able to cook, doesn't she?'

'No, not always. I employ a cook. I will go to London after Christmas and attend parties and balls and hope to find the right lady.' That was the plan. It had seemed perfectly sensible. It *was* perfectly sensible. It was how a gentleman found a wife.

'How will you know? Will she be pretty?'

'Perhaps she will.' *Blonde, blue eyes, tall. Cool.* 'How do you know when *you* like someone?'

'But it's more than liking, isn't it?' Joseph chimed in. 'You've got to live with her for ever and ever and have babies and love each other.' His voice trailed away. 'Until one of you dies.'

'We will have to like each other,' Hugo said briskly. 'Love could grow afterwards. And she will come from the same sort of background as me so she will know how to look after quite a lot of servants and tenants and a big house.' He was not sure who he was trying to convince, himself or the boys. *Or perhaps*, part of himself suggested, *they will tell Emilia and she will understand that really, this thing between us is just something that has sprung from the enforced closeness.*

'When do you exchange presents?' he asked. This was definitely the time to change the subject and presents was one topic guaranteed to secure their undivided attention.

'On Christmas Eve—tomorrow—before we go to the Feast.'

'Then shall I put the shelves up in your mama's bedroom while you distract her by calling her out to the stable?' he suggested. 'I'll go and pick them up and ask the carpenter for some nails.'

He tried to recall the process of giving presents when he was a child. His trustees would provide suitable amounts of money, then he sat down and wrote a careful note to each of the staff to wrap around their cash gift that would go on top of the new uniform they would receive every Christmas. His trustees would receive an immaculately penned letter of Christmas good wishes and thanks for their guidance during the past year, all under the supervision of his governess.

At school, and in the army, there were gifts for friends, of course, but those were easy enough. All that was involved was a little thought, a cheerful straightforward exchange. This business of plotting and worrying over the right present, of secrets and schemes, of really caring about finding the right thing for each recipient, this was new. A family thing, he supposed. He rather liked it, he realised as he turned back to the stable, Ajax nudging him in the back in a friendly way as they walked.

'Mama.'

'Yes, Nathan?' Emilia carried on kneading dough while she waited for whatever awkward question her sons were about to throw at her this time. She recognised the tone of voice for a Big Question. They had covered *where do babies come from*? At least, they had in as much detail as she felt appropriate at their age. And they had talked about how they knew Papa was in Heaven and why Johnny Pullin was such a bully. This was obviously another important topic.

'Why doesn't the major marry you? He's looking for a wife and you'd do very well, even if he doesn't need someone who can cook.'

'Why—? How on earth do you know?' Her hands stilled, sticky dough hanging in a lump in midair.

'We asked him if he was married and he said *no*. So we asked why not and he said he was going to look for a wife after Christmas, but he's already got a cook so that doesn't matter.'

'Indeed? And why would I do very well, might I ask?' Her pulse was all over the place. What on earth had Hugo said to them?

'He said it would be nice if she was pretty. And you are pretty, we think. And he said she should be from the same sort of background because of knowing all about servants and tenants and things. But I expect you could learn that, couldn't you, Mama?'

'No,' she said bluntly. 'When the major says the same sort of background, he means a lady from a big house, someone who already has lots of servants and probably a title. Now, please don't say any more about it because he would not like you discussing his personal business.'

They shuffled off, looking chastened. Emilia attacked the dough, feeling much the same. Of course the nosy little beasts had asked Hugo and, of course, he had guessed whatever he said would get back to her and so he had made it quite clear where his boundaries were. And the humiliation of thinking he might find that necessary was like coals of fire in her stomach.

Granfer Janes had promised the thaw would set in after Christmas Day and when it did Major Lord Hugo Travers, or whatever he was, would ride out of her life. Emilia scooped the dough out of the bowl and thumped it on to a floured board. That could not happen soon enough for safety, although she feared she was never going to get him out of her head. Or her heart.

* * *

Christmas Eve was a flurry of activity. There was baking to be done for the Feast, barrels of ale to mark and men to direct on which to take and which to leave. Neighbours called in to borrow flour or yeast or simply to take refuge from their own busy homes over a mug of ale.

Parcels were set out on the dresser. Sweetmeats, books, whistles and new coats for the boys from her, the neatly wrapped package of handkerchiefs, a mysterious large box for the boys from Hugo and a tantalising soft package for her with his *best wishes.*

A lumpily wrapped oblong was for Ajax from Nathan and Joseph and they had labelled a jug for Hugo. One sniff told her that they had traded some odd jobs for Granfer's lethal spirits. But there was nothing from the boys for her. Perhaps she had misunderstood Hugo's hints about the carpenter and that wasn't what they had been doing these past few days.

Hugo vanished, muttering something about helping at the barn. She had no sooner got the boys scrubbed and into their best outfits when they called her out to the stable. 'We've lost Ajax's bit,' Nathan explained. 'We were cleaning it and now we can't find it.'

'You will have to look for it tomorrow, we haven't got time now. I have to get changed and if you two grub about in here you'll get dirty again.'

'But, Mama!' Nathan sounded frantic. 'You have to help us. We don't want to upset the major.'

'Oh, very well, but hurry up.'

Ten minutes later there was still no sign of it. 'I can't waste any more time on this, I'm sorry.'

She was back in the house before the wails of 'But, Mama!' died away. There was thump from above her head, then another. *An intruder?* Heart in her mouth, Emilia seized the poker from the hearth, gathered up her skirts and was halfway upstairs before she realised that the village was still cut off and that, surely, none of her neighbours would be above stairs. It must be a cat, or a rat…

She flung the door open and there was Hugo, in his shirt-sleeves, standing in the middle of her bedchamber. 'What on earth do you think you are doing in here?' she demanded. Then she saw the hammer in his hand and, on the wall opposite her bed, a set of shelves painted blue with a jug on it full of holly.

'Oh! That's what the boys were doing! Oh, Hugo, thank you for helping them.'

He smiled, revealing half-a-dozen nails clenched in his teeth and dropped them into the palm of his hand. 'You gave me such a shock I nearly swallowed that lot. They've made a good job of it—and here they come.'

The boys pounded into the room. 'Mama, do you like the shelves?'

'They are lovely. You are both so clever!'

'Mr Daventry did the stars on the ends and the major helped with the painting,' Joseph confessed.

'All craftsmen have assistants to deal with some of the routine parts of the work,' Emilia said, inspecting the shelves carefully. 'You have made a wonderful job of these.' They came and hugged her and she bent for their kisses, and thought how blessed she was and how ungrateful to wish for anything other than this. 'I must get changed now. If you go down and make an early tea, then we can open our presents. Oh, and take the poker.'

That sent them scampering for the head of the stairs. Hugo started to follow them, then stopped at her side. 'You are very lucky in your family,' he said. 'Thank you for letting me share it.' And he stooped to kiss her.

If Emilia had not moved it would have landed chastely enough on her cheek as he had intended, but she half-turned and his lips found hers. He could not move, she seemed frozen, all but the heat of her mouth against his. Then the hammer fell from his hand with a thud and she started back.

'No!'

'I did not mean to kiss you on the mouth.' *Did I?* He didn't know what he wanted any more, except that it was tied up in a complicated knot of desire and lust and a deep aching need and somehow a sense of responsibility for this gallant woman whose hazel eyes held a mixture of desire and despairing anger.

How could he feel responsible for her? Was it simply years of being an officer, and of his early training to care for his staff and tenants? Hugo held out one hand and Emilia slapped it sharply away.

'Just stop it! I am not a nun, I am still young and I am lonely and I know I have no hope of marrying again.' Her face was stark, her hands clenched and the words were tumbling out as though a dam had burst, no less intense because of her struggle to keep her voice low. 'I am not one of the villagers and neither can I ever expect to be courted by a gentleman. I ache and yearn when you touch me, but I am not going to be your mistress, or any man's, and it is unfair of you to tempt me so!'

'Emilia—' Appalled by the outburst, he dared not touch her.

She turned away. 'It is I who should apologise. I landed myself in this situation, I broke my parents' hearts, brought disgrace on them. Sometimes I wonder if Giles would have been killed if he had not had to play that night to provide for us.'

'That is irrational,' Hugo said sharply. 'He was a gamester, the sort of dispute he found himself in was an occupational hazard.'

'I know it is irrational!' She spun back, seemingly as angry with herself as with him. 'Do you think that makes it any easier to think about in the small hours of the morning? When I wonder what I have done to my sons? And don't tell me that they would not exist if I had not eloped, I cannot cope with any more rationality.'

Hugo saw the anger ebb out of her leaving her a tired, brave young woman with too much on her shoulders and weighing on her heart and only love and will-power to keep her going. 'I was managing until you came,' Emilia said with an honesty that he could see was hurting her. 'You are so…male. And you fill the house and our lives. And I like you and I know you are a decent man and I wish I could forget about my conscience and my sons and make love with you. Just once.'

'Emilia.' What could he say? *Sorry* was utterly inadequate. The truth, that he wanted her just as much, was impossible. 'There is a thaw coming, I will be gone tomorrow.'

'Good,' she said, her voice flat. 'Now, let us go downstairs and smile and welcome Christmas into this house.'

Hugo followed her down the stairs and conjured up a smile with the same effort of will he employed to appear calm and cheerful before a battle when his guts were in a knot and his hands wanted to shake and he could show neither fear nor uncertainty before his men.

The twins were standing as close as they could to the pile of presents, their hands behind their backs as if they had to physically stop themselves touching.

'Which shall we open first?' Emilia said. The happiness in her voice was real, he realised. However desperate she felt, she could find joy with her sons.

'You first, Mama,' Nathan said and handed her the parcel Hugo had wrapped so carefully. He had stuffed his saddlebags with portable treasures brought back from France in case he yielded to the pressing invitations from his fellow officers and found himself needing to give gifts to his hosts.

She caught her lower lip between her teeth as she untied the twine and folded back the silver paper and then the tissue that enfolded the shawl. It was silk, a swirling pattern of gold and brown and reds like a drift of autumn leaves.

'Oh,' she breathed. 'Oh, how very lovely.' She draped it carefully around her shoulders and rubbed her cheek against its

softness. It brought out the rich brown in her hair and the gold in her eyes. 'Thank you, Hugo, I will treasure this.'

Joseph thrust the bottle into Hugo's hands. 'That's from us.'

He opened it and took a cautious sip, the spirit burning its way straight to his stomach. 'Thank you very much. I must treat this with care and make it last or I will be as drunk as a lord.'

That made the boys hoot with laughter, but Emilia sent him a steady, frowning look. Drunkenness was no laughing matter for her, it seemed. But she laughed when he unwrapped Ajax's present, a name board for his stable carved with rather uneven letters.

The boys were delighted with their sweets and the whistles, which they promised not to blow inside, and their very grown-up new coats. And that just left the box from Hugo, which they dived into to emerge with a wooden fort and an entire regiment of carved and painted toy soldiers.

'How on earth did you produce that from your saddlebags?' Emilia asked as they fell to their knees and immediately began to lay siege to the enemy positions.

'I bought the soldiers from one of my men who makes them as a pastime and I got your village carpenter to make the fort.' They watched in seeming harmony for a while, then Emilia whisked upstairs to change and Hugo was dragged into advising on strategy.

They needed cannon and an opposing regiment, he thought, amused by the boys' total immersion in their play. He could look through his old toys that must be stored somewhere in the attics at home. There were boxes of toy soldiers, he recalled.

And then he heard Emilia's footsteps on the stairs and realised that once he had left there was no coming back, no possible contact. He had ripped through the fragile walls she had built around herself simply because he had yielded to an impulse to hold her and then had not had the understanding to see what damage his kisses would do. And she in turn had rent some barrier he did not even realise he had erected and left him

vulnerable to emotions and feelings he did not know he possessed. Or perhaps he had not possessed them until he met her.

Hugo looked up as she came into the humble room and
thought she lit it up as though it was an elegant drawing room
lined with candles. She was wearing a green silk gown, simply trimmed with narrow lace around its scooped neck and at
the edge of the puffed sleeves. The shawl he had given her was
around her shoulders and her hair had been plaited and coiled
on her head like a coronet.

She looked beautiful even as she came closer and he saw
that the dress was faded and had darns in the folds of the skirt
and that the string of beads around her neck were the cheapest
polished pebbles. There was a small burn on the back of her
hand from the oven and he knew her hands were a little rough
despite the pot of cream by the sink. The shoes that peeped
out below her hem were not silken slippers, but simple leather.

But her cheeks glowed with colour, her lips were curved
into that generous smile that always made his heart contract
with pleasure and the smooth creamy swell of her bosom above
the narrow lace was as lovely as any Society lady could boast.
He wanted to tell her how beautiful she was, but he could find
no words that would not hurt her more than he had already.

'That's Mama's special gown,' Nathan confided proudly.
'The one she ran away with Papa wearing.'

'I can quite see why he wanted to run away with your
mother,' Hugo said.

Emilia laughed. 'You are all arrant flatterers, but I will
wager I am the only lady at the feast with three gentlemen to
escort me. Shall we go?'

He helped with boots and cloaks and lanterns, banked up
the fire safely and doused candles. He was reaching for his
own cloak when he found himself staring blankly into the
shadows of the taproom.

'Hugo?'

Emilia was waiting by the door with the boys. He shook off

the thought that this cottage was home and that he dreaded returning to the forty rooms of Long Burnham Hall, the dozens of servants, the comfort and the privilege. 'Coming,' Hugo said and picked up his lantern.

Chapter Seven

The snow was lit up by a dozen lanterns bobbing through the night as the inhabitants of the hamlet wound their way through the narrow trenches in the snow towards the barn. Voices called greetings and, despite his introspection, Hugo felt his spirits rise. The thought of a party composed of virtual strangers, with whom he had little in common, all with traditions he did not share, would normally have filled him with horror at the prospect of boredom and the unpleasant feeling of loneliness within a crowd.

But he found himself waving and smiling at the men he had met in the taproom, bowing to women he had come across when he had been out and about during the day. They grinned or waved or blushed as was their individual natures and he shepherded his little party into the barn on a wave of goodwill.

His first thought was to recall that he must explain this to the barn's owner on the morrow, the second that, even if they managed to burn the place down with all the candles and lanterns, let alone the roasting pit steaming outside by the wide doorway, it would be worth paying for.

Benches had been set up all round the walls with makeshift tables in front. An ill-assorted band was attempting to tune up in one corner: two fiddles, an ancient serpent that was probably part of the church's music, a flute and a drum. At the opposite end the women were laying their contributions to the feast on cloth-draped trestles and two barrels of Emilia's ale stood next to an array of mugs and beakers.

The smell of roasting beef drifted through the doors every time someone entered, the children were shrieking with excitement as they played tag up and down the central space and bunting and evergreens decorated every corner. From the central beam hung a great swag of mistletoe.

'Now this is what I call a party,' Hugo said to Emilia.

'You can help me with the special mulled ale,' she said when they had disentangled themselves and the boys from their outdoor clothing, changed their shoes and Emilia had tied her new shawl carefully around her shoulders and then behind her waist to keep it out of the pot. Two of the men brought the cauldron in from the fire pit.

'There are bottles of rum and brandy back there. I need one of each.' She was stirring in brown sugar, cloves, spices. 'All of both bottles,' she said with a grin as Hugo raised a questioning eyebrow. As he poured them in she stirred the pot and then grated nutmeg over the top, companionably close, nudging him out of the way as she reached for a spoon to taste.

Was he forgiven? he wondered and then realised that of course he was and that made no difference. Emilia would forgive him for his thoughtlessness, his clumsy failure to see what was in front of his nose and that forgiveness would make no difference whatsoever to the feelings he had stirred up in her and the loneliness those feelings threw into sharp relief.

'Mulled ale's ready, Billy,' she called to one of the men. He rang a battered hand bell and the adults began to crowd round and dip ale into their mugs.

'What happens now?' Hugo carried steaming, fragrant ale for both of them over to one of the benches.

'When the band sorts itself out they'll begin to play and there will be dancing for an hour until the roast is ready. Then we'll eat and people will take it in turns to sing or recite and then, once the feasting is over, they'll draw the boards and the dancing will start again until everyone is exhausted.' Emilia's eyes were sparkling with anticipation as she sipped her ale and the band finally stopped tootling and scraping and launched into a jig.

Hugo thought about the *ton* parties and balls he had attended and the carefully cultivated ennui of the ladies with their attempts to appear sophisticated. Emilia expected to enjoy herself and that showed in her smile and her laughter and her tapping toes.

He drained his mug recklessly and stood up. 'Come on, let's dance.'

'Do you dance?' She looked up at him. 'This sort of thing, I mean? It is hardly Almack's.'

'And thank heavens for that,' Hugo said with real feeling. 'One thing about fighting with Wellington, the man loves to socialise and he expects his officers to as well. We've held dances in hay barns, castles, inns and under the stars and the measures are more likely to be country style than anything else.'

There were a dozen couples making up two sets, enough not to make Emilia conspicuous dancing with him, he calculated. Once they formed up and were off, he realised that she did not care and, in any case, was probably set on dancing with every man present before the evening was out.

They wove and twisted, promenaded and spun, laughing when they bumped into people as more and more of the company came on to the floor and the rafters rang with the thump of feet on the beaten earth floor, the beat of the drum and the sound of laughter.

'The mistletoe!' someone called. 'Kisses as we go under!'

He looked down at her, worried about her reaction, but Emilia was laughing and held her face up for his kiss as they whirled underneath. Time stood still for a moment as their lips met and their eyes locked. Under his feet the floor of the barn seemed to shift. The onlookers clapped and cheered as they did for every kissing couple and then they separated and joined hands with the next pair.

An hour later, dizzy with dancing and mulled ale, Hugo collapsed on to a bench with his latest partner, the miller's buxom daughter. 'I am exhausted!'

'Here's the roast coming in,' she said. 'Cor, that's a fine beast and no mistake. Time to eat now, Major.'

He wondered whether he should sit away from Emilia, but the boys found him and towed him off to take his place with them.

'Enjoying yourself?' Emilia asked as they passed platters and forks along the table and then helped distribute the plates of food for everyone to help themselves.

'Very much.' He heaped steaming beef on the plates around him.

'You did not expect to, did you?' she asked, her smile quizzical and somehow sad.

'No,' he admitted. 'I thought I would feel out of place, that people would not truly welcome a stranger in their midst.'

'You are not a stranger,' she said softly. 'You have helped the old folks, worked and drunk with the men, and made this feast possible. They like you.'

He wanted to ask, *Do you like me?* She desired him, she had said so and her kisses told him so, without words. But perhaps she would feel the same about any halfway decent man who intruded so intimately into her life. She enjoyed being with him, he knew that. Emilia was too honest and too transparent to hide that she liked his company. She trusted him with her sons, and perhaps that trust was the hardest to win from her.

He wanted more and he did not have the words for it, only that strange tight sensation in his chest and a feeling of impending unhappiness. And that shifting sensation again, as though everything familiar was moving out of alignment.

Tomorrow he would be gone, back to his ancestral home.

Back to his duties and responsibilities. Back to the search for the right, the correct, the *proper* wife for the Earl of Burnham. Duty and responsibility. That was what he was good at.

They ate until they were stuffed and then sat comfortably digesting while the remainder of those willing to perform did their recitations, songs or, in the case of Mr Daventry, the carpenter, conjuring tricks involving coins in small boys' ears, a bemused chicken and vanishing playing cards.

Hugo cheered, laughed and clapped with the rest and then realised that the company was calling for Emilia to sing. She came out willingly enough, obviously used to performing. Her voice was clear, light, untrained, but very sweet and carrying. The songs she sang were all happy ones and yet Hugo found his vision blurring and realised, to his horror, that he was on the edge of tears.

He blew his nose under cover of the applause and thought he had himself under control by the time Emilia made her way back to his side, blushing a little.

'What is wrong?' she asked, cocking her head to one side the better to study his face. 'Was my singing that bad?'

'Nothing is wrong.' He cleared his throat. 'Your singing was very lovely, it is just this smoke. Look, they're starting the dancing again—shall we?'

She was still looking quizzical, but she gave him her hand and they launched into an energetic set of Strip the Willow, which was, Hugo discovered, quite sufficient to drive any maudlin sentimentality out of his head. Because that was what it was. It had to be.

An hour later, in dire need of a rest, he looked around for Emilia to see if she would like a drink and could not find her. The miller's daughter was catching her breath by the door. 'Have you seen Mrs Weston?' he asked.

'She went out ten minutes past,' she said and frowned. 'That's a while to be out in this chill.' The frown became a

look of concern. 'Come to think of it, Lawrence Bond followed her out. No harm in it, of course, only I wouldn't want
to be alone with him myself. He watches.' She gave a theatri-
cal shudder. 'Creepy-like.'

It was enough to give Hugo the creeps. 'Thank you.' He
turned up his coat collar and went out into the gloom.

'Mr Bond…Lawrence. I came out for a breath of air and now
I am cold and I really do not want to stand out here convers-
ing.' Emilia took a step forwards, expecting him to retreat, but
the smallholder stayed square in her path and the steep snow
banks were too high to let her go around him.

'It wasn't conversation I had in mind,' he said with the arrogant smirk she so disliked. 'I can keep you warm.'

She should never have come around the corner of the barn,
but she had wanted a clear view of the sky to see if it was beginning to cloud over, heralding the promised thaw. 'I told you,
I wish to go back inside.' It was ridiculous to feel a twist of
fear, not with all those people so close. But if she called out,
would anyone hear over the music and the talking?

'Come on, stop this coyness. If you can give it to that major,
you can give it to me. I see you watching me, batting your eyelashes and pretending to be so virtuous.'

'If I watch you, Lawrence Bond, it is because I do not trust
you! And I am a virtuous woman, you slimy-tongued lecher.'

'If you're not, then you can stop being coy and if you are,
then you'll be missing a real man between your legs.' Her insults just seemed to roll off him.

Emilia snatched a comb from her hair and gripped it. 'You
touch me and I'll rake your face with this,' she threatened.

'Oh, yes?' He was too big and too fast for her and her instinctive shrinking from violence made her slow to retaliate.

Emilia found herself lashed tightly into his arms, hard
against his chest as he sought for her mouth with his. His lips
were wet and his breath smelled of onions. She kicked out

and then suddenly he was gone, yanked backwards and then slammed into the knapped flint wall of the barn.

Hugo pulled him forwards by his neckcloth, rammed his right fist into his chin and tossed him into the snow bank. He looked at Emilia in the faint light, and she knew what he saw— her hair tumbled down her back, her dress askew. Would he think she had encouraged Bond?

'What did he do to you? Has he hurt you?' Hugo demanded. He was going to kill the lout. He had touched her, frightened her. *Emilia.*

'He wouldn't let me go, he tried to kiss me,' she stammered, dragging her hand across her face as if to obliterate the feel of Bond's mouth on her cheek.

He put his mouth on her and he had wanted more than that, would have taken more than that if he'd had the chance. My woman. He tried to ravish my woman.

Hugo bent down, dragged the snow-encrusted man to his feet and thrust his face close to his while he fought the killing rage. If Bond had been a gentleman, an officer, he would have called him out and put a bullet through him. Some faint trace of restraint penetrated through the red mist. He couldn't call him out and he could not beat him to a pulp in front of Emilia.

When he finally found his voice, it sounded as if he was speaking through gravel. 'You will apologise to this lady for your words and your actions and I might, just might, refrain from taking you apart.'

Lawrence sagged in his grip, too much a bully to have the courage to fight back, Hugo realised. 'Sorry,' he muttered.

'Try again.' Hugo shook him.

'I am very sorry, Mrs Weston.'

'That's better. Now, you listen to me, you snivelling lout.' Hugo punctuated each sentence with a brisk shake, like a terrier with a particularly large rat. 'Tomorrow I will call on Sir Philip and I will tell him how you have behaved, without naming the lady. And I will ask him, as a favour to me, to ensure that, if any complaint of such behaviour comes to his ears again, you are tried for assault and harassment. Is that clear?'

'Yes,' Bond muttered.

'Right, get out of here.' Another shove sent the man sprawling. If he held on to him for a moment longer he was going to go back on his word and dismember him. Bond scrambled away as a sudden gust of wind threw moisture into Hugo's face.

Emilia tugged at his arm. 'Hugo, it is raining, the thaw has begun.'

'Come here.' He pulled her gently into the shelter of his coat, opening the sides around her. 'We need to get you tidied up before we go back inside. I saw a lean-to around the side.' He could feel her heart pounding. Emilia allowed him to steer her around the corner and into shelter.

'I did not go outside with him,' she said and stepped away so they were no longer touching.

If he did not do something, he was going to yank her into his arms and kiss her until they both forgot every iota of sense. Hugo took the comb from her limp fingers and scooped up the fallen hair. *His woman,* and it had taken that lout Bond to make him see it. The thought of her with another man made him want to snarl with primitive male possessiveness.

'I realise that.' He managed to keep his voice calm. She would be terrified if she realised the raw sexual hunger he felt. 'There, your hair is respectable again. Just straighten your gown and no one will be any the wiser.'

'I…I want to go home.'

Her voice shook and for the first time she let him see her vulnerability. Something inside him shifted into certainty. *I love her. Oh, God, I love her.* So this was what it felt like? It was supposed to be a wonderful emotion, but he felt fear and longing and the vertiginous certainty that his entire life was slipping out of control. *I can't do this. I don't understand it. I'll hurt her.*

'Go and find the boys and get them into their coats.' He

gave her a gentle push. 'I'll watch your back, but I won't come in for a few minutes.'

He watched her along the path and into the spill of warmth and light and sound before he leaned back against the wall and swore viciously and inventively. He should leave her. He understood now that she needed love and trust and warmth and he did not know if he could ever break down those walls around his emotions enough to give her what she deserved.

But she was not safe. She was too pretty, too trusting, too vulnerable and unprotected, earning her living in a manner which exposed her to men, familiar or strangers, day and night. She had opened her door to him with complete trust and he could have been a thief, a murderer, a rapist, for all she knew.

He could speak to Sir Philip about Bond tomorrow, but while it might deter that individual it could not protect her from another and the thought made his skin crawl. He would be gone and she would be alone. Stamping the snow off his boots, he made his way back into the barn and found Emilia shepherding two yawning, but reluctant, boys in front of her.

'Major, we were just going back. I'll leave the door on the latch for you.'

'I will come, too,' he said. 'If you will just wait while I find my cloak and gloves.'

They tramped back through the drizzle, the path slippery and treacherous underfoot with the runnels of melting snow. Joseph was complaining that the snowman they had built with their friends would wash away and Nathan added to the gloom by pointing out that their lessons with the vicar would start again.

'And the major will leave,' Joseph wailed, suddenly realising what the disappearance of the snow would mean for their guest.

'And I am sure he will be delighted to be home after all this time,' Emilia said in a cheerful tone that Hugo was beginning to recognise. It was the voice she would use if they were on a boat sinking in the middle of the river surrounded by crocodiles, her *Mother is keeping calm, there is no need to worry* voice.

She doesn't want me to go either, he thought. He checked on the animals, made up the fire, then put the kettle on to boil, listening to the murmur of voices upstairs, the soft sound of Emilia's footsteps as she put the boys to bed. At last she came downstairs, her feet slow and hesitant on the steps as though she was unutterably weary.

'I've made tea.' Hugo held out the cup. 'Come and sit down and relax.'

'Thank you.' She curled up in her chair, hands tight around the warmth of the cup. 'You enjoyed the Feast?'

'Very much, especially your singing.' Such banal conversation. *Say what you feel.* But the words would not come. 'I am sorry it was spoiled for you at the end. Has Bond been a persistent problem?'

'No. He stares, but he has never tried anything like that before. I doubt he will again.'

She fell silent, gazing into the tea as though she could read the future in the brown depths.

Suddenly he knew what he had to do. 'Emilia, I need to talk to you.'

'Yes? I am sorry, I was drifting. You will want to have an early breakfast, no doubt, and be off at first light.'

'That was not it.' Now that it came to the point Hugo was not sure how to say this. It was hardly the sort of thing a man had practice in, unless he was very unlucky. 'Will you marry me?'

Chapter Eight

Emilia stared at Hugo. Surely she had not heard him correctly? 'Did you just ask me to—?'

'Marry me. Yes.' He might have been asking her to pass the salt.

'But why?'

It was his turn to stare at her. Perhaps she was dreaming. She was very tired, had drunk at least two mugs of mulled ale and Bond accosting her had been upsetting. It was her fantasy, this man proposing to her. But not like this—it must be a dream. Or a nightmare.

'Why? Because it is completely untenable you living like this. The work is too hard for you, the future uncertain, the boys are growing up fast. You have been born and raised a lady, you should not be here.'

'Forgive me, but what has that to do with you, Hugo? Or should I say, my lord?'

'How did you know I have a title?' As he asked it she saw the realisation dawn in those intelligent blue eyes. 'Ah, yes, that slip when we were all drinking here the other night.'

'Who are you, precisely?' There was a cold lump of misery in her chest. He was her dream and he was offering her marriage because a *lady* should not be working as an alewife. Her parents had rejected her because she had disgraced them, now this man was dismissing everything she had toiled to build up—her hard-won business, her independence, her plans—as demeaning, something to be rescued from by a gentleman doing his duty.

'I am Hugo Travers, Earl of Burnham.' Her reaction was obviously not what he had been expecting.

But of course, any rational woman would fall weeping at his feet in gratitude, she thought savagely.

'I hardly felt it appropriate to march in here proclaiming my title. It was irrelevant.'

'If you had dropped in for a mug of ale, then you could be Hugo Travers the night-soil carter for all I care.' Tears were stinging the back of her eyes, but she blinked them back furiously and set her cup down with a snap. 'You should have told me who you were instead of living in my house under false pretences. And then you have the effrontery to make me a proposal like this!'

'Like what?' he demanded. 'I am hardly offering you a *carte blanche*, Emilia. I made you an honourable proposal.' He hesitated. 'From the heart.'

Wonderful! He suddenly decides to introduce feelings into this! 'A completely irrational proposal, you mean. I repeat, what has my life and my circumstances got to do with you?'

He stood up, towering over her. 'I feel responsible for you.'

'Why? If that storm had not happened, you would not so much have passed my door. You would never have heard of me.'

'But it did happen and I am here and now I know you and I cannot simply ride away from here and trust that a few words to Sir Philip will keep you safe. And even if they do, you should not be labouring like this, working so hard, past your strength.'

'I am not your responsibility,' she said. So that was it. He would lead and nurture his troops, care for his tenants, rescue a drowning kitten because that was what earls did. *Noblesse oblige.* Presumably she came into the drowning-kitten category.

Emilia got to her feet, toe to toe with Hugo. She had to tip her head back to be able to look him in the eye, but it was better than cowering in the chair. 'You will ride away tomorrow, my lord, and you will forget me because I am nothing to you and I *can* be nothing to you. I might have been born a lady, but I threw my cap over the windmill, disgraced myself and my parents, lived like a gypsy with a gamester and now I am an alewife and a mother and I live in a little Hertfordshire hamlet.

'A lady would, no doubt, thank you for your obliging proposal. I, on the other hand, have the greatest dislike of being patronised and, having had the infinite blessing of being loved, I know what a proposal of marriage should be. And that, my lord, was not it!'

Memory and loss, and what she was very much afraid was a new, fragile love for this man, was suddenly too much to deal with. She had let herself dream, weave fantasies, feel desire and much more, knowing that those dreams could never come true. And now, here he was, the man of those dreams, offering her marriage because he felt responsible for her, because he thought she needed rescuing from the life she had built for herself.

'I have made a mull of this,' Hugo said, his mouth a hard line. 'I should have told you how I feel.'

'You, my lord, have made a complete pig's ear of it,' she retorted roundly. 'And I do not want to know how you feel.'

'I was abrupt and I have hurt your pride.' He was obviously working it out. Sooner or later he was going to come to the correct, humiliating conclusion—that the main reason he had hurt her was because she had been foolish enough to fall in love with him.

'I do not want to discuss this any further.' She tried to sidestep in the narrow space between his body and her chair.

'Emilia, there was something, surely? Something when we touched, when I held you.' He caught her by the shoulders, his big hands cupping bones that suddenly felt very frail. 'When we kissed. Under the mistletoe...' He bent and took her lips, gently, possessively.

It was so different from the other kiss she had experienced that night, *this* man was so different, that she found she could not move, only open her mouth to the urging of his, let his tongue sweep in to explore and tease and tantalise. She felt heat and found she had arched into his body, her own in its thin silk moulded to his. She could feel the muscles of his thighs, the strength of his chest, the erection that proclaimed beyond any doubt that, whatever else he felt, he certainly desired her.

Hugo's right hand slid down to cup her behind and he lifted her against that blatant ridge, moving his hips to tease and arouse. She moaned into his mouth, heat and passion and desire clamouring to break down the flimsy barricade that common sense and self-preservation were holding up against his sensual onslaught.

When he broke the kiss she simply hung there, quivering and tense in his arms. 'Let me show you, Emilia. Let me come to your bed tonight and prove we can be good together. You want to, you cannot hide it.' His hand cupped her aching breast, smoothed over the nipple that was pressing against the taut fabric almost to the point of pain.

His lips roamed over her jaw, down her neck, nuzzled into the angle of her shoulder, his tongue tracing heat and moisture as she shivered and the lights danced inside her closed lids and her body surged with the feminine power and longing and arousal that she had taught herself to ignore until she had believed it was dead. Until Hugo.

Emilia found herself lifted, swung up into his arms. For a moment of delicious surrender she let her head fall on to his shoulder, let her fingers sift into the thick dark hair, waited for the words that were the only ones that would make this right. They did not come, so she said, 'Hugo. I cannot do this.'

It was not because it was immoral, she was painfully aware of that. It was because she could somehow live with dreams

and might-have-beens, but she did not think she could bear to
know what it was to lie with him and then to lose him. Because soon he was going to recover from this quixotic fit of
gallantry and realise that, instead of the well-bred, reputable,
well-connected virgin an earl should be marrying, he had tied
himself to a disgraced daughter of a baron who had not even
the support of her own family behind her.

He was halfway across the room, but he stopped and let
her slide to her feet.

'Thank you,' Emilia said with as much composure as she
could muster. 'I will see you at breakfast. Please…do not let
the boys guess that anything is wrong.'

'I will endeavour not to do any more damage,' he said bitterly, turned on his heel and went into the taproom, leaving
her shivering in the middle of the kitchen.

Hugo flung himself down on one of the benches, put his el-
bows on the battered table and sank his head in his hands. He
wondered bleakly what the hell had he been thinking of. The
answer, quite simply, was that he had not thought at all. He
did not trust this new-found emotion of love, he did not know
how to speak of it, to express it. So it had been the old Hugo
who had proposed, the logical, controlled, disciplined man.
She was at risk, she was in the wrong place and working too
hard—those were arguments he could make without ventur-
ing anywhere near emotion.

And it was quite clear he had insulted and distressed her.
With surgically painful honesty Hugo began to analyse his
feelings in a way he never had before. He knew Emilia was not
his responsibility, so why pretend she was? Because Lawrence
Bond had aroused a violent male possessiveness in him? Yes, if
he was honest. Raw male sexual possessiveness, even though
she was not his possession, not a mistress or a servant whose
services were bought with coin.

He wanted her, physically, with a passion that was hard to

deny. But he was a mature man in control of his desires. He could walk away from that—he had just proved as much.

Emilia was unsuitable as a wife for an earl and yet that had not weighed with him for a moment. Didn't she realise what that meant? How was he going to make this right? Worn out with puzzling, Hugo let his head fall on to his folded arms and slept.

He woke in the small hours, cramped and stiff, blinking into the dull glow of the banked fire as he tried to separate jumbled dreams and reality. Making his bed before the hearth was routine now and he managed it without lighting the candle, then lay down and closed his eyes again.

She will not believe you if you tell her you love her now. Thoroughly awake now, he rolled on to his back and considered the situation as if it was a matter of battle tactics.

His friends who had made love matches had always been a source of mildly baffled amusement to their fellow officers, but he could understand them now. His happiness was tied up entirely in Emilia and what had seemed important, the fact that she was making her living running a village ale house, became utterly irrelevant.

He knew she had the courage and the intelligence to become a countess, to help him manage that great estate, to carve a role for herself. She could run a charity, manage a political salon, patronise artists, whatever she wanted, whatever would fulfil her.

If she wanted to. That was the rub. If she did not want him, could not love him, then he must let her stay here because it was her happiness that mattered, not his.

Hugo turned over and thumped the pillow. Somehow he had to convince her that he was sincere, that she could trust him, that perhaps, one day, she might come to love him, too.

But he had insulted her and she was quite right, he had patronised her, characterised the life she had made against all the odds for herself and her sons as something to be ashamed of, something she needed rescuing from. He buried his face in the pillow and groaned at the realisation that he had capped his insulting, and utterly unromantic, proposal with the suggestion that mutual desire was enough to make this all right.

Greeting Emilia tomorrow with the news that he was in love with her was only going to make things worse, he had enough sense to realise that. He must leave tomorrow and try to find a way back to her.

Hugo roused himself as the old long-case clock hammered out five strokes. He washed, shaved, dressed with the speed learned on campaign, groomed, fed and watered Ajax, put away his bedding, tossed the used linen into the wash basket and then gathered together his belongings to pack the saddle bags.

That was all, except for his holsters and his sabre. He stretched up to lift them down from the high mantelshelf and his cuff caught folded paper, sending it falling into the hearth. He dropped his sabre and grabbed for it, snatching it from the hot coals at the cost of singed fingers. It was a letter, folded, addressed, but unsealed.

Lord Peterscroft, Albany Manor, near Bedford.

Of course he should replace it where he had found it, but this, he guessed, was addressed to Emilia's father. If so, it might be the one clue he had to find his way out of this maze. Above his head he could hear Emilia stirring, the sound of feet moving about the bedchamber. He followed her in his mind for a moment, imagining her in her plain flannel nightgown, her hair in its heavy plait over her shoulder. She would be soft and warm from her bed, shivering a little in the chill of the room.

Hugo unfolded the letter and read it. Emilia had written it in a small, neat hand and he formed the impression that she had done so slowly, thinking through every word, every phrase.

Dear Mama and Papa,
I know you do not wish to hear from me, or see me, but

it is almost Christmas and I hope you will forgive one final effort on my part to reach out to you. I look at your two grandsons, Nathan and Joseph, and see how fast they are growing. I see so much of both of you in them—your eyes, Mama, your height, Papa.

They are good boys, intelligent, cheerful, hard-working and loving. Dare I hope that you would want to meet them, to have the chance to love them in return as I know they would love you?

All I ask is a word from you, I would not ask you to see me, just the boys. I hope you are both in good health and spirits,

Your loving daughter, Emilia.

Little Gatherborne, Hertfordshire

Hugo folded the letter, looked again at the address and re-placed it where he had found it. Then, schooling his face into an untroubled smile, he opened the door into the kitchen and met the onrush of the twins.

'Merry Christmas, Major!'

'Merry Christmas.' He scooped them up, one in each arm, and looked over their heads at Emilia who stood at the foot of the stairs. She did not look as though she had enjoyed a wink of sleep. 'Merry Christmas, Mrs Weston.'

She came into the room and glanced through the door at his stacked bags. 'Christmas greetings to you, Major. You are packed, I see.'

'I will be on my way immediately after breakfast.'

'Excellent,' she said, her smile serene, her eyes dark and unhappy. 'You must make good time towards home, for the roads will be heavily mired.'

'And I will call on Sir Philip as I pass to make all right about the barn, and the other matter.'

'Thank you. No, boys, stop whining, of course the major must leave. He does not belong here.'

Brutal but honest, Hugo thought as he ate and talked to the boys and managed not to indulge himself by glancing constantly at Emilia.

When he had saddled up and was standing in the yard, the twins stood beside their mother and solemnly held out their hands to be shaken. He had no trouble keeping a straight face as he did so, but when he came to Emilia and she held out her right hand he took it, turned it and brought it to his lips.

'Thank you for your hospitality, ma'am. I will not forget it, nor you.'

Her fingers were cold in his ungloved hand. They trembled a little, but she did not pull away. 'We will not forget you either, Major.'

The way she met his eyes, her own dark and shadowed, gave him hope, even while he castigated himself for taking comfort from her pain. Surely she would not care, would be only too pleased to be rid of him, if she did not feel *something* for him?

He swung up into the saddle and turned Ajax in the direction she showed him. 'That will take you to Longfield Manor and Sir Philip.'

He thought those would be her last words, but she ran forwards and caught the rein, reached up with the other hand to touch his knee. 'Be safe, Hugo. Be happy.'

Their fingers curled together and his tightened as if to pull her up on to the saddle in front of him. Hugo made himself release his grip. 'One of those wishes is in the hands of Providence, the other... I will see what I can do to bring that about. Goodbye, Emilia.'

Chapter Nine

'What are your New Year resolutions, Emilia?' The miller's daughter leaned against the kitchen-door jamb while Emilia counted out the coppers for the bag of flour she had brought.

'To finish the patchwork quilt I have been struggling with for two years, start a flower border at the edge of my vegetable plot and learn to fly like a bird,' Emilia replied with a smile, sending the other woman off into peals of laugher. *And forget about Hugo, which will be as easy as the flying.* 'What are your resolutions, Maudie?'

'Catch that Willie Carter and get him to propose,' Maudie said with determination. 'I'm tired of him flirting with every girl for five miles around.'

'Good luck, I am sure you can do it,' Emilia encouraged while she told herself that she would forget Hugo sooner if she had not taken his pillow case from the laundry basket and had been sleeping with it under her cheek every night since he had left. 'Have you time for a cup of tea?'

'Oh, that'll be a treat, if you can spare it.'

'Major Travers sent me a canister of it as thanks for taking him in during the snow at Christmas.' It was a wicked pleasure to talk about Hugo. He had not only sent the tea in its big black-and-gold tin, but also a side of bacon, a sugar loaf, a whole round of cheese and a shiny new spice box stuffed with cloves and three kinds of peppercorns with a nutmeg in the centre.

There was nothing that was not appropriate as a gift under the circumstances and the note was impersonal and respectful, of course, even if it was now folded in her underwear drawer, tied up with a scrap of ribbon.

They drank their tea and gossiped and speculated on the new curate's pursuit of the vicar's eldest daughter.

'I must be off,' Maudie said at last and Emilia came with her to the door. 'Look! Fancy that, some nobs have lost their way, I'll be bound.'

Emilia followed her pointing finger to where the track came round the barn and there, indeed, was a smart black travelling carriage with a pair of fine bays in the harness and, behind it, a big, raw-boned grey horse she would have recognised anywhere.

'Hugo?'

'Cor,' Maudie said with relish. 'I'll take myself off, then. Looks like you've got visitors.'

He spurred past the carriage and came down the hill, touching his hat to Maudie as he passed and reining in just short of where Emilia stood trying not to let her jaw drop and fighting emotions that ranged from delight, to shock, to anger.

'Good morning, Emilia.'

'What on earth are you doing here?' she demanded, too shaken for good manners.

Hugo swung out of the saddle. 'I have brought you some visitors.'

The carriage drew up and, with complete incredulity, she recognised the coachman. 'John?'

Hugo opened the door and lowered the step before the groom could jump down. 'We are arrived, ma'am.'

The woman who descended on his arm stood for a moment staring at Emilia then, with a sound between a laugh and a sob, held open her arms. 'Lia, darling!'

'Mama?' And then her father climbed down, bare-headed and startlingly grey-haired in the thin winter sunlight. 'Papa?' And then she was running into their arms and crying and being hugged and somehow they were all inside and Hugo was making tea.

'How did you get here? I was going to write and then...'

'After we did not reply to your other letter you decided not to send this one,' her father said sadly. 'I should never have written as I did, I cannot tell you how often I have wished those words back.'

'But I wrote three times, after we eloped and then when the twins were born and again when Giles was killed.' Her hands were locked tight with her mother's and she just wanted to lay her head down on that familiar, comforting bosom and weep for sheer joy.

'We only received the first and we had no idea where to find you. Oh, my dear, Hugo has told us about Giles. I am so very sorry, he was a charming man, even though he was so wild. But the boys! I cannot believe we have two grandsons, and twins, Hugo says.'

'But how did Hugo find you?' She took the cup he pressed into her hands. 'I never told him your name.'

'I read the letter, the one you never sent. It was on the mantelshelf and it fell off when I took my weapons down. It was unconscionably rude of me, but when I saw the address I guessed who it was for. I thought if your parents were hostile I would not tell them where you were, but they wanted to find you so badly. Can you forgive me for meddling?'

His eyes told her he wanted forgiveness for more than that. 'Yes,' she said and hoped he could read in her face that *everything* was forgiven.

Then the door flew open and the boys rushed in shouting for Hugo and demanding to know where the carriage had come from. They stopped dead in their tracks when they saw the two strangers sitting either side of the fire, tugged off their caps and executed, rather jerkily, their best bows.

'Sir, ma'am. Sorry to have made a noise.'

'Nathan, Joseph. These are my mother and father. Your grandparents.'

They were wide-eyed as their grandmother swept them into a hug and then their grandfather had Joseph on his knee and all four were talking non-stop. Emilia found she was being held very firmly in Hugo's arms and that she was weeping all down his beautiful linen shirt.

'Thank you,' she managed when he pressed a handkerchief into her hand.

'Don't mention it. This is one of a set of very beautifully embroidered handkerchiefs a lady of my acquaintance made for me.'

'Emilia.' Her mother stood up, one of Nathan's hands in hers. 'We are staying at the Sun in Hemel Hempstead. We thought the boys might like to come for a ride in the carriage and to have luncheon with us so we can get to know each other.'

'But, I can make luncheon here,' she began.

'I think Lord Travers has something he wishes to discuss with you,' her father said, straight-faced, although she could detect a familiar and much-loved twinkle in his eyes. 'We'll be back for dinner, shall we? Say, six o'clock? Then we can catch up on *all* the news.'

All? 'I…yes, if you can cope with them. Boys, you must be on your best behaviour for your grandparents.'

They were more than eager. Within five minutes Emilia was alone in the kitchen with Hugo. 'You are the most interfering, masterful, stubborn man I have ever met,' she said shakily. 'And I cannot thank you enough. I have taken that letter down every day since you left and then returned it. If I had sent it and nothing had come back I think it would have been the end of the dream that one day I would be forgiven. While it had not been sent, then I could still hope.'

'I think it is your parents who are asking for forgiveness. As I am.' He sat down at the table six feet from her with the board between them. 'I asked you to marry me in a way that could only insult your courage and your hard work and all you have achieved to make a living for your family and to bring those boys up to be the delight that they are.'

He looked up from his clasped hands. 'I spoke as I did because I could not express what I truly felt. When you turned me down I was forced to face what I was feeling and I knew I had to learn how to express those emotions. What I had come to feel for you, Emilia my darling—was love.'

'Love?' She sat down with a thump in the armchair. *Darling?*

'I could have killed Lawrence Bond, but that forced me to confront why I felt like that.'

'But you didn't say anything,' she protested, still unable to believe what she was hearing. 'You left.'

'I got up on Christmas morning and all I knew was that I had to go away and think about how I could convince you that I truly loved you, that I wanted to marry you and make you my countess. I sensed that to try to say anything after the night before would be a disaster.'

He grinned when she nodded, and she smiled back, a warmth spreading through her unlike anything she had ever felt before. Her parents forgave her, loved her, wanted her and the boys, and now Hugo was telling her that he returned what she felt for him.

'Then I found the letter. I thought that if I went and tried to reconcile your parents to you, if I could ask your father formally for your hand in marriage, then you might believe that I truly wanted to marry you.'

'I am twenty-five and a widow! I have no need of anyone's blessing,' she protested.

'But you would welcome it, I think?' Hugo was watching her, focused on her face, intent with what she realised was anxiety that she might not have forgiven him, might not feel anything for him.

'Should I fall in love again I would be happy to know that my parents approved,' she said, lowering her lashes, unable to cope with the realisation that dreams might, after all, come true.

'If?'

'They appear very taken with you—'

'Emilia.' He was on his feet, then kneeling by her side, her hands in his. 'I know I deserve it, but don't torment me. I will court you, take all the time you need, if you think that you might come to feel for me just a fraction of what I feel for you.'

'I don't mean to torment you.' She gripped his fingers as they interlaced with hers and found the courage to look deep into the blue eyes that had haunted her dreams. 'I just cannot believe this is true. I love you, how can I not? Why do you think I was so angry with you when I thought you were only proposing out of some misguided sense of gallantry?'

Hugo exhaled as though he had been holding his breath underwater. 'You love me and you will marry me? Emilia, I swear you will never regret this, nor will the boys.'

'I know. They adore you, but do you really want to turn your life on its head with a ready-made family?'

'Long Burnham Hall is a very big house. It echoes with emptiness and I cannot think of anyone better able to make it feel like a home than you and Nathan and Joseph.' He released his right hand and brought it up to caress the nape of her neck. 'So soft. Do you know I have been wanting to do that ever since you walked away from me that first evening, all hot and damp and glowing with the hair clinging to your neck?'

With a little sigh she bent to meet his lips and he knelt up, pulling her against him and she knew it had not been simply desire and loneliness—she really did belong in his arms. Hugo cupped her head in his palms and took her mouth with slow possessive sensuality, his tongue sweeping in to caress the sensitive sides, to tangle with her tongue.

When he finally released her she said, 'Hugo, I want you.'

'I hope so, after that,' he said, smiling, although his voice was husky.

'No, I mean now, upstairs.' She felt brazen and confident all of a sudden. Demanding and needing.

'Are you certain?' He wanted it, too, she could tell, only his essential decency and sense of responsibility was holding him back.

'I want to be where I was on Christmas Eve, in your arms with you about to carry me up to my bed.'

Hugo stood, scooped her up. 'Like this?' he asked as he began to climb the stairs.

'Exactly like that,' she murmured against his shoulder, inhaling the familiar smell of his skin, intrigued by the trace of a cologne that she did not recognise.

He set her on her feet and looked across at the bed. 'And what is that?'

'Oh.' Emilia had forgotten that he would see it. She could feel the blush rising, but there was nothing for it but to confess. He knew exactly what it was. 'Mistletoe, from the branch that you kissed me under at the Feast. I asked the boys to bring some home. I told them it was for luck, but really I would lie in bed and look up at it and remember the feel of your arms and the taste of you on my lips. And I would ache.'

'Aching can be good, but only if it can be soothed,' Hugo said. His fingers were busy in the knot of her apron. Clothes slipped off her as though by magic under his agile, urgent fingers until all that was left was her chemise. Emilia clutched it to her.

'Sweetheart, let me see you.'

'I...I am not a girl any more.' She was twenty-five, she had borne two sons and there was broad, unrelenting daylight coming in through the small, high window.

'No,' he agreed, stripping off coat and waistcoat and neck-cloth. 'You are a woman. My woman.' He stripped with haste and without shame and the body she had admired clothed, had fantasised about, was even more desirable naked. Muscled, lean, marked with the scars of war and magnificently aroused.

His mouth quirked as he saw her eyes widen and then they were on the bed and her chemise was gone and with it her fears. 'I love you,' Emilia said as he kissed his way over the swell of her breast and began to tease her right nipple. One hand speared into her hair, holding her head still while he plundered her mouth, the other slid purposefully down her body until he found the hot, wantonly wet core of her.

She gasped and arched up against him and he groaned and rolled on to her, fitting against her, cradled in her thighs. 'Emilia, sweetheart…'

'Yes,' she said, her fingers tight on his shoulders. 'Don't wait. I cannot wait. Oh, yes…*Hugo*.'

He felt so perfectly right, deep inside her, that she did not want to move, to breathe, to do anything to shatter the perfect moment. Hugo dropped his head until his forehead rested against hers and the tension grew and tightened until with a sigh he began to thrust slowly, powerfully, while her body tightened around him and her consciousness narrowed and narrowed until all there was in the universe was their joined bodies and the strength of him and the building pleasure and the sound of flesh against flesh and his breathing and her heartbeat.

And then when she thought her heart would burst, that she could not bear it any longer, the universe fell apart and she clung to him, calling his name, and he surged within her. *'Emilia.'*

When she climbed up from fathoms deep, where the storm of loving had tossed her, Emilia found Hugo had rolled on to his side and was holding her. 'Mmm.' She nuzzled into his chest, relishing the hot skin, the musk of their loving, the tickle of the crisp hair against her cheek.

'You've got to marry me now,' he said. The masculine smugness made her laugh and tickle his ribs.

'Ough!' He shifted and sat up. 'What the devil am I lying on?' He rummaged and pulled out a crumpled pillow case.

'Um…' She had just made love with this man in broad daylight—was there really anything that could make her blush now? It appeared there was.

Hugo spread it out. 'I recognise this. I came to know that darn very well.'

'I took it out of the washing basket and I have been sleeping with it because it smells of you,' she confessed.

'Darling Emilia, that is the sweetest thing.' He took her hand and kissed the palm. 'I do love you.'

'I love you, too,' she murmured, giving in to the temptation to stroke the nape of his neck, exposed as he bent over her hand. 'Shall I make some tea? I suppose we had better get up and—'

'Why?' Hugo rolled her back on to the pillows. 'We have until six o'clock.'

'Hugo! We cannot make love all day! And I have to make dinner…'

'Five o'clock, then,' he conceded with a grin. 'And I have every intention of making love to you all day today. And then I will become a respectable fiancé and master my impatience until we are married.'

'But that could take weeks,' Emilia protested. 'Mama is going to want me to have a wedding with a lot of fuss.'

'I know. You will just have to make it up to me afterwards, my love. I have never made love to a countess before.'

'And today is the last time you will ever make love to an alewife under the mistletoe,' she said, surrendering to the delicious inevitable as his body came over hers again and his kisses made promises enough for a lifetime.

* * * * *

TWELFTH NIGHT PROPOSAL

Lucy Ashford

Dear Reader,

I just love Christmas. I always tell myself I'll be sensible and cut down on the cards and the decorations, but by mid-December I'm eating mince pies, humming carols and hanging tinsel on the tree as happily as anyone.

In the Peak District of Derbyshire, where I live and where this story is set, there are often heavy snowfalls in winter and everything grinds to a halt, just as it did back in Regency days. But the wintry weather has its advantages and there's something quite magical about a Christmas walk across snow-covered hills, as my story's hero, Lord Dalbury, discovers. Something magical, too, about the old traditions the beguiling local girl Jenna describes to him, though Theo realizes that if he's not careful Jenna is just as likely to vanish from his grasp as the melting snow.

Don't forget to visit me and learn about my other books for Harlequin Books at www.lucyashford.com.

With seasonal best wishes,

Lucy

Chapter One

December 1817

This was desolate countryside indeed. Pulling up his horse, Theo gazed all around for something—*anything*—other than mist-shrouded moorland. Maybe December wasn't the best of months to leave the comforts of London.

Or maybe—and Theo's grey eyes narrowed—it *was*.

Last night, after two days of travelling through endless rain, he and his loyal groom Henry had finally reached the hilly spa town of Buxton in Theo's curricle and four. This morning Theo had decided he would head on alone, while Henry returned with the curricle to London, for the last stretch of the journey had proved beyond doubt that Theo's high-sprung conveyance wasn't built for Derbyshire roads. Henry had examined it tenderly this morning, then glanced at the sombre hills that surrounded the highest town in England.

'If I was you, milord,' Henry pronounced dismally, 'I'd be thinkin' of doing exactly the same.'

'What? Head back to London?'

'That's right. In fact, milord, I wouldn't have set out on this fool's errand *at all*.'

Theo, Lord Dalbury—around six foot tall and muscularly lithe—looked at his diminutive groom with some amusement.

'That's what I like about you, Henry. Ever the optimist, and completely bereft of respect. But damn it, I'm going to get to Northcote Hall today if it's the last thing I do!'

Henry's pursed lips told Theo that in his humble opinion it quite probably would be. But since Theo was already securing his waterproof saddle pack to the big roan he'd hired, Henry wisely limited his comments to simply bidding his master farewell. 'And you'll be back in London, milord…?'

'Soon, Henry. Very soon!'

And with that Theo set out into the wilds. With very little idea, really, of where he was going, or what, exactly, he'd find there. But perhaps that was the story of Theo's life.

On his father's death many years ago, he'd inherited a minor barony, that came with a small income and few responsibilities—luckily so, since Theo, an officer in Wellington's army, wasn't accustomed to spending much time in England anyway. In fact, after Waterloo, as soon as the final peace was signed, he'd set off with his old army friend Gilly to Cairo and Constantinople and beyond, because nothing in particular awaited him back home.

Or so he'd thought.

Just three months ago Theo, now twenty-seven years old, lean and bronzed from his travels, had got back to London to find a letter from a lawyer telling him that in fact his prospects had changed quite considerably. Which was why he found himself here, heading out into the hills in the gathering December dusk, with nothing but the rain, the interminable rain for company. As for the Derbyshire roads…

'Did you call them "roads", milord?' Henry had queried politely yesterday when their curricle had got stuck in a pothole yet again. There was mud. There were sheep. And miles of grey-stone walls, criss-crossing bleak hillsides.

Sighing, Theo urged his nag on, wondering if he really was heading in the right direction for Northcote Hall. Mist was closing in now, as well as darkness; he was hard put to see the road ahead, let alone any sign of habitation…

But wait. Suddenly he saw some tiny specks of light, bobbing about in the dark. What on earth were they? In the war he'd seen similar lights by night in the marshlands of Spain—will o' the wisps, the soldiers called them—and though a studious young lieutenant had explained they were caused by marsh gas the locals and the soldiers still muttered they were the spirits of the dead.

Steadying his horse—which was as spooked by those lights as the soldiers used to be—Theo carefully got out his pistol. Then he heard voices. *Children's* voices.

Theo lowered his gun, incredulous.

Carefully he guided his horse towards them. The mist parted, briefly; the ghostly lights glimmered more strongly, and he saw that indeed there were a dozen or so children, the smallest carrying old glass jars with string tied round the necks and tallow candles burning inside.

So much for the spirits of the dead. Some older, bigger ones dragged a rough two-wheeled cart. What on earth were they doing out here when it was practically dark? Up to no good, of course. Yet clearly they knew where they were going, which was more than he did. 'Hey!' he called out, urging his horse closer. 'Hey!'

They swung round. The smaller ones looked absolutely terrified, and a couple of them started to run. But the tallest of them—a youth in a long coat and cap, who'd been leading the way—called out to them in a clear voice, 'Stop. He's not one of them! Stay by me, while we find out his business!'

Not one of them. Theo carefully put his pistol away. What in Hades was going on?

The youth was coming towards Theo's big horse warily, hands thrust deep in pockets. And Theo's preconceptions were kicked in the teeth. Not a lad, but a girl of eighteen or so, with tousled blonde hair that escaped from her scruffy boy's cap, and an uptilted nose, and big brown eyes framed by thick lashes. Yes, she was wearing a baggy old coat far too big for her, and a man's breeches and boots. But she was quite definitely female and—unlike all the women *he* was used to—going to great lengths to hide it.

'What do you mean,' he said to her sharply as he leaned down from his saddle, 'that I'm not one of them?'

She met his gaze defiantly. She was rather striking, by God, and... *Just another country lass, Theo. Control yourself.* 'They thought you'd come to stop them taking the holly from Hob Hurst's Gate,' she answered. She gestured to the cart and he saw it was laden with prickly sprays of holly. 'It's got the best berries for miles. Hewitt and his greedy friends always want it all for themselves, to sell it at Buxton market. But it belongs to *everyone.* It's every villager's right to collect it, for Christmas!'

Christmas. Sentimental nonsense, Theo muttered to himself. 'And where are you taking this precious holly?'

She hesitated.

'Tell him, Miss Jenna!' urged one of the children. Their initial fear had been replaced by wide-eyed curiosity. 'Tell him!'

'Very well.' She spoke reluctantly, Theo thought. 'We always collect holly for every cottage before the Christmas season. And some of it's for the plague well.'

Theo caught his breath. *'Plague* well?'

She nodded, her gaze steady. 'When the plague raged around here, it was the only well whose water stayed pure, so the villagers decorate it every December in thanksgiving...' She must have seen his eyes narrow at the word *plague,* because she added, almost pityingly, 'Don't worry. All that was hundreds of years ago. Where are you heading? You're a long way from the road to Buxton.'

'I've actually come *from* Buxton. I appear to have lost my way.'

'And where did you want to be?'

Back in London, in the comforts of my own home... No.

Not that. Hell, that was why he had *made* this journey—to get away!

Theo eased himself in his saddle, feeling the cold mist penetrate his caped riding coat. He said, 'I'm trying to find Northcote Hall.'

He saw the ripple of surprise that ran through the girl and all her little band. 'Why?' she asked. 'The old lady is dead. And besides, she never visited the Hall, ever...'

'I know she's dead,' said Theo softly. 'That's why I've come.'

The girl stepped back, the candlelight flickering on her high cheekbones and wide, startled eyes. 'You're the new lord?'

'Yes.' *And what a way to arrive.* Theo sighed and reached into his coat pocket to pull out some coins. 'Here. Two shillings for you to share between you, if you'll guide me to the Hall.'

The children chattered excitedly at the sight of his money, but the one called Jenna tilted her chin stubbornly, Theo tried not to notice how her coat had fallen back and her boy's shirt strained across her small but full breasts. 'We don't want your money!' she declared. 'But if you really are the new lord, I can tell you what we *would* like. We'd like a promise that the holly can always be collected by everyone, every winter, from Hob Hurst's Gate!'

Theo was getting irritated. 'Have you tried asking Hob Hurst?' They all fell back, aghast. God, what had he said now?

'*You're* the one whose promise we need,' she said with emphatic patience. 'Is it so very much to ask?'

Yes. Yes, it certainly was! Plague wells, holly, a troop of lantern-bearing little pagans; this was getting ridiculous!

And then, suddenly, something else happened. Something rather mundane, but disastrous. A black-and-white sheepdog, barking furiously, appeared from nowhere and rushed towards Theo.

The girl lunged after it. 'Bess!' she cried. 'It's all right, Bess—down, girl, down!'

Too late; Theo's horse had panicked and was rearing up.

Theo, realising its floundering hooves were about to come down lethally on several small children, did all he could to pull it away and succeeded. But the horse gave one last, almighty kick which threw Theo from the saddle—and galloped off into the darkness.

Jenna ran to the fallen figure and gazed, stricken. 'Bess,' she scolded the dog that was whining and sniffing around him. 'Oh, Bess, what have you done?'

When he'd appeared out of the darkness on his big horse, she'd thought, *Here is another enemy.* A man, an arrogant man, and their new lord…

He'd had a knock on the head, that was all. He was big and strong, he'd quickly get over it. And then he'd be ruling the roost, as gents like him always did.

But…*his face.* He had a face you wouldn't forget, with a long, straight nose and a mouth that would look lovely if it was smiling. His hair was dark and unruly; beard growth was starting to shadow his lean jaw, and…

And men were trouble, always. And best to be avoided at all costs. Resisting the inexplicable urge to smooth his dark hair from his forehead, she turned and calmly said to the children, 'Help me, Jed and Simkin, to lift him on the cart. The rest of you, take the holly out—carefully!—and carry it to the village.'

'What are you goin' to do with him, Miss Jenna?'

'I'm going to take him to Northcote Hall, of course.'

Where he was expected. She, of all people, knew that.

And a rough ride in a handcart would certainly put this new arrival in his place.

Chapter Two

Theo opened his eyes to find that he was being bounced about on something very hard and very uncomfortable. He turned his head sideways to realise he was lying in a handcart, being trundled into the forecourt of an ancient manor house.

My God. By the illumination of a few faintly lit windows, Theo could see the place was completely unkempt, with ancient chimney pots clustered atop steeply angled roofs and tangles of ivy growing haphazardly up an old stone turret.

Everything came flooding back. The children. The girl, Jenna—a rustic maid in a man's coat, whose scorn for him had been transparent. That barking dog, and the horse throwing him...

He struggled to sit up. The girl, her voice very clear, was saying, 'We're here, my lord. Northcote Hall.'

Theo heaved himself out of the cart, stretching each limb to make sure nothing was broken and touching the bruise on the back of his head rather carefully. He noticed that the children had vanished into the darkness with the greenery and their lanterns, all except for a young lad who hovered by the cart, and the girl, of course, and—the dog.

The blasted dog.

The girl must have seen his expression; she said, 'I'm sorry about Bess—she thought you were threatening us, you see.

But we've brought you here safe, so will you still promise to do what you said?'

Theo's head momentarily spun. He began, 'It depends on what…'

Her face changed. Those thick-lashed eyes looked stricken; her fists were clenched. 'You'd break your promise!'

'All right,' he said curtly. He couldn't even remember what he'd promised, if indeed he had—it was about holly, or wells, or something equally pagan. 'All right.'

Suddenly he jerked his head round as the great front door of the Hall began to open. The dog—Bess—growled softly. Theo frowned, reaching for his pistol. A man—a rough-clad, black-bearded man—strode out into the yard.

'What in thunder—God's teeth, it's *you*!' He was glaring at the girl. 'What the devil brings you here?'

The girl stood there, pale but proud. The dog was alert at her side. 'I have someone for you,' she answered him. 'Someone you've been expecting, Hewitt.'

Theo frowned. Clearly the girl knew, and despised, Hewitt; and now it was the man's turn to go pale. 'Hell. Not Lord Dalbury!'

Theo stepped forwards to stare him down. 'I'm Dalbury, yes. Who the devil are you?'

It was the girl who answered. Tossing her head scornfully, she said to Theo, 'This is Joseph Hewitt—*supposedly* the steward of Northcote Hall. Which accounts, my lord, for the state you see it's in.'

Hewitt looked enraged. 'Why, you…'

Theo looked at him, then turned to the girl. 'And you are?' It had occurred to him a while ago how well she spoke for a rough country girl.

'I am Jenna Brook,' she answered steadily. 'I live with my mother in Northcote village, half a mile from here.'

'And you're a damned troublemaker,' Hewitt was muttering.

She spun back to Hewitt, anger sparking. 'I've spoken with

his lordship, Hewitt. And he agrees with what I've always told you—that the land at Hob Hurst's Gate belongs to the people, and it's their right to collect greenery every Christmastide! Is Aggie there?'

Just then a plump, grey-haired woman wearing a big apron and white cap came rushing out. 'Miss Jenna. I heard Bess, and… Oh!'

Her eyes had alighted on Theo.

'Lord Dalbury,' said Jenna swiftly, 'this is the housekeeper, Aggie. Aggie, you will see that his lordship is well looked after, won't you?'

The housekeeper was blushing and curtsying. 'Oh, my lord! You're welcome indeed. If you'll come this way…'

Theo followed, but turned one last time to look at the girl, who was still in altercation with Hewitt.

'You *knew* he was coming,' she was accusing the steward. 'Yet you've done nothing, and you made poor Aggie's life a misery when she tried to prepare the place…'

'I never thought he'd really arrive mid-winter!' Hewitt was muttering. 'I just thought his lordship's letter was maybe one of yours and Aggie's tricks!'

The girl answered scornfully, 'If you'd ever learned to read properly, Hewitt, you'd have known *exactly* what that letter said. And I hope that one of the first things his lordship discovers is what an incredible rogue you are.'

With that she went to join the lad waiting by the cart and together they began to pull it across the cobbles and out of the yard, with the black-and-white dog trotting behind.

Clearly there was more going on here than met the eye. That girl had spoken to Hewitt with scorn, and even authority— *why*? Once inside Theo took his time gazing round the huge hall with its vaulted ceiling and stone-flagged floor. The place was chilly and distinctly damp. The few candles that had been lit showed furniture and wall-hangings that looked as old as the building itself.

Aggie, the housekeeper, was saying anxiously, 'I've kept it as clean as I could, my lord! But it's difficult… If you'll excuse me, I'll just go and light a fire in your bedroom.'

'By all means.' As Aggie headed off up the big staircase Hewitt sauntered in, scowling; an odour of mingled tobacco and brandy hung about him.

'She's a local troublemaker, that girl Jenna, milord,' he muttered. 'Her mother was a foreigner, came from Germany…'

'Germany?' Theo was surprised.

'Aye. Came here to pick up what she could.' Hewitt spoke louder. 'She was nothing but a whore, and the daughter's set to go the same way—you don't want to go believin' a thing she says!'

'I want the fires lit down here, Hewitt,' interrupted Theo. 'The place is freezing. And you're the steward, is that right? I want to see all your accounts, now. Including the rent books.'

'Now? But…'

'Right now, if you please.'

Hewitt sloped off, muttering under his breath.

Aggie had come down again. She, unlike Hewitt, was desperately anxious to please. 'I've just lit the fire in your bedchamber, my lord, and should I set some food out for you in the dining parlour? There's soup I can heat, and cold mutton pie.'

'That sounds wonderful,' said Theo. 'Thank you. Did Lady Hasledene never visit you here?'

'Why, no, my lord,' said Aggie. 'Nor ever sent anybody for the last ten years, just her agent now and again. Which is why… Well, things aren't as they should have been.'

She led him up to his bedchamber—a chilly, dark-panelled room almost filled by an ancient four-poster bed—then fussed around, lighting candles. 'Will this do for you, sir?' she asked anxiously.

He gave her a brief smile. 'Aggie, I've slept in far worse places than this, believe me.'

'We heard you were an officer in the army, sir. But…' she hesitated '…were you closely related to the old lady? None of us knew she had family.'

'She didn't,' said Theo. 'But she knew my father.' He eased off his big coat and slung it over a chair.

'Knew your father. I see, sir.' Then Aggie went downstairs, clearly not seeing at all, and she wasn't alone there, because Theo was equally bemused by what had happened to him in the last few weeks.

Quite simply, Theo had got back to England with Gilly to find that he'd inherited a fortune. From a very awkward, very old aristocratic spinster called Lady Hasledene—who wasn't even a relative, but had been godmother to Theo's long-dead rake of a father.

Theo himself had only met Lady Hasledene once. It was when he was on leave from the army; she'd asked him to call on her at her Grosvenor Square mansion, and either he or his uniform had made quite an impression. For that mansion was now his, together with a considerable fortune, and a place in Derbyshire called Northcote Hall.

For Theo, son of my godson, her will had said, *who is so clearly everything that an English gentleman should be…*

An English gentleman? Theo felt he was certainly typical of his kind. Like many of his army comrades, several close brushes with death meant that he took life, money and women lightly. With no vast fortune to pass on, he'd been in no rush to marry; he'd intended to go travelling again come spring, but now…

Now, everything was different. He washed quickly, then went downstairs to eat alone at the big oak table in front of a reluctant log fire. When Aggie took away the final dishes and asked if he wanted anything else, he took a quick look at the scruffy account books left on the table for him—by Hewitt, presumably—and said, 'Yes. I want to talk to you. Who was that girl who brought me here?'

She tensed. 'Just a village girl, my lord. A *good* girl, whatever Hewitt says!'

'Why do she and Hewitt detest each other so?'

Again, the hesitation. 'Mr Hewitt, my lord—has he said anything?'

Yes. Hewitt told me she was the daughter of a whore—a German whore—and was set fair to go the same way... 'What should he have said?' Theo enquired evenly.

'I doubt if he'd tell you anything like the truth, my lord!' Aggie said bitterly. 'But the fact of the matter is that Miss Jenna's mother was housekeeper here at Northcote Hall, 'til the old lord died ten years ago and Hewitt threw Miss Jenna and her dear mother out! Lord Northcote used to keep Hewitt in his place, you see—but once his lordship was gone there was no stopping Hewitt. Such a lovely little girl, Miss Jenna was... I used to be cook here, sir, then I took on the post of housekeeper, and my son, Rob—he's a good lad, but a little slow, my lord—does the heavy jobs round here. I don't know where else we'd live, if...'

'You won't lose your job, Aggie,' Theo told her.

'But Mr Hewitt—'

'I think,' Theo cut in icily, 'that I have rather more to say on that matter than Hewitt.'

'I hope so, my lord,' said Aggie. 'Indeed, I very much hope so! I hear your horse ran off, sir. My Rob'll find it for you first thing in the morning, never fear!'

Theo thought of the miles of deserted moorland and raised his eyebrows. Aggie gave him a tentative smile, bobbed a curtsy and left, with her arms full of dishes.

Theo took his glass of brandy and went to sit by the fire, deep in thought. So Jenna's mother had been Lord Northcote's housekeeper, and a foreigner—that German heritage went some way, perhaps, towards explaining why the girl puzzled him so.

In fact, he'd been intrigued by her the minute he saw her, trudging through the mud in her boots and long man's coat, with her blonde hair falling carelessly round her shoulders, and that expressive face that at times looked so scornful, at others almost—vulnerable.

She was just a country wench who'd got ideas above her station because her mother used to be housekeeper here. Yet how could Lady Hasledene have abandoned Northcote Hall to the care of a man like Hewitt?

Why had Lady Hasledene left Theo—amongst everything else—this ancient pile that she'd not bothered to visit, ever?

Because she had the fickle power of the truly rich, that was why. In the last few months Theo had rapidly found that, with money, the world was a different place and not necessarily a better one. Before, he'd been carefree. Now he was rich, with a fortune carefully invested, a London house full of servants and all the damned hangers-on in the world.

As for the women—well, Theo and Gilly had broken many a heart between them in the past, no denying. But Theo's parents' own marriage had been a total disaster—in fact, his mother had been driven to an early grave by his father's drinking, womanising and steady gambling away of the estate.

No marriage for me, Theo had always sworn. *Not until I've had as much fun as I want.*

But since September he'd found himself under siege from the matchmakers. Gilly had offered practical advice. 'Tell the girls and their mamas you're not in the market yet for marriage, old fellow. Keep the women at bay—and you've got 'til spring before the Season really gets under way.'

But that autumn Theo had found, to his cost, that quite a few eager parents had hit on the idea of giving their daughters early come-outs, to steal a march on next spring's batch of debutantes. All of these marriageable misses had their eyes firmly fixed on Theo, Lord Dalbury. And the worst of them was Lady Celia.

It had been the simpering Lady Celia's latest ploy, when he was foolish enough to attend her parents' November ball, to lure him into the conservatory on some pretence of helping her find a missing cat. Cats! He loathed the things! Then she had told him her gown had slipped from her shoulder and asked him to attend to it—at which point, just as Theo was about to beat a *very* hasty retreat, Lady Celia's mother had burst in, and…

'I'm going to Derbyshire,' he'd announced to Gilly later that night as they sat morosely over their brandy.

'Derbyshire!' Gilly had looked aghast. 'Of all the bleak, benighted places! Why, Theo, on God's earth… Unless there's hunting?'

'I'm not interested in hunting.' Theo shrugged. 'But I've got an estate. Or so they tell me. And, Gilly, it's a long, long way from London.'

Gilly frowned, then brightened. 'So's India. How about India?'

Theo struggled. 'I really ought to visit this place first.'

So here he was, and the sooner he sorted it, the sooner he could leave this decaying relic of a house. So when Aggie came in to see if there was anything else he needed, he told her he'd sit by the fire for a while and examine the estate's papers.

'Where's Hewitt?' he asked. 'I'd like to see him about these accounts.'

She hesitated. 'At the village alehouse, my lord. He usually goes there around nine or so. He'll be back soon. But…'

He'd be drunk, Theo surmised, and in no fit state to talk about anything. 'I think I've got all I need, Aggie. I'll see you in the morning.'

'Then I'll wish you a good night, my lord.'

A good night? Theo would sooner have been camping out in the mountains of Spain with Wellington's army—but at least he was away from London and Lady Celia.

His mouth set in a grim line as he turned back to the accounts. But Theo found his concentration lacking greatly as Jenna's face played over and over in his mind. She intrigued him, and not only with her beauty. Jenna piqued Theo's curiosity.

Because of various errands, night had truly settled in by the time Jenna set off for Northcote village, alone. She had plenty to think about as she tramped the familiar path homewards.

Jenna had hoped, so much, that the arrival of the new lord at Northcote Hall would mean that old wrongs would at last be put right. But she had been foolish to hope. Just as foolish to let something strange churn at her insides when she'd seen him lying there, thrown from his horse. She'd felt pity, and something else—almost fear—when she struggled with Simkin and the others to get him on that cart.

He was so big, so *male*. Yes, a fine-looking man and the local girls' hearts would be all aflutter for him. But his lordship would doubtless turn his back on Northcote Hall just as soon as he could. Why should he stay? And anyway, men were trouble—she only had to look at her poor mother's life to see that.

She was almost home. Their cottage lay a little off the track, with a garden for chickens and vegetables, and some apple trees. The eggs and produce, together with her mother's beautifully delicate embroidery, brought in just enough to live on. They'd been there ten years now, and she'd have known the way blindfolded...

But now—dear God, she could smell smoke. She could see flames rising from behind the trees. And soon she was running.

Those flames—the bright golden flames that she could see so clearly now—were crackling around what was left of her home.

Chapter Three

By eleven o'clock Theo gave up on Hewitt and went to bed, where he fell asleep almost immediately, only to wake a little later, wondering for a few dazed seconds, where on earth he was. Northcote Hall, at the back of beyond, that was where. And—what on earth was that racket out in the yard? He glanced at his watch. Half-past eleven. Heaving on his breeches, aware of his head still aching from his fall, he strode to the window to look out.

Hewitt. Back from the tavern with his friends. They were clearly drunk and making a din fit to wake the devil. And then he saw that the girl was there. *Jenna.*

She was wearing that man's coat again; the moon shone pale on her long, loose fair hair. And she was confronting those men—all five of them.

'I've been waiting here for you, Hewitt,' he heard her say, her fists clenched. There was more, but Theo couldn't make it out. Something about her mother, and their cottage...

'So you've come here to appeal to his fine lordship, have you?' jeered Hewitt. Theo could hear *his* voice all right. 'Already plannin' on playing the same sort of tricks as your mother, is that it—?'

He broke off. The girl had flown at him and hit him. She

would have hit him again, Theo thought as he rapidly buttoned his shirt, if Hewitt's cronies hadn't held her back.

'You are a wicked, ignorant creature, Hewitt!' she cried, still struggling. 'And I've come here to tell you that you will *not* get away with it!'

'Oh, I'll deny everything, my pretty,' Theo heard Hewitt say in a dangerous voice. 'And now I'm going to show you what I think of you, givin' yourself fancy airs…'

'No! You'll not touch me!'

But Hewitt was starting to take his coat off and his friends were gripping her more fiercely than ever, grinning.

Good God. The girl was about to be raped down there. Theo had pulled on his boots and was charging down the stairs and out into the yard. 'Tell your men to get their hands off the girl, Hewitt,' he breathed.

Hewitt's men had already backed away. Hewitt was unrepentant. 'She's just asking for it, my lord! Was waitin' here for me…'

'Waiting for you to *assault* her? You think I'd believe that? Get out of here, yes, and the rest of you!' Hewitt's friends were already slinking away towards their tethered nags, but Hewitt was in a dangerous state of inebriation, Theo realised: angry, resentful and just beginning to wonder if he should stand up to his new master.

'I mean it, Hewitt,' went on Theo warningly. 'I want you gone from this place, for good. I'm dismissing you as of now.'

'You cannot do that!' Hewitt's eyes were ugly, his fists already clenching. 'You fancy young lordling, you…'

Theo planted him a facer that sent him sprawling. By the time Hewitt had staggered to his feet, his friends had ridden off hastily into the blackness of the night. Hewitt, clutching his tender jaw, muttered, 'My things…'

'I'll have them put them out in the yard,' said Theo curtly. 'You can come and collect them tomorrow. If you dare.'

As Theo watched Hewitt ride off he was breathing hard,

mentally damning the man to hell and back. Then he realised that the girl was still there, watching him.

'He fights dirty,' she said tonelessly. 'Beware.'

'For God's sake,' said Theo irritably. 'You don't think I'm scared of *him*? But what were you doing here at this hour? No wonder you found yourself in trouble!'

'I came here to find him because he's burnt our house down.' She stared up at Theo, her gaze defying him to doubt her.

'He's what?'

'He set fire to it. I came to tell him I *know* it was him, though I don't suppose anyone will take any notice.'

'You're sure it was him?'

She shrugged. 'Who else? But I've no proof—he's careful like that.'

Theo knew she was most likely right; it would be the devil of a job to prove it. At least some justice had been done in that the rogue had now lost his own home and livelihood. He said, 'Listen. I know your mother was housekeeper here, to the old lord…'

He saw her tense again. 'Who told you?'

'Aggie. She said your mother was dismissed, when Lord Northcote died ten years ago. Surely Lady Hasledene wouldn't have intended her to lose her job and her home?'

Jenna shrugged. 'Lady Hasledene probably didn't even know my mother existed. My mother was given her notice, and Hewitt took over.'

Her big coat had fallen apart and Theo was once more aware of the slenderness of her female form beneath her loose shirt and breeches. Of the way the dim lights from the windows fell on the pale curve of her cheek, the softness of her dark lashes…

Hewitt had muttered words to the effect that her mother was a whore and that Jenna was set to go the same way. Theo felt a sudden stab of interest and stifled it at birth.

She was clearly trouble. And it was damned cold out here,

especially if your home had just burned down. 'Where will you stay? Where will you live?'

'My mother's taken shelter with a neighbour.'

'Did you walk here?'

'Yes, and I'll walk back.' She was buttoning up her coat. 'My mother will be waiting and worrying.'

Hardly surprising. Damn it, damn it, he didn't come here to saddle himself with fresh problems… He said curtly, 'Tell her I'll find you both somewhere before I leave.'

Those eyes flew to his. 'You're leaving?'

'Very soon, yes.'

'Before Christmas?'

'Most likely.' *Most definitely.* 'But you'll be all right,' he said.

She looked at him. As if to say, *How on earth can you know that?* Then she shrugged her shoulders again and walked off quickly into the night.

Damn. She shouldn't be setting out there on her own, but clearly the last person she wanted was him! Suddenly Theo became aware that a young, strapping lad had just emerged from the house, looking anxious.

'Rob?' he asked sharply.

'Aye, my lord. That's me!'

'Go after the girl, will you? See that she comes to no harm.'

Rob nodded, already hurrying off. Theo went up to his room. *Her face, when he told her he was leaving…*

Hell. Why should he feel guilty? A few days would give him enough time to put things to rights here—he'd already started, by sacking Hewitt! Christmas—they all went on about it, but Christmas for Theo was simply something to be got through as quickly as possible. It brought back far too many painful memories.

India, with Gilly, would have been a *much* better idea.

Jenna hurried home—home? she had no home!—feeling as if her world was collapsing around her. She'd known

straight away Hewitt must have set fire to their house tonight
to punish her for what she'd said about him, in front of Lord
Dalbury. Frightened though she'd been, she *knew* she had to
stay strong—men like him thrived on fear and she sensed that
the best place to confront her enemy was at the Hall. For she'd
foolishly harboured the faintest, just the faintest hope that perhaps things might be about to change. But, no.

Hewitt had been dismissed—but Lord Dalbury was leaving.
And…she was being followed. She swung round, heart banging
against her ribs. '*Rob!* Oh, Rob. Thank goodness it's only you.'

'His lordship sent me after you, Jenna!' Rob was a friend—
a playmate from her youth. 'He was worried about you. He
seems kind. P'raps things are going to get better for us all!'

'How, Rob?' She gazed at him in despair. 'How, when he's
leaving?'

Her mother was waiting, tearful and afraid, in the thatched
outhouse a neighbour had offered. Jenna soothed her. 'Everything will be all right, Mama.' Soon her mother was asleep,
on the old straw mattress in the corner.

But Jenna was awake, her thoughts in raging turmoil. He
was going—and in many ways he'd left them in a worse mess
than ever. Because she'd just lost Hewitt his job and Hewitt
would want revenge.

Chapter Four

What, in God's name, was that? The next morning Theo rose abruptly from his bed and went to the window to haul back the ancient curtains. The church bells—half a mile away, but how the sound travelled out here!—were in full peal. It was Sunday and there was no way he was going to get a lie-in here.

He washed himself vigorously in cold water and wondered what Gilly and his other friends would be doing in London. They'd probably only just got to bed after a Saturday night spent roistering around London's clubs.

'Are you going to church, Lord Dalbury?' asked Aggie timidly as she served him sizzling hot ham and eggs. 'The neighbours will be eager to see you. *Glad* to see you.'

Not when they learn I'll be turning my back on this crumbling old place just as soon as I can, thought Theo.

Rob had miraculously found Theo's hired roan—it had turned up at a neighbouring farm—but Theo had decided to walk to the church to get the lie of the land and he slid into a back pew just as the first hymn was beginning.

Was Jenna there? He found his eyes wandering during the service, but saw no sign of her. Having your house burned down wouldn't, he supposed, encourage you to go and give thanks to God the next morning.

He didn't linger after the final blessing but went out to wander around the ancient graveyard, where he found a memorial to Lord Northcote. Theo knew already that he'd never married, had no children or relatives other than his distant cousin Lady Hasledene. But… Theo drew closer, for he'd seen that a fresh wreath lay on his grave, of holly and ivy interlaced with winter jasmine. The delicate yellow flowers cast a sweet scent into the bleak winter air.

The congregation was starting to come out now and the vicar together with the more prosperous locals hurried to greet the new lord of Northcote Hall, while the poorer ones eyed him with wonder from afar. Suddenly he realised Jenna was there after all, emerging from the church with her mother. The likeness was unmistakable; she had the same proud carriage, the same high cheekbones as her daughter, though her skin was etched with fine lines of anxiety around her mouth and eyes.

Jenna was saying something to her, reassuring her. If Jenna had seen Theo, she didn't betray it. In fact, she'd moved away to talk to a small group of women nearby. Her mother—the former housekeeper at Northcote Hall—stood steadfastly by the church wall, but she looked as if a strong wind would blow her away.

Theo found himself walking towards her. 'I was sorry to hear about your house burning down,' he said.

'Lord Dalbury?' Her face lit up. 'You must be Lord Dalbury. My daughter told me you would help us—and she says you've got rid of Hewitt. I am so glad! He was such an evil man…'

She had a musical voice that was still coloured by her German origins. Theo wondered if Jenna had told her mother how the brute almost attacked her last night. He said, 'I'm only sorry that Northcote Hall has been unvisited by its owner for so long.'

'Since Lord Northcote died. But you have come to visit it already—that bodes well for its future, my lord!'

Jenna had come back and was helping her mother to fasten her mantle. 'Lord Dalbury has to leave again very soon, Mama. His home is in London.'

Theo saw the sudden fading of hope in the woman's eyes. 'Before I go,' he said, 'I'll find someone to replace Hewitt as steward, someone decent. And I'll appoint an agent in Buxton to keep an eye on things.'

'That is what Lady Hasledene did,' Jenna informed him flatly. 'The agent was a crook, hand-in-glove with Hewitt.'

Theo felt suddenly angry. What right did this poor country girl have to assume his negligence from the start? He said, 'Well, I'll see that things are done differently.'

'You'll have to arrange it all from London, though, since you're leaving so soon.'

'I'll spend a few days looking round the estate,' he answered coolly. 'Tomorrow I was thinking of taking the gig around the tenant farms.'

A glance from her, some faint hint of amusement. 'Are you quite sure you won't get lost again, Lord Dalbury?'

'Not if you come with me,' said Theo.

Now, where the hell had *that* come from? He cursed himself inwardly; she was looking at him with startled surprise, and no wonder. 'I mean it,' he went on. 'You can show me the way. And at the same time we could look for a suitable cottage for you and your mother.'

She hesitated, no doubt analysing his motives. Damn it, what *were* his motives? Well, it was useful that she seemed to know everyone and everything around here. And—he might be able to pay her. Yes, that was it. He would pay her, for her time…

'Very well,' she said at last.

He nodded. 'Shall I pick you up here at the church, in the gig at noon tomorrow?'

'If you like.'

He was aware of people watching him as he walked away. Speculating. Which they'd do even more, once he'd gone visiting the farms with her tomorrow… Damn. For all the good he'd be able to do here, he'd probably have been better off not coming at all.

* * *

The next morning Theo asked Aggie to show him round the Hall and he made a mental note of the repairs that needed doing. She didn't show him the old turret, but when he mentioned it Aggie laughed dismissively. 'You'll find nothing of interest up there!'

Then he was diverted by Rob coming in to tell him he'd got the gig ready and Theo set off to pick Jenna up and make his tour of the Northcote estate.

There were five farms altogether, and as they approached each one, Jenna told him about the families who lived there, and how Hewitt had wronged them.

'Hewitt always raised the rents twice a year or more,' Jenna explained without expression. 'And he bought the farmers' crops at low prices then sold them on for more than twice the cost, keeping the profit. Once he took on Farmer Fairlie's daughter as maid at the Hall, and tried to—'

'I get the picture,' said Theo grimly.

'I hope so, my lord,' she replied calmly.

The farmers all looked delighted to see Theo and their faces brightened even more when they heard Hewitt had gone.

'Amen to that!' said one stout farmer's wife. 'So you'll be takin' over the running of it all, my lord?'

They looked at him hopefully.

Jenna said, in her clear, steady voice, 'Unfortunately Lord Dalbury has to return to London almost immediately.'

'But you'll stay for Christmas?'

'I'm afraid not,' Theo replied.

Their faces fell.

Theo noticed that they all knew Jenna and she them. They'd heard about her cottage catching fire and muttered darkly about who was to blame. Sometimes children would come hurrying out to greet the gig as it rolled into the farmyards and he thought he recognised some small faces from the holly procession. From Hob Hurst's Gate, he remembered.

'Who *is* Hob Hurst?' he asked Jenna as they drove away from the last farm. By now the sun was beginning to set and a chill wind blew from the east.

'Hob Hurst? It's the locals' name for a mischievous goblin. As Hewitt said, the people round here are all rather pagan at heart.' She was pointing into the distance. 'Look, you can see it from here. That pile of rocks up on the western ridge is Hob Hurst's House. And Hob Hurst's Gate is in the field below, where in spring hiring fairs are held.'

'Hiring fairs?'

'That's when the farmers take on labourers for the season. Hob is supposed to help with the work around the farms by night, when everyone is asleep...' She glanced at him sideways. 'No doubt you'll find our country ways primitive, my lord. When you get back to London you'll be able to entertain your friends with them.'

The hint of challenge in her steady gaze sent warning signals racing through his blood. Damn it. This country air must be doing something to his wits. He was actually finding this wench alluring, with her full lips and soft skin...

'I doubt my friends would be interested in Derbyshire customs,' he said coolly. Why was he feeling so ridiculously *guilty* about leaving this place? For God's sake, he couldn't wait to see the back of it!

Though he was, he acknowledged, just a little sorry to be seeing the back of Miss Jenna Brook.

Suddenly he exclaimed, 'A cottage. We haven't found one yet, for you and your mother...'

'Pray don't trouble yourself, Lord Dalbury,' she said stiffly. 'We'll find somewhere.'

'At least you must allow me to pay you for your time today!'

Silence. The faint colour rising in her cheeks told Theo he'd made another blunder.

She said, 'Will you stop the gig, please?'

'What?'

'I said, will you stop? And—I do not require any payment, thank you!'

He hauled on the reins; she was already getting down, in a huff, damn it, thought Theo. 'But you need whatever you can get, surely? Aggie told me that you had a smallholding and your mother earned a little money for her needlework. But you lost *everything* in the fire… How are you going to live, now?'

Standing at the side of the gig, she looked up at him and said, 'Let me put it this way, my lord. If you hadn't deigned to come here you wouldn't even know of our existence, let alone our plight. So let me venture to suggest that you return to London and resume your state of blissful ignorance—*so* much easier for you, Lord Dalbury!'

Theo said, 'God damn it, you can't walk all the way. It must be at least a mile…'

'Oh, I *much* prefer to walk!' she said sweetly. And she set off down the track, her pert behind swaying enticingly.

Was it deliberate? Hardly. She'd certainly made it plain what she thought of *him*.

Damn it, swore Theo in exasperation.

It was Theo's intention to write up everything he'd learned about the farms before his evening meal, but Aggie was on him almost immediately to say there was a message—a letter— waiting for him. She handed it to him with floury fingers; he opened it with a slight frown.

He read it once, twice, then a third time. It was from Lady Celia's mother.

My dear Lord Dalbury, We have been invited by his Grace the Duke of Devonshire to Chatsworth House for the approaching seasonal festivities—and since we realise your own

Northcote Hall is a mere seven miles distant, we are on pins to pay you an afternoon visit on our way to the dear Duke's abode...

Theo couldn't believe it.

We will arrive, went on Celia's mother, *on the 24th at around midday, and later that afternoon we shall travel on to Chatsworth. Oh, and we will have friends with us...*

Theo clutched his head. Celia's mother had boasted often about some connection with the Devonshires, but he'd ignored her.

Hell's teeth. To evade them once—as he had in London— might pass as a mischance. To evade them twice would look downright devious, and besides, any letter he sent now might not reach them in time. Today was the nineteenth of December. He had no choice but to stay on for a few days in this godfor- saken place—but how was he going to manage, with no staff except Aggie and her son?

It was then that he had his idea.

'Miss Brook,' Theo said the next morning, 'it looks as though I'm soon going to have a few unexpected visitors.'

He'd ridden out to Northcote village to find Jenna, causing much wonderment amongst her neighbours as he asked for directions. He'd found her in the yard of what was little more than a hovel, pegging out some washing. Winter sunlight spar- kled on her loose fair hair and creamy skin. Underneath her baggy clothes, Theo could see the outline of alluring curves. *She shouldn't be doing work like that,* thought Theo, frowning. *She shouldn't be dressed in that shapeless old gown.*

Suddenly the dog that had startled his horse—Bess—came dashing out and began to bark.

'Quiet, Bess!' Jenna called sharply. The dog lay motionless at her feet, eyes on Theo.

Jenna put down her pegs and said calmly, 'Unexpected? So

they have invited themselves, my lord? Isn't that a little forward of them?'

'It is,' declared Theo. 'They're not staying overnight—' for which he was heartily grateful '—but it's too much for Aggie to cope with. And I've been thinking. Your mother used to be housekeeper there, so would the two of you consider moving in again and helping out? I did say yesterday that I'd like to provide you with a—' he glanced at her present abode '—a *proper* home before I leave.'

She'd gone very still. 'You mean—move into the Hall?'

'Yes,' he said. 'Is that so strange? I'm simply offering you what you used to have. A home and a job, helping Aggie.' Good grief, he didn't dare to raise the topic of money again.

She had become rather pale. 'My mother can do very little now by way of work—she is not well—'

'I wouldn't expect her to do a thing,' he cut in. 'In fact, you can hire extra staff, if you wish. It's purely a matter of expedience, Miss Brook—you needn't be afraid I'm offering charity. After all, it saves me the trouble of finding you and your mother a cottage.'

Blast, that sounded selfish. But since she went all hoity-toity at any hint of condescension, what else could he say? 'We'll discuss everything in more detail,' he went on, 'when you move into the Hall.'

'Tomorrow?'

'Why not? The sooner the better.'

She still looked perturbed. 'Can Bess come, too?'

'What?'

'We can't leave her! She's usually so well behaved, and she'll be no trouble to you, since you're leaving anyway!'

'But I… Oh, very well.'

And Theo rode away from the village with the feeling that things hadn't gone quite as he'd planned.

She could, he thought, have at least shown some gratitude.

Chapter Five

Theo spent some time the next morning working his way through the estate's neglected paperwork, then got Rob to saddle up the roan so he could survey the rest of his estate. A chill drizzle began to fall, which did nothing to improve these desolate moorlands, and he got back in need of dry clothes and a blazing fire. But...

Once inside he froze to the spot. He'd been out for—what? Two hours, three at most—but everywhere had been freshly swept and dusted; the old oak furniture had been polished till it gleamed. And there was greenery everywhere. Even the mantel shelves were festooned with yew branches and pine cones. Was there no escape from the looming festive season?

He was suddenly aware of a couple of girls in large aprons stealing looks at him from the kitchen doorway, then Jenna was there. He felt his breathing hitch slightly. She'd pinned up her long blonde hair in a way that defined her pretty cheekbones and had tied an apron round her waist, ensuring that what had been a shapeless grey gown fitted her slender yet feminine curves rather alluringly.

God, he'd only been out of London a few days, and his wits were already wandering, if he was finding this simple country girl enticing.

'You've arrived, I see,' he said.

She coloured and tilted her chin. 'You said to, my lord! You said to find some extra staff and to make the Hall ready for your guests!'

'Yes, indeed. But…'

His voice trailed away. He'd meant to make it spick and span—to sweep the floors and clean the windows, that was all.

'They'll be arriving on *Christmas Eve*!' she went on, a note of desperation in her voice.

'Of course.' He saw her crestfallen face. 'You've shown—initiative.'

'I've been talking to Aggie,' she went on, 'about everything else that needs doing. I know your guests aren't staying overnight, my lord, but nevertheless we should prepare some upstairs chambers for the ladies to remove their cloaks and have some privacy. Is it all right if I keep the two Harris girls on for the week to see to the various tasks?'

'Very well.' Clearly she'd inherited her mother's skills as housekeeper. 'Do what you think fit, Miss Brook. Which is a very *English* name, by the way.'

'It's Bruch, actually.' She spelled it for him. 'That was my mother's name. This afternoon, then, I'll ask the girls to start on the upstairs rooms. You've thought, no doubt, about food, my lord? There's the market in Buxton tomorrow. I could go there and order it all…'

Time for him to take a hand. 'We'll *both* go,' said Theo firmly.

Her eyes looked stormy. 'There is really—'

'I've business in Buxton myself.'

Looking far from happy, she left. Suddenly he was aware that the dog had loped into the room. Bess gazed at him, head on one side, then padded closer, nuzzled at his booted leg and let out a sort of little sigh.

Theo found himself reaching down to stroke the soft place behind its ear. At least, thought Theo wearily, *someone* was glad he was here at Northcote Hall. God's teeth, this was a

devilish hole to have landed himself in—and he was still hot
and uncomfortable from his ride. He needed clean clothes,
but first…

He remembered spying an old pump in the backyard. Now,
easing Bess away, he strode out into the secluded yard and,
following old army habits, pulled off his shirt, cranked the
handle and doused his upper body and head in icy-cold water.

Only to look up moments later, with icy rivulets streaming
through his hair and down his chest, to see that Jenna was there.

She held a large copper pan in each hand. She looked as if
she would never move again. 'I—I needed these pans from the
outhouse,' she stammered. 'I'm sorry, my lord.'

And she ran inside.

Theo swore softly.

Jenna ran up to the tiny bedchamber that used to be hers and
slammed the door, trembling. She should never have agreed to
this. This was disastrous. Lord Dalbury had found her efforts
to make the Hall fit for his visitors simply laughable. He'd tried
to hide it, but she could tell.

She'd had no trouble finding girls to help here for the next
few days. 'We saw his lordship at the church,' chattered the
Harris girls, 'and he's *ever* so handsome!'

Handsome? He was utterly—beautiful. That was the only
word for him. She'd thought so on first seeing him—but how
could she ever forget what she'd seen just now? He'd been like
a vision, all sinew and muscle, with the water gleaming on his
smooth skin and the crisp, dark hairs on his chest… She'd seen
men half-stripped before, of course, working shirtless in the
hot fields in summer or wrestling at the fair, but none of them
had ever struck her as being, quite simply, beautiful.

Stop it. If he felt anything at all for her, it would be pity. *My
lord Dalbury is possessed of a handsome face, nothing more,*
she told herself. *A handsome face, a winning smile—and he*

cannot wait to get away from here. He would have left already, were it not for these visitors of his.

But—Hewitt would still be around.

The next morning Theo drove the two-wheeled, sturdy gig into Buxton, while Jenna sat beside him, wearing a cloak and an ugly bonnet.

Theo had decided that the best way to get over yesterday's embarrassing incident in the courtyard was to pretend it had never happened. Jenna appeared of the same mind, and—apart from the slight awkwardness caused by the narrow width of the gig's seat and the fact that, every time they went round a corner, she was thrown slightly against him and had to jump back again—Theo began, almost, to enjoy himself.

He noticed that this morning a crisp frost had whitened the fields and hedges. Even the bare-branched trees looked rather striking against the clear blue sky and he had to acknowledge that perhaps this wild place did have a kind of beauty.

He suddenly realised that the girl at his side was speaking. 'My lord, what kind of food did you have in mind for your guests?'

'Oh, keep it simple,' he said.

'You're sure?'

'Quite sure.' Inspiration struck. 'Go for local specialities. After all, they'll only be here for one meal.'

She said calmly, 'Unless it snows.'

What an appalling thought. 'If it snows, they won't even get here, will they? And I was thinking, Jenna. We'd better have some entertainment—music, perhaps.' It would kill some time and drown the sound of Celia chattering. 'Can you arrange that, do you think?' Theo was rapidly finding out that the demurely clad, softly spoken Miss Brook— Miss *Bruch*—knew everything and everyone in the vicinity.

'I shall see to it,' Jenna said calmly. 'What will *you* do in Buxton, my lord?'

'Take a look round the town. Purchase some wine.'

'Don't go to Mayfield's,' she said. 'Mayfield is hand-in-glove with Hewitt—he charges the estate double for the wine he delivers each month, then Hewitt and his friends drink it all.'

'How do you—?'

'It is the way of things,' she said calmly, 'to know everything around here.'

Theo dropped her off at the food market with her list, then went to stable the gig at a nearby inn. Damn it.

He told himself the girl and her ailing mother would be right as rain once he'd gone, back in what was after all their old home. And someday, perhaps, she'd marry a good local farmer, or someone like Rob….

Married to Rob? The idea struck him as ludicrous, but why? It was because of the way she spoke. The way she walked, slender and graceful, holding her head high…

Theo pictured her suddenly at a London ball, dressed in a pale pink silk gown, with her blonde hair loosely arranged and jewellery adorning her neck and arms.

A pity there wasn't a nearby pump to stick his head under. Instead Theo went to sort out the wine merchant—Hewitt's friend—who'd been swindling the estate for years. Hell, was everyone in this godforsaken county determined to steal from the inheritance he'd never wanted in the first place?

She wasn't, that little voice said.

Chapter Six

Theo extracted a grovelling apology from Mayfield and a promise of reimbursement, starting with several cases of excellent claret, which Theo had loaded in the back of the gig. Then he visited a lawyer whose name had been recommended in London, who promised to embark straight away on finding a trustworthy local man to act as agent in Theo's absence.

Finally Theo made one last, impulsive purchase and went to meet Jenna again. She didn't see him at first. She was standing at the corner of the square, her drab cloak completely shrouding her slender figure. She'd taken off her ugly hat to do something with her long blonde hair; fix the pins in it more securely, he suspected, so she could hide every single strand of it under that atrocious headgear.

Why was she so determined to disguise her femininity? Because of men like Hewitt and his friends, was the obvious answer. But why hadn't she and her mother left the area altogether? Jenna would surely have been able to find *some* kind of work—as housekeeper, or companion to a lady—in one of the nearby towns or cities.

A sudden buffet of wind tore her hat from her hands and she dashed after it. A passing tradesman got to it first and handed it to her with a look of open admiration in his eyes. Theo watched her thank him; the man positively blushed with pleasure. *She is so pretty. Damn it, she's far too pretty to be stuck in this rural backwater for the rest of her life.*

By then she'd seen him coming in the gig. She'd got her wayward hair securely back under her bonnet and had tied the strings tightly under her chin.

'Did you manage to see to the food?' Theo asked.

'Everything, my lord. It's all ordered.' She was already scrambling up on to the seat by his side.

He nodded towards her basket. 'What's in there?'

'Apples for the children,' she said quickly, 'and a few sweetmeats for them on Christmas Day—they gathered all the holly and pine cones yesterday, you see, to decorate the Hall. I hope you don't mind? I told them how pleased you were with them and Lord Northcote used to give them small gifts. Children crossing the threshold on Christmas morning is supposed to bring luck, you see.'

A chill easterly wind was blowing in from the moors and the sun was already starting to sink as they left the busy little market town behind them. 'Jenna,' Theo said, 'do you actually believe these superstitions? No, seriously. I'm not mocking. I knew soldiers in the war who swore these old customs kept them going. Some kept a lock of a loved one's hair close to their heart. Others would wear sprigs of rowan.'

'Rowan's a lucky tree,' she said. 'Did those poor men believe their tokens would keep them alive, my lord?'

He was concentrating on guiding the pony and gig off the main road for the track that led to the Hall. 'Certainly the tokens gave them hope and the belief that what they were fighting for was a righteous cause.'

'And wasn't it?'

'I used to think so,' Theo said quietly. 'Now I'm not so sure. So many lives ruined. Not just those of the soldiers, but the ordinary people, whose homes—whose *countries* were destroyed.'

She was looking straight ahead. 'My mother's home was not

so very far from the border with France, my lord—her father
was a Prussian army officer. During the war, armies were for-
ever marching through, destroying everything.'

'How did she end up in Derbyshire?'

'Her father died fighting the French when she was about my
age now. She had no other family and her home was razed to
the ground. Like many others she fled for England—London.'
Jenna hesitated, then glanced up at him. 'She worked there as
a housekeeper.'

Where she was seduced by Jenna's father, perhaps? Jenna's
next words confirmed his suspicions.

'That job did not—work out,' continued Jenna. 'She travelled up here because she'd heard some distant relatives had
come to Derbyshire to work in the lead mines. She found no
trace of them, but Lord Northcote hired her as his housekeeper.'

'Did she enjoy the job?'

'Oh, yes!' For a moment her guard was down. 'My mother
made the Hall beautiful, especially at Christmas, bringing in
the greenery and a Yule log. But…' Her voice trailed away.

'But then old Lord Northcote died,' said Theo quietly. 'Leaving the Hall to Lady Hasledene, who never once came to view
her property.'

She said steadily, 'That is the way of things. After all, *you're*
leaving very soon, aren't you, my lord?'

She made it sound like an accusation. Yes. Yes, he was getting away from this godforsaken place, but who could blame
him? At least he'd already set about seeing the estate was run
properly, after years of neglect!

He urged the horse into a trot. 'You could find better work
in London, Jenna,' he said. 'You could be a governess, perhaps.
Or I could help you set up some kind of business—'

He broke off, because she'd twisted round suddenly on the
narrow seat to face him. 'No. My mother *cannot* move far
from here!'

Hell's teeth. She was stubborn, awkward—and damnably

attractive. Sitting like this on the narrow seat of the gig, he'd become aware that her slender leg was unavoidably pressed against his own hard-muscled one, and his body was reacting in a way it definitely should not.

What had that devil Hewitt said about her mother? *She was nothing but a whore and the daughter's set to go the same way.* Her mother had been labelled thus presumably because she'd arrived here from London either pregnant or with her baby. But what the hell had Jenna done to invite Hewitt's insults? As far as Theo could see, the girl did everything she possibly could to repel anything in the way of masculine advances!

Now he said, through gritted teeth, 'It's up to you, of course, Jenna, whether you stay at Northcote Hall. I was just thinking that, given half a chance, you might prefer somewhere with a bit more *life* in it!' With a sweep of his arm he indicated the chilly, deserted moors. 'And somewhere a bit warmer, for God's sake.'

She shook her head, biting that full lower lip he was noticing too often. 'I told you,' she breathed. 'I cannot leave here.'

Theo said nothing else and thought her quite perverse in her tastes. But then, as the gig climbed to the top of the ridge and they saw Northcote Hall lying in the valley ahead with its pale grey walls almost rosy in the low rays of the winter sun, and the faint glimmer of candles already shining from its leaded windows, it looked almost welcoming.

Only because everywhere else looked so damned bleak, Theo muttered to himself.

After that Jenna made herself scarce. Theo had reluctantly decided the pump in the yard was too public, but he damned well needed *something* to calm his restless blood. As luck would have it, Bess was lying hopefully in the hallway by the door, so Theo, keeping on his greatcoat, whistled to her and went out into the fading afternoon light for a short walk up on to the moors.

He shouldn't let the girl trouble him so. But he couldn't push from his mind her tousled blonde hair, her endearingly tip-tilted nose, and those strikingly high cheekbones. Damn—his loins were tightening at the thought of her. It was doing him no good being stuck out here in this backwater, with nothing but sheep and peasants in sight.

And, in two days' time, Lady Celia's party would be arriving—now, there was a female who *definitely* doused any erotic imaginings. How Gilly would grin at his predicament.

Theo threw a stick or two for Bess, then whistled her to his side to go back down the hillside, considering himself suitably purged of lust. From up here, he suddenly realised, he could see the far side of the old turret, that Aggie had informed him was never used. But—there was a light gleaming from its single high window.

His first action on getting back was to take a candlestick up the twisting staircase to the turret, where he opened the heavy door at the top.

It was—or had been—someone's study. The walls were lined with books and there was an old oak desk, complete with pens and a replenished ink well. It had been recently polished with beeswax; the fragrance still hung in the air. And there was another familiar scent, beside the beeswax. Hung on the back of the door was a small wreath of holly, woven with the delicate yellow flower-spikes of winter jasmine.

Theo went downstairs again. He put more logs on the fire and sat with Bess at his feet. He thought of London, of his friends there. But…London seemed a hell of a long way away. The girl Jenna was very near. *Too near.* And this place bewildered him more by the minute.

Chapter Seven

The next morning Theo worked steadily on the estate's papers until Aggie told him, when she brought him coffee, that Jenna was about to set off to Buxton to collect the food she'd ordered yesterday.

Theo confronted her in the cobbled yard, where Rob was helping her get the gig ready.

'Jenna. You're not going by yourself, are you?'

'And how else did you expect the food to get here, my lord?' She said this in a mild voice that couldn't be described as insolent, but…

'I thought it would be delivered.'

'Out *here*?'

Of course. Stupid idea, to expect small market traders to come all this way. His eyes narrowed. She was dressed as he'd seen her that first day, in a man's scruffy coat, with boots and her long hair thrust under a cap. It was as if she was determined to show him she wasn't seeking his, or anyone's, attention. Except that somehow, with her small hands thrust in the pockets of that big old coat, and with her wide brown eyes blazing defiance, she looked more enticing than ever…

Hell, swore Theo. He'd asked after Hewitt in Buxton and been told he'd left the area; as well, or he'd have seen the wretch in gaol. Now he said, 'Take Rob with you.'

'Impossible! Rob has to collect firewood from the North Wood.'

'Take Rob with you and stop arguing,' ordered Theo.

Lips pressed tight, she climbed up on to the gig and took the reins; Rob clambered up beside her and they rattled out of the yard.

Theo went round the house room by room, making a list of repairs that needed doing, horribly aware that tomorrow— Christmas Eve—his guests would arrive. When he heard the sound of the gig clattering into the courtyard a couple of hours later, he made himself stay where he was for a while.

Then he went into the kitchen. The big table was laden with provisions and he examined each item with dawning incredulity. 'What on earth…?'

Jenna had come in carrying one last big parcel. She'd taken off her coat and cap, and her long blonde hair hung loose. She saw his face, and her eyes grew stormy. 'You said!' she accused him. 'You *told* me to get traditional Christmas fare!'

'I know,' Theo said. 'But what on earth is it?'

She pointed at everything in turn. 'This is brawn. Here are chitterlings and Derbyshire oatcakes. These are pigs' heels. And here…' she unwrapped her parcel '…is a boar's head.'

'A boar's… Dear God, you're joking.'

She stared at him a moment, then she started to gather it up again and push it into her assortment of wicker baskets. 'Very well, my lord. I shall take it all back!' The boar's head was heavy; Theo saw her stagger and hurried to take it off her.

'No,' he said, 'leave it.' He was thinking of Celia's face. She would most likely faint when she saw the boar's head, and… Good God, the boar had little, puckered-up eyes like Celia's mother's!

He was trying not to laugh. 'We'll keep it,' he said. 'I think we're going to give my visitors tomorrow an experience they won't forget for a long, long time.'

Jenna's face was shuttered. 'I must go and get changed, my lord,' she said very quietly and hurried off upstairs.

Damn it. He'd upset her again.

A few moments later Aggie came in, having clearly encountered Jenna. 'Miss Jenna's tired after her journey, my lord,' she told Theo in a reproachful voice, 'so I've told her to have a rest. Now, these pies can go in the pantry and the pig's head, too. The brawn I'll put in stone jars, to keep nice and moist... What've you done to upset our Miss Jenna, my lord?'

'Nothing,' lied Theo.

'I just hope you haven't made mockery of all this food she's bought. 'Cos no one works harder than our Miss Jenna, my lord—and I should know!'

Theo heaved in a deep breath. 'You've been here over twenty years, haven't you? Jenna told me.'

'Aye, my lord,' Aggie said proudly, 'twenty-four in all! I served the old lord fourteen years, and Maria—that's Jenna's poor mother, sir—had been here for almost ten when he died. So sad it was...'

Theo frowned. *Almost ten years? But that would mean...* 'I thought,' he said, 'that Jenna's mother arrived here with her baby?'

Aggie froze. 'Of course, sir. Me and my silly head, I've got it all in a muddle—I'm no good with dates.'

Theo said sharply, 'Aggie. Do you know who Jenna's father was?'

Aggie was carrying a big pie towards the pantry, but she turned, still rather pink-cheeked, and said, 'She shouldn't be skivvying, sir. That's all I know. The poor lass shouldn't be skivvying.'

'I can tell that,' said Theo. 'I want to help her.'

'Do you, indeed?' declared Aggie. 'I'm sorry if I'm speaking out of turn, but she's a lovely lass, is our Jenna—and is your *help* going to do the poor girl any good at all, my lord, when you go back to your fancy life in London?'

* * *

Theo had taken Bess out for a walk. All his best-laid plans—
escaping from London and Lady Celia, offering Jenna and her
mother security in their old home—were going badly wrong.

He'd only just got back, and was putting more logs on the
fire, when Jenna came in.

She was wearing that shapeless grey gown and a huge apron.
The drabness of her attire smote him.

'My lord,' she said quietly, 'you asked me yesterday if I
could find some musicians to entertain your guests tomorrow.
There wasn't much time, but while I was out this morning—'

He interrupted her, eager to show approval. 'You've found
some? Excellent, Jenna! Can they come tomorrow afternoon,
when my guests are here?'

'They're here *now*. So you can listen to them.' She hesitated.
'But I'll quite understand if they're not suitable.'

'Of course they will be!' Theo said heartily. But his cheer-
fulness faded a little as they came in.

As entertainment for Lady Celia, her mother and friends,
they looked—unpromising. There were five of them altogether.
One had a fiddle, three carried wind instruments of some sort,
and the fifth had—

Bagpipes. Lord help us.

'Festive greetings to you, your lordship!' said the burly man
with the fiddle. 'Now, then, what tune would you like?' Jenna
hovered by the door, looking apprehensive.

'Oh, anything,' said Theo, sitting down. 'But make it seasonal, you know?'

They began. The noise they made was extraordinary, registered Theo in astonishment; sounded, in fact, as if a cat was
being strangled, very slowly. And that was before they started
singing.

It was dreadful. Just as astonishing as the food…

A rather wicked idea began to form in Theo's mind. 'That's
enough,' he said, standing up. He was aware of Jenna watch-

ing him, dismayed. He went over to the man with the fiddle and shook his hand heartily. 'Just the job. Can you come and play here tomorrow at around four o'clock?'

'On Christmas Eve, your lordship?'

'Exactly. I have some rather special visitors and I'll pay you well.'

Broad beams spread across their faces. 'Well, if you're sure, your lordship! Some of them fancy London folk, they say Ned's bagpipes do hurt their ears!'

'Ned's bagpipes are just fine,' said Theo stoutly, escorting them to the door. He turned back to where Jenna hovered, uncertain.

'I'm sorry,' she whispered. 'They were dreadful, weren't they? I—' She broke off suddenly. 'You're laughing! Why are you laughing?'

He shook his head, still smiling. 'They're perfect,' he assured her. 'Inspirational, in fact!'

She was backing away from him. 'You're making fun of us all again. Mocking us...'

'No!' His hands were suddenly on her shoulders. 'No, Jenna, it's my *guests* I'm laughing at, not you!'

She'd frozen beneath his touch, but he could feel the warmth of her beneath that drab dress; could see a faint pulse flickering in her slender white throat.

'Your guests? But—' her voice was little more than a whisper '—your guests are rich, fashionable people from London, and you surely want to impress them.'

'No,' he said earnestly. His fingers were moving down her arms now, in an instinctive caressing movement. *I'm just comforting her,* he told himself. *Reassuring her.* 'Listen to me, Jenna. I don't even want them here, but I couldn't say no.'

'You—'

'I don't like Christmas. In fact, I detest Christmas—but everything you've done, the decorations, the food, and now this

music—will mean my guests can't get out of here fast enough!
You're—*inspirational*, Jenna!'

With his hands round her waist, Theo picked her up without thinking and swung her round—she was so light in his
arms, so slender—then he put her down. She was trembling;
he could feel it, because his hands still spanned her waist. Her
eyes were lifted to his, with something he didn't understand
in their depths; her face was very pale.

She twisted from his grasp and fled from the room.

Theo sighed and slumped in the armchair by the fire with
Bess at his feet. What had he done now?

*Nothing, except pick her up in my arms and feel the soft
slenderness of her, the delicious curves hidden beneath her
ridiculous clothes. She's done something to me that I damned
well shouldn't have allowed to happen.*

Tomorrow, Lady Celia and her party would spend a brief interlude here and hurry on their way. Then he, Theo, could prepare to leave—and the sooner the better for everyone, clearly.

Jenna's mother was sewing by the light of a candle in her
room next to her daughter's. 'Is everything ready, my darling,'
she asked, 'for Christmas? It will be like the old days—do you
remember? Sit here beside me, and we can talk of the old days.'

Jenna forced a smile and pulled a small chair close to her
mother's. 'You must not tire yourself, Mama.'

'I'm not tired at all. Because everything is going to be all
right!'

She talked on, in her softly accented voice, of the
Christmases when Jenna was little, and of the happy times
when she herself was a child in Germany, before the war came.
Jenna listened, but inside her heart was a knot of pain.

To Lord Dalbury, she was nothing, but Jenna had let Lord
Dalbury come to mean far too much to her. Seeing him under
the water pump that day, half-stripped and splendid, had sent
riotous emotions through her that she hadn't known existed.

All her emotions—all her senses—were fine-tuned to his voice, his movements. To the way he dragged his hand through his dark hair when exasperated, or burst into reluctant laughter when his irritation turned to amusement…

Soon he would leave and forget her completely. But—when he'd swung her round in his arms just now, she'd wanted to melt into his warmth and strength, and lift her face for his kiss, and beg him for…

No. Impossible!

And Lord Dalbury wasn't her only problem. When she'd set off to Buxton this morning his lordship had ordered her to take Rob, which she did—but only as far as the North Wood, where she'd left him, despite his protests, to get on with chopping the firewood needed for the Hall over Christmas.

Soon she was regretting her decision bitterly, because on her way back from Buxton with all the food, she'd been accosted by Hewitt and a couple of his rough friends on horseback, who'd pulled out in front of her on a lonely stretch of road.

'Well, well. If it ain't our jumped-up little Miss Jenna,' Hewitt had said nastily. 'I've come to ask you how you're going to pay me back for makin' me lose my nice comfortable job!'

'You deserved to lose your job years ago, Hewitt,' said Jenna steadily. 'Move aside.'

'Or you'll what?' He was edging his horse closer. 'Set his lordship on me? Then I'd tell him the truth. That you're the local whore's daughter…'

'Don't!' she cried. 'Don't you dare to tell him such falsehoods about my mother!'

'Aha! Is *that* the way the land lies?' crowed Hewitt. 'Opened your legs already for Dalbury, have you? Then I guess we'll have to leave things alone for a while.' He drew very near, so she could smell the stink of his breath. 'But just wait till his fancy lordship's gone. Then me and the lads, we'll come creepin' up to the Hall one night and give you a time you'll never forget…'

'You are scum, Hewitt,' breathed Jenna. 'Get out of my way.'

Hewitt pulled back his horse, laughing. 'Just wait till your lordling's gone. Oh, aye, just wait...'

As she drove on home she'd kept her head high. But her hands had been trembling.

No wonder her mother's mind was fragile—for scarcely a week after Lord Northcote's funeral Hewitt had pressed himself upon her mother and warned her that it was no good at all complaining to the authorities, because she was a foreigner and a whore.

Jenna had been a child—eight years old—but she'd remembered her mother's terrible, terrible silence: a silence that endured for months. And she'd learned the lesson, loud and clear, that men brought you heartbreak if you loved them and ruin if you refused them.

Wait till he's gone. Hewitt's words sent sick shivers up and down her spine.

The next day—Christmas Eve, Aggie reminded Theo, as if he could forget—passed slowly. Jenna was quite clearly avoiding him, though he glimpsed her from time to time, busy around the house with the two Harris girls. By midday Theo was expecting any minute to see two, possibly three carriages containing Lady Celia and her companions coming down the rough road to the Hall. But midday came and went.

At two Theo ate a cold lunch. He did some more work on the estate accounts. When daylight began to fade, he started to feel—what? Relief?

No, because if they were much later, they'd have to stay overnight—a truly awful thought. Then the musicians arrived, just as he'd told them to.

'I'm afraid I don't need you after all,' Theo told them.

'You mean—you don't want us to play, my lord?' Joe, with his fiddle, was crestfallen.

'No, because my guests aren't here yet. I'll pay you, of course.' Already he was reaching in his pocket, handing out coins.

The festive decorations mocked him.

When Theo heard the sound of a horse's hooves clattering into the courtyard a couple of hours later, he hurried outside to find a liveried groom. 'Message from Chatsworth House, my lord!'

The groom held out a note from the Duke's secretary. The Duke had received a letter today telling him that Lady Celia's party hadn't even set off yet from London, because Lady Celia's mother had a sore throat! *Talking too much*, thought Theo. They would, however, commence their journey north on the twenty-sixth, spend two nights on the way and would hope to call at Northcote Hall on the afternoon of the twenty-eighth of December, if that was convenient.

Theo ground his teeth. *No.* Not convenient at all. He'd hoped to be off just as soon as Christmas was over and travel was feasible again. But—what could he do? If he sent a letter today, it wouldn't reach them until after they'd set off!

Damn.

The groom departed.

An hour later Theo was sitting at the dining-room table, the steak-and-ale pie Aggie had served him going cold at his side, when Jenna came silently in.

He looked up at her. 'They're not coming,' he said flatly. 'Not for another four days.'

Jenna felt her heart jolt. *That meant he would have to stay.*

But—he hated it here. She could see it in his face.

'I'm sorry, my lord,' she said quietly. 'To spend Christmas on your own here cannot be what you would have wished. You must be used to celebrating the festive season with all your family, all your friends—'

He interrupted her. 'Christmas is about as enticing to me as it is to a Norfolk turkey,' he said.

She shook her head in bewilderment. 'As enticing...'

He pulled out the chair next to his. 'Have you a moment?'

'Of course, my lord.'

'Then please——sit down.'

And he told her. He didn't know *why* he told her, this woman whom he scarcely knew; he didn't know why he should confess to her what he'd told nobody else. He hadn't even been drinking, for God's sake. But he told her basically how, as a child, he'd been left at his boarding school every Christmas because his father didn't want him at home.

'How old were you, my lord?'

'I scarce remember. I think I was seven when I was sent away.'

She listened, her lovely face lambent with sympathy. 'Didn't your father love you? Didn't your mother?'

'My mother died when I was four. My father was busy being a rakehell, gambling away what was left of his estate. I didn't fit in with his plans.'

'I'm sorry. So sorry...'

Theo poured himself wine. 'Don't waste your sympathy on me. That was long ago, but I'm just trying to explain why Christmas for me has never held much appeal.'

She hesitated. 'I believe you were in the army for some years, my lord. Surely you got the chance to celebrate Christmas with your officer friends?'

Theo smiled at the memory. 'In Spain Wellington always had us retreat to our fortresses during winter, so we weren't actually fighting. But Christmas Day didn't mean a great deal. An extra rum ration for the men, an extra portion of meat if they were lucky and something the army cooks called plum pudding.'

'But plum pudding's delicious!'

He grinned. 'Not by the time our army cooks had finished with it, believe me.'

Ruefully he remembered the doughy mess pretending to be plum pudding boiled up in huge cauldrons by the army's slovenly cooks. In the evening some soldiers might try singing a carol or two, until the others started throwing things at them. Theo and Gilly used to talk rather longingly about London, where the festive season at least served the purpose of being an excuse for party after party. They used to fantasise about their return home, and talk about the beautiful women who'd welcome them...

But—it hit Theo like a thunderbolt—the most beautiful woman he'd ever met was sitting here at this table with him. And all he wanted to do was gather her in his arms and kiss her, and tell her he would make everything all right for her. But he damned well couldn't, because...

He couldn't, for a thousand-and-one reasons, and it was cruel to even let her start to guess the impact she'd made on him in this strange, lonely place.

'Jenna,' he said, touching her hand—hell, he shouldn't even have done *that*, she jumped as if he'd struck her—'Jenna, when I leave, I'll see that you and your mother are safe here, I swear it.'

'Of course,' she said steadily. 'You told me from the beginning you weren't staying long—no one could expect you to. But...'

Her voice trailed away. It was important. He could *tell* it was important, from the way she looked at him, from the way she lifted her sweet face to his.

'But what, Jenna?'

'Some people,' she whispered, 'face Christmas with *nothing*. You know that, don't you, my lord? With barely enough food to exist, perhaps not even a roof over their heads. My mother's home in Germany was devastated by the war.'

'Yes,' he said quietly. 'Forgive me for my selfishness. I've seen what war can do.'

'Of course.' She drew her hand away, still anxious. 'My lord—this sounds presumptuous—but what would you *really* like for Christmas Day tomorrow?'

You, Jenna. The thought surged through him like a rip tide. He wanted this lovely girl in his arms, in his bed, damn it... He put his head on one side, pretending to think hard. 'I'd like...a long walk over the hills.'

'You're getting the idea,' she approved. 'With Bess?'

He grinned back. 'With *you.*'

That wiped her smile away. 'No—tomorrow morning I'll have so many jobs to do...'

'I'm your employer,' he reminded her gently. 'Please come, Jenna. You want me to enjoy Christmas Day, don't you?'

'I'll come.' She smiled again; he felt his breath catch in his throat. 'And you never know, my lord—your Christmas might not be as bad as you think.'

She slipped away from the room before he could reply.

Theo leant back in his chair, breathing deeply, Enjoy Christmas? *Him?*

But—something about the girl cast enchantment on whatever she touched. Careful, he warned himself. Be very careful.

Chapter Eight

The next morning Theo was awoken by the clamour of church bells. He turned over and tried to cover his ears with a pillow, but then he heard something else. The sound of children's laughter.

Children?

He heaved on his clothes and went downstairs into the kitchen. Jenna was there, surrounded by at least a dozen small children, who chattered gleefully as she handed out little paper parcels wrapped in string.

When the children saw Theo they ran off into the yard like frightened chickens. Theo said, 'Good morning, Jenna.'

'Good morning, my lord. And a merry Christmas to you!'

Theo grinned back. 'Merry Christmas. I'm sorry about the children—I didn't mean to scare them witless. What were you giving them?'

She looked defensive. 'Oh, it's something my mother used to do, when she was housekeeper here, with Lord Northcote's permission, of course. It's an old custom, from Germany, you see?' She unwrapped one of the paper parcels for him. 'There are a few nuts and dried fruits, and pieces of marzipan—a tiny treat, but the children adore it. You must be ready for breakfast, my lord? Christmas Day breakfast?'

She was already leading the way into the dining room,

where the oak table was laden with ham, cheeses and bread. She started pouring him coffee. 'There is cold food, as you see. Or should I cook you some bacon and eggs, my lord?'

'The cold food looks good. But what's that?' He was pointing at a long, rich-looking loaf, bursting with fruit and almonds.

'It's called *stollen*,' she said. 'I made it early this morning, with Aggie; it's still warm. My mother taught me how to make it—they have it on Christmas Day in Germany. I—I baked another one for the children, but they've eaten it. I do hope you don't mind?'

'It sounds an excellent idea,' Theo said. 'And next is that long, long walk we talked about, remember?'

'I'll be ready for you in an hour, my lord.' She bobbed a quick curtsy and hurried off, while Theo carved himself a thick slice of warm *stollen*. Which was actually one of the best things he'd ever tasted.

They climbed up to the rocky ridge that crested the moorland, where Jenna showed him how you could lean with your arms spread out and catch the strong wind like a sailing ship. Theo tried it, too, laughing with her, but really he was noting how lovely she looked with her fair hair blowing around her face.

Then they walked along the ridge for two miles, while ragged clouds played hide-and-seek with the mid-winter sun; they heard the distant, joyous sound of yet more church bells ringing for Christmas, then they sat a while and Jenna told him about a bottomless pool high on Kinder Edge, where if you went up in the light of the full moon a mermaid might rise from the dark depths and predict your future.

'Have you ever been to see her, Jenna?'

She turned to him, suddenly serious. 'Me? I know my fortune already, I hope—to stay with my mother and keep her safe. I haven't thanked you enough, my lord, for allowing us to move back into the Hall.'

'You've thanked me,' he said. Suddenly he caught her hand and pulled her up. 'But what about *you*? What about marriage and children, Jenna? What about—love?'

Just at that moment the sun went behind a cloud. She shivered and her hand, so warm in his, pulled away. 'That's for others.' She shook her head. 'Not me.'

'But—why?'

Already she was marching on, Bess bounding at her heels. Theo, frowning, strode after her. She was heading down the hill now, along an ancient paved way. 'What's this?' he called.

'The lead miners used it, centuries ago,' she called back, the wind snatching at her words. 'Some say it was built by the Romans.'

'Where does it go to?'

She waited for him with a mischievous smile that did something strange to his insides. 'It leads the way, my lord,' she said softly, 'to a party. And I hope you are going to be pleasantly surprised. The party is at—Northcote Hall.'

For once, Theo was speechless.

Afterwards, Theo remembered the party as a series of vivid, almost riotous images. He remembered farmers, villagers and children all gathered in the lantern-lit courtyard as he and Jenna returned. He remembered the almost fearful silence that fell, until Theo called out, 'Merry Christmas to you all!'

'Merry Christmas to you, my lord!' Their greetings resounded in the crisp winter air.

Then he heard something else—Joe's fiddle, tuning up. Theo was already backing away as the band of musicians set about a jig, but…

'This time,' he said wonderingly to Jenna, 'they don't sound so bad.'

'They were nervous of you, my lord, when they played for you in the Hall,' she answered quickly. She'd been watching him, wary of his reaction. 'I hope you don't mind the party,' she rushed on, 'it was presumptuous of me, I know! But I thought, there's so much food and it's what Lord Northcote used to do...'

'Jenna,' declared Theo, 'you're amazing. Truly amazing.'

Somehow they were alone here in this shadowy corner of the courtyard. Everyone else was dancing to the merry music, even the children. Theo wanted to kiss her, wanted to do much more than kiss her, God damn it. Desire was thumping hotly at his loins.

He simply took both her hands and asked, 'May I have the pleasure of this dance?'

When everyone was hot and worn out from the dancing, Rob and some of the village lads hauled out two trestle tables and Aggie and the two Harris girls brought out huge platters of cold meats and fresh-baked bread, with spiced ale for the grown-ups and milk for the children.

Theo sat at the head of the bigger table. Jenna, he saw, hardly sat down at all, but was busy organising, making sure no one was left out. Theo talked to his neighbour, a jolly farmer, but he was never more content than when he could see the sparkle in Jenna's eyes, or hear the soft lilt of her laughter as he watched her graceful form weaving amongst the guests.

Afterwards, when the stars shone overhead, the children sang some old Christmas carols, then everyone started to reluctantly depart, the men shaking Theo by the hand.

'Just like old times,' they were saying fervently. 'The best Christmas for years—everything's going to be all right, now you're here, my lord!'

What would they say, Theo wondered, if he told them it was the happiest Christmas he had spent in his life?

Aggie and the girls were already clearing away the dishes. Theo helped Rob put the tables away, then went inside. Jenna was about to begin on the washing up, but Theo beckoned her aside. 'Come with me a moment. Please.'

'But—'

'Aggie's got plenty of helpers. I want to show you that I'm not *entirely* bereft of Christmas spirit!'

She followed him almost shyly to his study. 'Have you enjoyed yourself today, my lord?'

'Enormously,' he said and her sweet face brightened. Inside his study, he lit a candle; he suddenly noticed that she was wearing a gown that actually showed her figure and her hair must have fallen from its pins during the dancing.

He dragged his eyes away from her and unlocked a drawer. 'I believe gifts are traditional at Christmas, aren't they? Look. I got this for you the other day in Buxton. A small seasonal token of gratitude.'

He lifted from the drawer a small package wrapped in silk; he watched as she opened it.

It was a small coral bracelet. It wasn't expensive—he hadn't wanted to embarrass her. But…

'No,' she breathed. 'I cannot take it.'

He saw how the shadows from the candles were flickering across her face, making it difficult to read her expression. 'Why?' Theo asked softly. 'Don't you like it?'

'Yes. Yes, it's lovely, my lord.' She swallowed. 'But I shouldn't…'

'Why not?'

'I've bought you *nothing*, and…'

She tried to say more; her full lips trembled slightly as she sought words that wouldn't come.

'Jenna,' he said. 'You've given me a precious gift. A Christmas Day that was not only endurable, but…'

'But what, my lord?'

He saw a pulse beating at the base of her throat and placed his finger there, softly. 'But was one of the most magical days of my life,' he breathed. Then he touched her tender cheek, cupped her jaw and lifted her face to his.

Her lips had parted slightly—in question? In protest? He wasn't sure. And he didn't wait to find out.

He kissed her. He'd been wanting to kiss her for so long— ever since he saw her on that hillside on the day of his arrival, in her man's coat and breeches. He'd been wanting to kiss her ever since he'd realised how full her lips were, and how much he longed to taste them.

He felt the utter shock rippling through her as his mouth touched hers. He knew—just *knew*—that she had not been kissed before. Gently he caressed her mouth with his and drew her closer. Knowing he should not be doing this. Knowing he could not stop doing this.

As for Jenna, she felt the heat surging through her veins at the first touch of his lips. And all the time, his strong warm hands were pulling her closer, pressing her against the lean length of his hip and muscled thigh, filling her with tremors of desire. Her breasts ached with something she couldn't name; they felt soft and full, wanting to nestle further against the hardness of his chest… *No.*

She shuddered violently in horrified awareness of how deep was her longing for this man, and how dangerous. If just his *kiss* could do this to her, then what else lay in store? How far would he take her, if she let him, into the hot velvet darkness of that place she had never been? Her insides were melting and no wonder, because now his hand was cupping one of her breasts through the thin fabric of her gown and his touch on her nipple—stroking it between thumb and forefinger—shot pangs of scarcely bearable longing through her. His mouth was on hers again, a possession, a caress, drawing her deeper under his masculine spell. Weakly she leaned into him, burning at the sensation of her own soft flesh against his hard muscle.

She broke away with a low cry. 'No. This is not right…'

Theo said huskily, 'It could be right. It could be *very* right.'

Her breath froze in her throat.

'I would look after you,' Theo went on, his grey eyes raking her. 'I would pay you a generous salary to continue helping Aggie here. You would have everything you wanted—clothes, food—and I would visit regularly.'

'You—you are asking me to be your *paid mistress*?' She pulled herself away; Theo saw the colour had drained from her face.

'Jenna,' he said almost harshly because his body was fiercely—painfully—aroused. 'We both want each other—you know that. You would be secure here, you and your mother!'

'Is it so very obvious?' she whispered.

'What on earth do you mean?'

She didn't answer; she'd already turned, and was hurrying away.

'Jenna!' he called. 'For God's sake…'

She'd disappeared, up the stairs. Theo cursed. Damn it, she'd enjoyed his kiss all right—she'd melted into him with all the sweetness of a young and eager temptress! Painfully he fought down his arousal. The rich new lord of Northcote Hall had come to pay a Christmastide visit, and she was making the most of it, before he left…

Wrong, Theo. He ground the heel of his palm against his temples. He was utterly and completely in the wrong. Wasn't it bad enough that he'd tried to seduce her? What possible grounds did he have for putting the blame on her, when it was all his fault in the first place, for luring her into trusting him, then lunging at her like some skirt-starved trooper?

The bracelet lay on the floor where she'd dropped it. Sighing, he picked it up. God, that kiss. The incredible sweetness with which her mouth had opened to his… This had gone too far. He had thought to make things plain between them by asking her to become his mistress, but the words he'd intended to use to distance himself from any emotional commitment had actually rebounded on him. The look in her eyes as he'd made his offer—the look of sheer, raw *hurt*—had pierced his defences in a way he hadn't thought possible.

And in three days' time, his unwanted guests were arriving. *You fool. You idiot.*

The next day Theo had glimpsed Jenna from time to time working around the house, organising the giggling Harris girls. He had carried on drawing up his list of improvements to be made on the old Hall after these years of neglect, then had gone out riding. He was still furious with himself for the mercenary offer he'd made to Jenna; was still scarcely able to control the fierce desire for her that was burning him up.

When he got back to the Hall at last, it was almost dark. And he saw that once more a light was on in the turret room.

He stabled his horse, then walked to the foot of the twisting stairs that led up there.

Someone was singing up in that small room.

Softly he climbed the stairs. The door to the room was ajar. And he saw Jenna's frail mother, Maria, in there, humming to herself in a sweet, low voice. She had a cloth and a pot of beeswax, and was polishing everything—the bookshelves, the old carved oak desk—with exquisite care and tenderness.

Theo went very quietly downstairs again, wondering.

The next couple of days passed uneventfully. It was clear that Jenna was making sure she was never alone with him, and Theo had taken Bess for so many walks that the dog was in seventh heaven. He'd heard nothing more from Lady Celia's party, but that morning he was barely back from his walk when Aggie came rushing out to him.

'My lord! My lord! A serving man's just ridden here, with a message!'

Cancelling again? *No such luck.* Breathlessly Aggie told him that Lady Celia, her mother and a party of a dozen friends would reach Northcote Hall in less than an hour.

Theo went to the kitchen, where Jenna was taking some hot, scented loaves from the oven. When she realised he was there, she swung round quickly and gave him a bright smile.

She was dressed—in black. Yes, her apron was white, and she wore spotless white cuffs over her slender wrists. But she wore *black*, and her lovely hair was covered by a hideous cap, of the kind old spinsters wore.

His face must have expressed his astonishment.

She bobbed a curtsy that irritated him beyond measure. 'We're all ready, my lord, as you'll see. Sarah! Joan!' The two Harris girls presented themselves also, and curtsied low—all in black, except for their aprons and caps.

'You look ready for a funeral,' Theo said heavily.

Jenna kept that bright smile pasted to her face. 'But, my lord, we don't want you to be ashamed of us country folk,' she said softly. 'Is there anything else we should be doing to prepare for your guests?'

Hell's teeth, she was playing games. He wanted to rip that stupid cap off her head and kiss her. Instead he just said, 'Everything is absolutely perfect, Jenna. Though—do you think you could send for those musicians to come this afternoon?'

'Presumably so your guests can laugh at them, my lord?'

'Look.' He drew a deep breath. 'I thought I'd made it clear. I didn't invite these visitors and they're the kind of people I left London to get away from, for God's sake!'

She said nothing. He rubbed his temples. 'Jenna—what age was old Lord Northcote when he died?'

'He wasn't old at all, my lord,' she answered quietly. 'He was thirty-five.'

'Then—Jenna!'

But she'd already gone to speak to Rob, who was bringing in logs from the yard. Theo sighed and went to get changed.

Outwardly calm, Jenna saw that all the food was ready. She checked again that the girls' black dresses were tidy and their aprons clean, their hands and faces spotless. She looked at herself, in a mirror on the wall. Some locks of her fair hair had strayed. She pinned them tightly under her cap again, because she was, after all, only a servant.

She would soon be waiting on those rich people from London. Loud, confident men and beautiful women amongst whom Lord Dalbury, despite his protests, would be at ease. With whom he would talk and laugh…

He'd kissed her. He'd asked her to be his mistress, and when she'd refused, he'd been angry, perhaps thought she was angling for more. When all she could think was that his touch melted her, his kiss had been the sweetest thing she'd known, and for more of those moments in his arms, she would have given anything, anything at all.

He would be leaving, very soon. Yet since the day he'd arrived, her life had changed. Her world had changed.

You should have accepted his offer, you fool.

But he didn't really mean it. He couldn't mean it. Look at the way he'd poured scorn on everything here—the customs, the music, the food. And as for his kiss, he was just like all men. Quickly aroused, wanting to bed her then and there—but he'd soon forget her, as she must forget him.

And yet, the certainty of him leaving here was like a dark chasm opening up before her. *As long as you don't let him know it,* she told herself rather desperately. That was all that mattered now. *As long as you never let him know it, you will manage, somehow!* But she wasn't even sure of that, when his friends arrived.

Chapter Nine

Lady Celia's party arrived soon after one. It had grown colder during the last day or so, Theo had noticed; the ground was iron hard, and the blackbirds were clacking in the woods as they hopped from branch to branch searching for the last shrivelled berries.

Theo welcomed them all in the big entrance hall, where Aggie and Jenna and the two girls, in their black gowns and hideous caps, waited to take their coats and mantles. The guests exclaimed in wonder over the hall and the roaring log fires, and the greenery everywhere.

'Why, it's positively *medieval*, darling Theo!' cried Lady Celia in her shrill voice. She was only nineteen, but already sounded exactly like her mother. 'There *must* be ghosts!'

'No ghosts,' said Theo flatly, but Celia's mother, wandering down the passageway, had already spotted the winding stairs to the turret and gave a squeal of delight. 'Theo, please—'

'*No,*' said Theo with unexpected sharpness. 'Don't go up there.'

The women pretended to cower with fright. 'Why not, Theo? Oh, don't say there really is a ghost and you're not telling us?'

Theo barred the way. 'The stairs are unsafe,' he said and ushered them towards the dining hall with gritted teeth.

* * *

Two hours later Theo was forced to acknowledge that all his plans had gone completely, hideously wrong.

He'd thought the ancient hall would horrify them—but they loved it. He'd relied on the food to make them recoil in fastidious distaste. But instead, as Aggie, Jenna and the Harris girls brought in course after course, they applauded with delight. The brawn, the chitterlings—he still wasn't sure what they were, and didn't really want to know—and finally the boar's head, with an apple stuck in its gaping mouth—they adored it all.

'When we reach Chatsworth tonight,' exclaimed Lady Celia, 'we can tell the dear Duke that we have had a positively enchanting time!'

When Jenna came in to whisper that the musicians had arrived, Theo hurried out to speak to them. 'In you go, lads. Make it as loud as possible, will you?'

'Right you are, your lordship!' grinned Joe. 'We'll tune up first, shall we?'

'God, no,' said Theo. 'Those bagpipes of yours, Ned—my guests can't wait to hear them. In fact—I'm depending on all of you.' *You don't know how much I'm depending on you.*

One by one the musicians traipsed in, clearing their throats and shuffling bashfully. There was a startled silence from Theo's guests as they began a wassail song. Theo began to hope.

Then the song ended, and everyone except Theo broke into rapturous applause. 'Wonderful!' cried Lady Celia's mother. 'So thoughtful of you, dear Theo, to arrange such *authentic* entertainment for us!'

The musicians started up again, delighted with their reception. Theo, with a muttered 'Excuse me', went out to the kitchen.

Jenna was there, preparing the next course. Damn it, it

wasn't *fair* that she should have to slave like this. She might be penniless, but…

He suddenly realised she was looking at him with apprehension. 'My lord. Is anything wrong?'

'No,' he said quickly. 'But can you just—you know—hurry the food on a little?'

She looked puzzled. 'But what if your guests haven't finished?'

'Just clear their plates anyway,' Theo said breezily. 'Whether they've finished or not. After all, they won't want to be late leaving.'

She raised her clear eyes to his. 'My lord, were you aware that it has started to snow?'

Apprehension froze his gut. 'Just a few seasonal flakes, I trust?'

She was shaking her head. 'I'm afraid it's falling steadily,' she said.

By the time the musicians trailed home, their stomachs full of warmed wine and mince pies from Aggie, the snow was several inches deep. Their stout clothing and knowledge of the local paths meant that their short journey would be no problem.

But for everyone else travel was impossible. It snowed steadily all evening and a stiff wind piled it up in drifts. Theo's guests took the news calmly; in fact, Theo would have sworn that Lady Celia's blue eyes positively gleamed.

Not one to miss her opportunities, our Lady Celia, Gilly would have said drily.

Aggie and Jenna hurried round all the bedrooms, swiftly lighting fires and putting stone hot-water bottles between clean sheets. The three grooms and two coachmen who'd brought the visitors took up quarters in the attics, their horses fed and rugged up well in Theo's stables.

Theo went outside to fetch in more logs from the store in

the barn and he met Jenna by the back door, carrying some fresh candles for the bedrooms.

'You're quite sure you can manage?' he asked her. Hell, this was his fault—he should have sent a resounding 'no' to his self-invited guests the moment he received that first letter!

She replied calmly, 'My mother would tell you, my lord, that every winter a house like this has to be prepared for severe weather.'

Her mother. That reminded him... *Not now. Leave it, you fool, for now.* 'Of course. What else needs to be done?'

He saw her hesitate. 'We could do with the coppers being filled from the pump in the yard, so we can take hot water up to the bedchambers when your guests retire. But Aggie and I can manage.'

'You will do no such thing,' Theo said grimly, heaving up a huge copper pan from its place by the back door. 'And to be quite honest, I'd rather be of some use than sitting in there with them, exchanging London tittle-tattle. Does that shock you, Jenna?'

'No,' she said slowly. Her eyes met his properly for the first time since he'd kissed her.

Theo put the copper down abruptly and caught her by both shoulders. 'Jenna. I have not been kind to you.'

'My lord—'

'Please,' he said, 'just *listen*. I'm sorry, about you having to do all this extra work. And what I'm most sorry about is my insult to you on Christmas Day. When I offered you money, to...'

And he'd upset her again, he could see, damn his clumsiness! He could feel her tensing as his fingers caressed her shoulders; he could see emotion darkening her wonderfully expressive eyes as she breathed, 'Please. Let me go, my lord.'

'That Christmas Day was magical, Jenna,' he whispered. 'Quite magical.'

He could feel her trembling. He let his hands fall and she hurried off; she had more sense than he did. If she'd stayed, he would have kissed her senseless and let his guests go hang.

Theo went to fill the heavy coppers, which was a kind of penance—but not nearly enough. And he still hadn't asked her the one question he needed to ask.

After absenting himself for as long as he could, Theo reluctantly rejoined the men. The ladies had retreated to the parlour, to partake cosily of tea and gossip by the fire there; he hurried past the open door before they should catch sight of him.

The men were addressing Theo's good brandy in a determined way. 'By God, Dalbury,' drawled Sir Charles Rollaston, 'you've found yourself a strange old pile out here!'

Theo had known Rollaston briefly in the army and couldn't stand him. 'Being away from London has its attractions,' Theo replied evenly.

'I'll wager there's a woman!' another man exclaimed. 'Dalbury must have a sweet little country lass hidden away! Have you heard the saying?

Derbyshire born, and Derbyshire bred—
Give 'em a penny, they'll drag you to bed!'

Oh, how they roared with laughter. Theo felt his fists clench with the effort of not hitting them. Rollaston said, 'Perhaps we'll come up here for the shooting next season, eh, Dalbury? You could set up a house party—get together a bunch of our old army comrades and a few willing girls, what?'

Theo gave a chilly smile. 'Sorry to disappoint you, Rollaston. But I'm not even sure that I'm keeping the place.'

'You're selling up?' they chorused. 'But you can't! It's priceless, Dalbury, really priceless! Never been so entertained in our lives as we were by those fellows who call themselves musicians! And the food—God save us, the *food*...'

Jenna heard it all, because she had just come to the door with the mulled wine they'd demanded. *Give 'em a penny, they'll drag you to bed!*

They'd laughed. All of them. Theo's back had been to her, but she knew he'd have joined in. And his words couldn't have been clearer. He was selling up. He'd lied to her.

She backed away and crashed into a small table set against the wall. She dropped the tray. Theo was out there in an instant.

'Jenna. Here—let me help…'

'No! I can *manage*! Leave me alone!'

She was already kneeling to pick up the tray, but the mulled wine spread like blood across the flagstones. He reached out, to touch her shoulder. 'Never mind about them, or the wine. Just—'

She struck his hand away and ran upstairs to her room.

Afterwards, after Theo had sold the place, Jenna didn't know what she'd do. Whoever bought it wouldn't want her and her frail mother here. And Hewitt would be waiting for his revenge—they'd have to go where he couldn't trace them. Yet her mother would be shattered not to be within sight of this place.

Give 'em a penny, they'll drag you to bed!

So unfair. But—the colour rushed to her cheeks, and her breath caught in her throat—Lord Dalbury didn't have to give her a penny, even. From the moment she'd first seen him, she'd lost her stupid heart.

But she must never, ever let him know it.

For another day and night, it snowed. On the third day it stopped, leaving a glittering, silent world of white-clad hills and frosted trees. The roads were impassable for carriages, but Lord Dalbury's guests were enjoying themselves enormously, playing old-fashioned parlour games like charades and spillikins. Jenna saw that Lady Celia clung to Theo's side from morning 'til night. Once, when Jenna was cleaning out the grate in Lady Celia's bedchamber, Lady Celia herself came in unexpectedly.

Jenna scrambled to her feet. 'I'm sorry, my lady. I'll come back another time…'

Lady Celia put out her hand to stop her hurrying from the room. 'No! I've only come for a shawl.' Her hand suddenly dropped; she looked pale. 'I rather feel it's I who should apologise to you.'

'My lady?'

Celia sat on the edge of the bed. Jenna, watching her, suddenly realised that she was possibly only a year or two older than herself.

'We've put you all to such inconvenience,' Celia whispered. 'And Mama and her friends—they are *hateful* to you all.'

'You are Lord Dalbury's guests, my lady,' said Jenna steadily. 'It's our job to serve you.'

'Perhaps.' Celia gave her a wan smile. 'But Theo didn't really *want* us here, did he?'

'My lady…' Jenna didn't know what to say.

'It's my mother, you see.' Celia gazed up at Jenna. 'She's desperate for me to marry Lord Dalbury, and…and I like him so much, but I don't think he can bear the sight of me!'

Jenna stood frozen. Celia was blowing her nose with an exquisite lace-edged handkerchief. 'I'm sorry, so sorry! I shouldn't even be telling you all this, but you're young, too, you look as if you'd understand…' Celia's tears were flowing down her cheeks now; Jenna took a step forward.

'Can I do anything, my lady? Bring you a cup of tea, perhaps? Or fetch your mother?'

Celia's sobs turned almost to laughter then. 'My mother? Oh, no. One thing you *can* do is keep her away from me! And—please don't tell anyone about this, especially Theo… Will you promise? *Please?*'

'I promise,' said Jenna quietly, and left the room, closing the door behind her.

Chapter Ten

Aggie told Jenna she looked as if she needed some fresh air, so Jenna went out in the crisp snow, walking up on the moors in the sun, trying not to even think about Theo. But on the way back, when the Hall was just half a mile away, she saw a familiar figure striding towards her through the snow.

Lord Dalbury. *Please, please let me be strong.*

'Aggie told me you'd gone out on your own,' he said.

'I've done all my jobs!'

'I'm sure you have.' Theo saw she was wearing her man's coat and hat. 'And you wanted to get away from my guests, no doubt. But, Jenna, I'm sick of the sight of them, too, and a couple of hours ago I walked over to the village, to hire every able-bodied man I could find to dig out that blasted road over the hills. As long as it doesn't snow again, the way should just about be clear by now for their carriages.'

Poor Lady Celia. Jenna gazed up at him, still defiant. 'And when are *you* going, my lord?'

'Me?'

'You're selling up,' she said bitterly. 'I heard you say you were selling up just as soon as you could. You hate it here, don't you?'

'No. I don't hate it at all. In fact, I think it's rather beautiful... Look, you'll be getting cold standing here. Walk back with me and tell me about yourself and all the things you used to do at Christmas. I told you about *my* childhood Christmases, but you hardly told me a thing about yours. What was it like, living at the Hall?'

She'd already set off, her hands thrust deep in her coat pockets, and Theo matched his stride to hers.

'Oh, I was just like any other child from around here,' she said airily. 'We'd go round the cottages on Christmas Eve, tormenting the villagers to give us festive treats like gingerbread men and toffee. And all the way through to Twelfth Night we'd sing heathen songs and believe in all sorts of superstitious nonsense about goblins and mermaids...'

'Jenna,' he said warningly, 'Jenna...' But there was a spark of dancing amusement in his eyes.

'Sometimes,' she went on, 'we'd go hunting for Hob Hurst, because over Christmas he was supposed to grow fat and slow from the extra food the farmers' wives left out for him. Often we'd pinch Hob's food, especially if it was leftover Christmas pudding. But if we were caught, we'd be chased away with curses and snowballs, because it's cold and grim up in these northern parts, my Lord Dalbury!'

Theo was choking with laughter. She laughed back, then was running away from him, round the back of an old stone barn against which the snow had drifted several feet deep.

She couldn't go any further.

Theo followed her. *Now*, he told himself. *Now* was the time to ask her, about her mother, and... 'Jenna—'

Too late, he saw that she'd bent to pick up some snow in her gloved hands and, with a mischievous grin on her face, she hurled it. It caught Theo smack on the chest, exploding into shards of ice that tickled his nostrils. 'Why, you little *imp*!' he called.

She was scooping up some more snow. 'Not up to a battle, Lord Dalbury?'

'I most certainly am.' He was already picking up snow; soon

they were running like children around the barn, laughing and stumbling in the deep drifts, pelting each other with snowballs.

It came to a sudden end when Theo tripped over some hidden obstacle and went crashing face-down in the snow.

'Oh!' Jenna ran over to help him. The smile had vanished from her face. 'Oh, Theo. Are you hurt?'

He pulled himself up. 'Not in the least,' he said. *She'd called him Theo. She'd...*

She was dusting him down, trying to get the encrusted snow off his coat, his sleeves. 'You will catch cold,' she was saying worriedly. 'Look at you, my lord, you look like a snowman, you will be *freezing...*'

'Jenna,' he said softly. 'Jenna.'

'What...?' Her voice trailed away. He wiped some snow from her delicious tip-tilted nose and suddenly his strong arms were around her. 'I'm not cold at all,' he whispered. 'Try me, Jenna.'

And suddenly his lips were on hers, as warm and wonderful as she remembered. His hands had stolen round to the back of her waist, trapping her, and through her garments she could feel the heated power of his body. The frosty air nipped at her ears and nose, but flames of desire uncoiled inside her. The soft, feathery kisses he bestowed were followed by the teasing lick of his tongue; she gasped and resisted, but Theo raised a hand, his fingers drifting across her cheek before they glided to the nape of her neck, holding her ready for what came next.

A *real* kiss.

Jenna barely had time to draw in a shaky, fractured breath before his lips met hers in a passionate caress that instantly flared out of control. Her response was instinctive, inevitable, as was his; he pulled her closer, deepening the kiss. He pushed her coat apart, to run his palms over her shoulders through the thin lawn of her shirt; then his big warm hands moved on to cup and cradle the weight of her breasts until they ached almost painfully for so much more than his touch.

With a groan from somewhere deep in his throat, Theo swung her up in his powerful arms and carried her into the small barn. He kicked the door shut on the cold air and the outside world. He wanted her. He didn't know how the devil he was going to make this work out, but he wanted her more than he'd ever wanted anyone, or anything.

He set her tenderly on her feet in the hay-scented barn. He started kissing her again and this time she responded fiercely, her hands finding his warm body beneath his coat, her sweet lips caressing and coaxing in return. Theo was easing off her coat, unbuttoning her shirt, kissing her swollen lips again while letting his hands slip down to her breasts and tease their tightening peaks until a long, deep shudder ran through her.

Dangerous, a little voice whispered inside her. *Impossible.* She simply could not afford to feel like this. But *he* wasn't to know that. And—she wanted him. She wanted him so badly, even if it was only for a short while. *Something to remember, for the rest of her life.*

He was strong, tender and honest—at least he'd made no false promises of 'for ever'—and if this was all she could get, so be it. To long for love was a weakness she'd resisted since childhood—yet she had never felt so safe, so cherished as she did when he drew her to the hay-strewn floor in his arms, his kisses and caresses bringing her to a fever pitch of need. Soon his mouth was on her breasts, spearing sensation straight to her womb. She gripped him tightly, her hands roving across the tense muscles of his back. She heard herself softly moaning as his fingertips grazed up her thighs, tormenting her. 'Theo. Please...'

He buried his free hand in her hair, his dark eyes fiery with passion. 'Jenna. Say now if you want me to stop. Say it, now. I can tell you've never—'

But she interrupted, whispering, 'I want you, Theo. I *need* you.'

Already he was easing himself into her, gentle yet so strong as his mouth pressed kisses to her face. She gasped and went very still when she felt the blissful wonder of him inside her. Filling her. *Completing* her.

The joy as they moved together took her breath away. She had never known anything so shatteringly beautiful existed. Wave after wave of ecstasy built inside her as he continued to pleasure her, his eyes burning into hers; his husky voice telling her how beautiful she was, how adorable. Then his mouth moved, hot and warm, over her breasts, and she was crying out his name as he took her to the peak of pleasure and beyond. He rode out his own powerful climax, then Jenna pressed her face into his shoulder as the afterwaves of pleasure continued to ripple through her.

He held her close. Wanted to hold her close for ever. *Hell.* He had never felt like this about anyone before in his life. He simply couldn't bear to let her go. What use was his wealth without this beautiful, passionate girl, who'd shown him that possessions—riches—were nothing without responsibility, and love?

'You are mine, Jenna,' he breathed almost harshly. 'Mine.'

She wrapped her arms around him. *No one else's, ever, my love.* She wanted to kiss him again. She wanted this never to end.

But Theo was already on his feet, straightening his clothes and striding to the door. 'I hear voices,' he muttered.

Two men were coming up the hillside, Rollaston and his friend. 'Hey, Theo!' they called.

Theo hurried back to Jenna. 'I will make this all right, believe me,' he said fiercely, taking her hand and kissing it. 'Stay in here.'

Theo went to meet them, buttoning up his coat. 'Gentlemen.'

'Theo,' smirked Rollaston, 'what have you got in that barn? Or should I say—who? Is it by any chance the pretty fair-haired wench who works in your kitchen? Are you averse to sharing, old fellow?'

'Shut your mouth, Rollaston, or I'll shut it for you.' Theo's expression was dangerous.

'God, Theo.' Rollaston backed away. 'Nothing to make a fuss about, bedding a serving wench. Nothing to even *think* about. Marriage, now, that's a different question. We all know you've got to marry well, within the next few months, or you'll lose your new-found fortune, isn't that right?'

Silence fell.

'Do you know,' Theo said, gritting his teeth, 'I've a feeling the road from the Hall might be cleared of snow at last. And I think it would be an extremely good idea if you got on your way by daylight. Don't you?'

They looked at him, frowning, but Lord Dalbury seemed to be in an ugly mood, so they nodded quickly. 'No need to get in a lather,' said Rollaston. 'We'll just go and tell the ladies and get our things together.'

As soon as they'd turned to head down the hill, Theo hurried back to Jenna. She was shivering as if she'd never get warm. 'Is it true?' she whispered. 'What they said?'

'Jenna, *listen*. You must take no notice of them, they're idiots and fools...'

'Do you take *me* for an idiot?' she cut in. 'Is it true, that you've got to marry soon or you'll lose everything?'

He closed his eyes briefly. 'It was a condition of Lady Hasledene's will, yes. But Jenna—'

'You *knew* all this. Yet—' she waved towards the barn '—you let all this happen. And what did you intend to do with me next, pray? Keep me here, readily available, while you choose your new bride and bed her also? Will you marry poor Lady Celia? Is she—*highborn* enough for you, even though you despise her?'

'Please, Jenna, listen—'

She was pushing him aside, cramming her hat over her tangled hair and heading for the door. 'Leave me alone, damn you, Theo!'

'Jenna!' He thought he'd seen tears in her eyes. He tried, one last time, to think what he should say. But by then she was gone, hurrying and stumbling through the snow.

Oh, Theo. I was going to accept your offer, Theo. I was going to agree to become your mistress—because I thought at least you were being honest with me!

Sheer pain fractured Jenna's heart. This was unbearable.

Theo returned to Northcote Hall to see his guests' carriages being loaded in the courtyard. Lady Celia was alone in the parlour, dressed for the journey. When she saw Theo, she moved hesitantly towards him.

'Theo,' she said, 'thank you so much for everything.' She tried to smile, but her voice betrayed her. 'Though I know that you never really wanted us here.'

'Lady Celia,' he began.

But she put her hand on his arm. 'Be happy, Theo,' she said, then turned with a sigh at the sound of her mother's voice.

'Celia, there you are! Theo, my dear, we'll see you in London soon, I trust?'

Theo made the usual comments of a polite host as he saw them on their way. But all the time, he was thinking of Jenna.

She knew now, about the one condition Lady Hasledene had laid on her heir. *Marry well, within the next few months, or you'll lose your new-found fortune.*

Lady Hasledene's ideal gentleman was, she'd stated quite specifically in her will, one who was married—or about to marry—a young woman of suitable breeding and virtue. Up and down the country marriageable misses had latched on to the fact that the newly rich Lord Dalbury was in urgent need of a bride.

Lady Celia was merely the most persistent of their number.

Hence his flight to the wilds of the Derbyshire hills, to give himself time to decide whether he wanted to be part of Lady Hasledene's machinations or not. Then he had met Jenna.

He thought he would never forget first seeing her as she led those children down the hill with their holly, in her man's coat and boots, with her long fair hair just starting to stray from her man's cap, and those lovely gold-brown eyes wide with apprehension as she watched him approach…

Jenna. His blood raced at the memory of their lovemaking in the barn. At the recollection of her soft, low cries as she clung to him and surged towards rapture…

Planning on playing the same sort of tricks as your mother, is that it?

Those ugly words—Hewitt's, on the night he and his friends had intended raping her—hit him like a punch in the gut. Her mother. He had to speak to Jenna, about her mother.

And her father.

The minute his guests had left, he went hunting for her, but found no sign. He hurried up to that little room in the turret, but it was empty, and the jasmine wreath had vanished.

He found Aggie, in the kitchen. 'Aggie. I need to know where she's gone.'

Something in his voice made Aggie step back from him a little. 'Oh, my lord. You've guessed it all now, haven't you?'

'I know that Jenna's father was Lord Northcote. But why didn't anyone *tell* me?'

'My lord,' Aggie faltered, 'I think Jenna thought you might not allow her and her mother back here, if you knew. She felt she brought shame to the place…'

'Far from it,' breathed Theo. 'Did Lord Northcote treat her mother well?'

'In his way he treated her well, my lord. But he was often elsewhere, you see. He used to forget how important he was to her.'

Like me, thought Theo bitterly, *and most of my kind.* No wonder Jenna had refused to be Theo's mistress. She had guessed he would just use her, as her father had used her mother. 'And he left them nothing in his will?'

'No, my lord! As I say, he was a busy man, and he died suddenly, in a riding accident. Jenna's mother was devastated by his death—she was blind to his faults. But then Hewitt was put in charge here, and what he did to Jenna's poor mother… It was *unspeakable*, my lord. She was never well after that, never strong…'

And lately, Hewitt had turned his evil attentions on Jenna. Theo was breathing hard. 'Aggie. This is important. Where has she gone?'

'She wouldn't tell me. She and her mother, they've taken the gig, my lord—she said she'd get it back to you. But I don't think she plans, ever, to return!'

Theo stood outside, where the moon flickered ghost-like on the snow-covered roofs and gables of the Hall. Bitterly he recollected all his own mistakes. Most of all he remembered Jenna's horror when Theo asked her to be his mistress, and she'd whispered to him, *Is it so very obvious?*

He'd not understood those words then, but he did now. She'd meant, *Is it so very obvious that I'm a whore's daughter?*

He simply had to find her. For the first time in his life, he'd found a place and a person worth fighting for. The arrival of Rollaston and the rest had been simply an ugly intrusion into a world he'd realised was truly precious. Looking round the courtyard, he felt he could still see the farmers and their wives merrily dancing beneath the stars at the Christmas Day party, could hear the children sweetly singing carols, could feel Jenna in his arms.

This place was beautiful, and so was she. He needed her—he *loved* her—and he was going to do his damnedest to get her back, this time for good.

Chapter Eleven

'Look, Mama.' Jenna was carefully lighting a fire in the little grate. 'I bought some coal this morning, and soon we'll be quite cosy here.'

She had found a garret in Buxton for them to rent, but even with the fire the room was damp and cold. Out in the streets the sun was starting to turn the packed snow to slush, but the air was still raw. Her mother was distraught.

'I promised him I would stay close to the Hall, always,' she kept whispering. 'I promised I would always remember him...'

Jenna calmly took her frail hand and warmed it with her own. Her poor mother thought Lord Northcote had adored her, when really, in his thoughtless way, he'd simply used her, leaving her penniless on his death, and prey to anyone—especially Hewitt.

They had to get away from here now, because Hewitt had sworn revenge. But where could they go? How could she earn a living for them both? Whether she tried for posts of governess, companion or anything else, no employer would welcome the encumbrance of her poor, sick mother.

Yet all this paled into insignificance, compared to the fact that her heart was broken.

In meeting Theo, she'd felt the rebirth of hope. She'd begun to believe that perhaps he really was what he'd seemed to her from the first—a man of courage and honesty, who wanted to put his neglected estate to rights, and who did not give a fig for what society thought.

She'd been wrong. His own interests—chiefly, his inheritance—came first. *We all know you've got to marry well, within the next few months, or you'll lose your new-found fortune...*

Within months! That was what really hurt. Even while he was making love to her—oh, her insides helplessly melted just at the memory—he knew he would be getting married soon. To whom was clearly not a matter of much importance to Lord Dalbury—and neither was she.

A hard lesson learned.

Her mother was asking for tea, but Jenna had forgotten to buy sugar, so she hurried out to the market only a street away and was on her way back when two children ran eagerly up to her. 'Miss Jenna! Miss Jenna!'

They were from Northcote village; they'd been with her on the holly-collecting expedition when she'd first seen Theo.

For a moment she felt she could scarcely breathe, such was the raw emotion in her chest. 'Jack. Ellie.' She forced a smile. 'What brings *you* here?'

'We've been looking for you, miss! Here's a letter!' they cried excitedly.

Quickly she unfolded the sheet, then turned back to the children. 'Who gave you this?' But they had gone.

She looked at the letter again. She read it slowly, aloud. It was an old-fashioned word puzzle, a riddle.

My first word's not false,
My second's not hate.
My whole you shall find—at Hob Hurst's Gate.

I understand you are looking for employment. Be there on Twelfth Night, at seven o'clock.

Her pulse was racing. Could it be Hewitt, up to his tricks?

But it wasn't his crude writing, and it was delivered by the children, who detested Hewitt and his men. Who, then?

On Twelfth Night she left her mother alone, after telling a kindly neighbour that she was going out for an hour. It was a clear frosty evening and the stars sparkled overhead. Dressed in her man's coat and boots, she climbed steadily up from the town to the place that was known as Hob Hurst's Gate. She gazed all around.

No one. Nothing. Just for a while she'd hoped… She'd been a fool to come. Someone was playing a trick, that was all.

Suddenly she heard footsteps crunching up the path behind her. She whirled round, her heart thumping with apprehension. *Theo.*

He stretched out one lean hand, then stopped. Stayed where he was, a few feet away from her. 'Jenna. I owe you an apology.'

'No. No, you owe me *nothing*,' she whispered. 'Those children. It was you?' She'd known it was him all along—who else? Oh, this was going to be difficult. She'd thought she was strong; she hoped she was immune to him, but…

'Yes. I asked them to find you. Jenna, I didn't expect you to leave the Hall so suddenly.'

She shivered. It was no good. The moonlight on his tall figure made her weak with wanting him. But weakness now was something she could not afford.

'Didn't you?' she shrugged. 'I thought I might become—inconvenient.'

'Oh, Jenna.' He stepped closer. 'I was a selfish fool, to ask you to play the role of servant to my truly hateful guests. Even more a fool, to try to make a more intimate bargain with you.'

'I hope you're not going to offer me money again.'

He caught his breath. 'No. God help me, no. That was one of the worst of my mistakes. An unforgivable insult…'

'You know, don't you?' she said steadily. 'That I'm Lord Northcote's daughter. I assume you got Aggie to tell you?'

'I worked it out for myself—though I should have realised it far, far earlier. And the wretched man left you and your mother in poverty!'

Jenna stood very still. Theo found that he wanted to hold her tight. Wanted to pull her into his arms in that ridiculous old coat of hers. He wanted to kiss the sheer *hurt* from her sweet face and her haunted eyes.

'You think you understand. But you don't,' she whispered, her voice husky with emotion. 'My mother lived for the times he came to stay. She loved him, so much.'

Theo drew in air sharply. 'He left her—and *you*—without money or a home. Prey to villains like Hewitt.'

'She loved him,' Jenna repeated steadily. 'And she believes that he loved *her*. I will not let anyone take that belief away from her!'

'No,' he said. 'I understand. Oh, Jenna.' *No wonder she didn't trust men.* Whether they were villains like Hewitt or rich lords offering impossible promises, she'd seen the ruin they could wreak.

'Jenna,' Theo went on urgently, 'the Hall should be yours and your mother's by as much right as it is mine. For God's sake, I wasn't even related to Lord Northcote, or to Lady Hasledene!'

'I will not take charity!' she declared.

Theo stared down at her. Raw hunger clenched his insides, because he'd simply never seen her looking so beautiful—never seen *anyone* as beautiful as her.

But it was more than mere sexual hunger. He wanted her as his companion. Wanted her to talk with, to laugh with, to cherish and love throughout his life. He said calmly, 'I'm not talking about charity. Would you do me the very great honour, Jenna, of marrying me?'

Slowly the colour left her cheeks. '*No*, Theo. You would lose your inheritance. I heard those men saying you had to marry well, or forfeit everything!'

Somehow he'd taken her hands and was kissing her cold fingers into warmth. Jenna shivered, but her blood was pounding hotly in her veins, and the usual helpless longing was starting to seize her body in its grip. This man meant the world to her. This man had *become* her world. *Impossible.*

On the day he'd made such sweet love to her in the barn, she'd realised that she was powerless to resist him. She'd known, and accepted, that she would take anything he offered, anything that meant she could just be a part of his life, however small. But—she couldn't let him give up so much, so very much, for her!

Then she realised. He was *laughing.* Laughing with that familiar, husky chuckle that melted her very bones. 'I care for that inheritance,' he said steadily, 'about as much as I care for the so-called friends who imposed themselves on me at Northcote Hall. In London that damned will brought me nothing but misery. Then I came—*here.*' His voice was suddenly softer. 'Where I met a beautiful and intriguing girl called Jenna, who has quite simply stolen my heart away.' He took her hand and pressed his lips to it. 'Please marry me, Jenna.'

She was trying so hard to be strong. 'Oh, Theo. This is madness. Society would shun you…'

'My real friends won't give a fig when they see how happy I am. And as for that cursed inheritance—I've got enough for us to live on quite comfortably. Enough to buy up Northcote Hall, if we want to.'

'Buy up… But I thought you hated it!'

He shook his head emphatically, eyes glinting. 'I'm beginning to think it could be the most wonderful place in the world,' he said softly. 'With you by my side. By the way, did you work out the riddle I sent you?'

The colour was stealing softly back into her pale cheeks. 'The riddle... I don't know. I wasn't sure that I got it right.'

'Weren't you? Say it,' breathed Theo. He was holding both her hands now, drawing her closer until she was in the shelter of his strong, warm body. 'Just say it, Jenna.'

She began hesitantly. *'My first word's not false.'*

'Go on.'

'My second's not hate...'

'Which must mean?' There was a teasing warmth in his eyes which made her heart leap and bound.

'Love,' she whispered. 'True love. Oh, *Theo...*'

He held her very tightly. 'That's what I'm offering you, my darling. True love, for ever and always.'

Jenna felt her heart tumbling about inside her. A rush of exhilaration was starting to melt her insides. But still she scarcely dared to hope. 'Are you sure? To give up so very much...'

'I've told you. That Christmas Day, for the first time in my life, I felt like I truly belonged somewhere. I love you, Jenna. I want you to marry me. Will you?'

And suddenly the pure, simple truth of what he was saying wrapped itself around Jenna's heart like a tender embrace, just as his arms enfolded her, and his warm lips pressed kisses to her forehead.

She tried to push him away so she could think straight, instead of being driven to madness by the delicious feel of his lips. 'Theo, you might regret this, terribly. You will have to introduce me to your family...'

'Haven't got any.'

'But there's society!' she pressed on rather desperately. 'We'll have to go to London and face society some time, won't we?'

'Listen to me.' He held her close. 'I won't hide a thing about you when we go to London, because I won't need to. My real friends—and yes, I do have quite a few—will adore you. Marry me.'

Happiness was just starting to pour through her like honey. Her eyes danced. 'I can see you're not going to take no for an answer, are you, Lord Dalbury?'

'You're damned right I'm not.' He grinned.

She nestled into him with a little sigh. 'Oh, Theo. When I saw you with Lady Celia, I hated her enough to murder her! Then I felt sorry for her...'

'She'll get over me.' His finger was tracing the soft line of her throat. 'So your answer is...?'

Her voice came through shaky laughter. 'Theo, I adore you. Of course I'll marry you.'

He let out a sigh of relief. 'Thank God. That means I shan't have to face the London marriage mart again.'

She pretended to squeal with indignation, but Theo pulled her close, his deep laugh rumbling in his chest. And his kiss, tender and cherishing, reminded her deliciously of what lay ahead. Reminded her that, whatever the years might bring, she would have this man at her side, for Christmas and for ever.

At last he reluctantly pulled away. 'It's starting to snow again,' he said.

Jenna gazed around, still in a daze from the magic worked by his beautiful lips. A snowflake landed on her nose, and he kissed it away.

'Oh, I should be getting back to my mother!' she cried. 'She'll be so worried...'

'Your mother,' he told her, 'will be safe at Northcote Hall by now. I sent Rob with the gig for her and a message to explain you would be there.'

'You mean—you knew I'd say *yes*?'

He was suddenly serious. 'I was counting on it,' he said quietly. 'You don't know how much I was counting on it, my darling.'

She stood on tiptoe to kiss his cheek gently. 'I love you, Theo,' she said, her eyes full of yearning. 'Please take me home.'

Home indeed, thought Theo in wonder. Hand in hand they walked down the snow-covered hill together, to the welcoming lights of Northcote Hall. To a new life full of hope, and love, to explore—together.

* * * * *

CHRISTMAS AT
OAKHURST MANOR

Joanna Fulford

Dear Reader,

When I was asked if I'd like to contribute a story for this anthology I jumped at the chance. The only proviso, apart from the Christmas element, was that the story must have a snowbound theme. That suggested all manner of possibilities. The one that stayed with me was a Regency country-house party—it would allow for a lot of social interaction, which seemed appropriate for the festive season, and the snow theme would, conveniently, keep everyone together. Of course, if all the guests were comfortable with each other that wouldn't be a problem. But what if they weren't? What if circumstances brought two old flames together after a traumatic parting ten years earlier? What if being confined in this way was the last thing either of them wanted? How would they deal with the situation, particularly when they've brought another decade's worth of emotional baggage with them? What would happen if the magic was still strong but trust wasn't?

Answering these questions gave me the basis of my story. My hero and heroine may still be attracted to each other, but they're also older and wiser this time around. They've had years to come to terms with what happened before, and they both know that only a fool makes the same mistake twice.

I had great fun writing this tale, so I hope you'll like the result. For maximum enjoyment I would also suggest the addition of a comfy chair, a cozy fire, a bar of your favorite chocolate and, possibly, a glass of wine. Happy Christmas.

Joanna

For Alma and Eunice with love

Chapter One

Vivien Hastings regarded her reflection with a critical eye. Although the neckline was modest and the style demure, the lilac gown did at least flatter her figure and colouring. A matching ribbon was threaded through her blonde curls, her jewellery restricted to a gold pendant. The effect was simple and elegant, eminently suitable for a widow eighteen months made. She sighed. An impoverished widow with two children and an uncertain future.

In the shorter term her life was about to become even more complicated, something she hadn't known when she'd accepted Eleanor's invitation to spend Christmas at Oakhurst. They had been taking tea in her friend's private sitting room the day before, when the conversation turned to the forthcoming celebrations and, not unnaturally, to the guest list. Vivien had already met most of the Dawlish family and was looking forward to renewing the acquaintance.

'Best of all, Andrew will be joining us as well,' Eleanor continued. 'You will recall me speaking of him. He's Charles's youngest brother.'

'Ah, yes. The brother who has been out in India, I collect.'

'That's right. He has been away nine years and is but lately returned.'

'I'm sure your family will be delighted to see him again,' said Vivien.

'Indeed we shall.' Eleanor smiled. 'Not only that, he is bringing another guest with him, a friend from India who returned on the same ship. I never met the man but I'm sure that any friend of Andrew's must be agreeable.'

'No question.'

'His name is Max Calderwood.'

Vivien suddenly felt as though all the air had been driven from her lungs, and she stared at her friend in stunned silence. Max coming here? It couldn't be. There must be some mistake. Perhaps it was a different Max Calderwood, and not the man she had once known.

'Are you all right, dearest?'

'Oh, yes, quite all right,' she lied.

'Only you look rather pale.'

'It's nothing, really.'

There was no way to explain how she felt just then. She was hardly sure herself. It was an emotion compounded of alarm and dismay and, underneath it, something more elusive that resisted definition. Gradually it gave way to relief: at least she'd been forewarned. She would have a little time to prepare herself.

Except that, somehow, it hadn't worked like that. If anything, she felt even more nervous now...

These reflections were interrupted by a discreet knock at the door. It opened to reveal a middle-aged lady in a pale green gown, complemented by a beautiful Norwich shawl. Greying mousy hair framed a face with no pretensions to beauty. She glanced into the room, regarding its occupant with anxious brown eyes.

'Are you ready, my dear?'

'Yes, Aunt Winifred. Quite ready.'

Ready was the last thing she felt but there was nothing for it now but to put a bold face on things.

'Only I should not like to keep our hostess waiting,' her aunt continued.

'No, indeed.'

'Shall we go down then?'

They reached the drawing room a short time later. Seeing them arrive, their hostess excused herself from the conversation and came forwards to greet them. Eleanor Dawlish was a pretty brunette with a ready smile and vivacious temperament that made her appear younger than her thirty years. A near neighbour and close friend, she had been insistent on Vivien spending Christmas at Oakhurst: *Charles and I would like it above all things. Bring the children as well. It will do you all good to get away for a while.* Initially Vivien had thought so too. Now she was far from sure.

'Vivien, you look very elegant as usual. Miss Pritchard, what a lovely shawl.'

Aunt Winifred smiled timidly. 'It is most kind of you to say so, Lady Eleanor. The shawl was a gift from Vivien. She is very good to me.'

'I am sure she is.' Eleanor returned the smile. 'Come; let me introduce you both to my newly returned brother-in-law.'

Vivien inclined her head in acquiescence, knowing that there was no alternative. Eleanor led the way, pausing to greet Peter and Jason Dawlish and their wives Annabel and Mary. Sir Digby Feversham and his sister were there too, talking to the local magistrate, Sir Arthur Hurst. Eleanor continued on until she reached the little group across the room. Her husband smiled as they approached. Vivien returned it. Charles had been unfailingly kind and helpful, particularly since her husband's death, and she was grateful for it, just as she was for his wife's unstinting friendship.

'What fortunate timing,' he said. 'My brother is most desirous of making your acquaintance.' He turned to the man beside him. 'Andrew, I'd like you to meet Lady Vivien Hastings and her aunt, Miss Pritchard.'

Major Andrew Dawlish was just above average height, and possessed the same light brown hair and blue eyes as his siblings. He also had the same impeccable manners. He bowed and favoured them both with a charming smile.

'Delighted, I'm sure.'

'I believe you are but lately returned from India, sir,' said Vivien.

'Just a week ago, ma'am. I must say it's good to be back.'

'It's good to have you back,' replied Charles. 'Nine years is too long.'

'I do hope you had a pleasant voyage, Major,' said Aunt Winifred.

'Tolerably good, I thank you. Of course, I was fortunate to be travelling with an old friend.'

'That *was* fortunate, sir.'

'Even better, I persuaded him to spend Christmas with us at Oakhurst.' Major Dawlish touched the shoulder of a tall gentleman standing nearby. As the man turned round, the Major continued, 'Allow me to introduce my friend, Mr Calderwood.'

Vivien took a deep breath, mentally gathering herself. Then she was face to face with Max Calderwood. Always tall and athletic, the lean frame she remembered now had the hard-muscled strength of a mature man. His hair was still as black as a rook's wing and framed a face whose clean lines and square jaw were entirely lacking in classical beauty. Yet it possessed the kind of rugged good looks that took her breath away. Withal he had undeniable presence. The handsome youth of memory was gone and in his place was this dangerously charismatic stranger.

Cool grey eyes met and held hers. For a brief moment they registered surprise and disquiet. Then he bowed.

'Lady Hastings, this is a most unexpected pleasure.'

With an effort she managed to keep her voice level. 'Indeed it is, Mr Calderwood.'

Charles looked from one to the other. 'Have you two met before?'

'It was a long time ago,' she replied. 'In London.'

'Ten years,' said Max. 'The Harlstons' ball. We danced together.'

Charles regarded him in frank astonishment. 'You have an excellent memory, sir.'

'For some things.'

Vivien's pulse quickened a little. The Harlstons' ball was the last time they had ever danced together. The recollection was bittersweet. It was also dangerous ground and she sought for a change of subject.

'I understand you are but lately returned from India, sir.'

'That is correct.'

'Is this a visit only or do you mean to remain in England?'

'It is my intention to remain—and settle,' said Max.

'Do you have anywhere in mind?'

'Not yet, but I'm sure the right property will present itself.'

'I'm sure it will.'

Charles beamed. 'What a fortuitous meeting this is. I'm sure you'll have much to talk about over the next few days.'

Vivien summoned a polite smile. For the life of her she couldn't imagine what she could have to say that would possibly interest Max Calderwood. However, there was much she would have liked to ask him.

Before either of them could say more they were joined by Digby Feversham and his sister. The former was in his mid-thirties. Of average height, he was not entirely ill-looking, with a florid complexion and light brown hair carefully arranged in a Brutus to disguise the onset of baldness. He smiled warmly, his brown eyes surveying her appreciatively.

'A pleasure as always, my lady.'

Vivien wished she could say the same. His attentions had

become more pronounced in recent months, despite her efforts to discourage them. Just then she could have wished him at Jericho. Unfortunately, courtesy required her to acknowledge his presence.

'Good evening, Sir Digby.'

'What a delightful interlude this festive season promises to be.'

Delightful was not the first word that leapt to mind, but agreement was the only possible response. Then she turned towards his sister and greeted her politely.

Cynthia Vayne's voluptuous figure was currently shown off to advantage by a low-cut evening gown of Pomona green silk, in the first stare of fashion. Brown ringlets framed a face that was striking rather than beautiful, and dominated by dark, assessing eyes whose gaze until then had rested hungrily on Max. Recalled by the mention of her name she assumed a smile.

'Lady Hastings, I am delighted to see you again.'

'What a pretty dress, Mrs Vayne.'

Cynthia preened, her gaze flicking dismissively over Vivien's lilac gown. 'How fortunate you are to be able to wear that colour, but then widows are obliged to entertain such sober hues, are they not?'

Max frowned and shot a swift glance at Vivien. 'I'm sorry. I didn't know.'

'How should you?' she replied. Then, deciding he might as well hear the rest, added, 'My husband died eighteen months ago; pneumonia following a chill.'

'My sincere condolences.' The tone *was* sincere, like the accompanying look, and both were unexpectedly warming.

Cynthia shot him a sideways glance and then adopted an expression of sympathy. 'And how are your children, Lady Hastings?'

'They are both well, I thank you.'

'They must be such a comfort to you.'

'Yes, they are.'

'They must be quite old now.'

'John is eight and Rachel six.'

'No wonder you look tired. Children are such a huge responsibility, are they not?'

Vivien saw which way the game tended. Max was being informed in no uncertain terms of how much baggage she was carrying. However, she had no wish to hide it and, on the whole, it might be better if he did know.

'Yes, they are a big responsibility,' she replied, 'but I will not tire of it.'

Max surveyed her steadily. 'The sentiment does you much credit, my lady. It cannot be an easy situation.'

'No, it isn't, but we play the hand we're dealt.'

Cynthia's gaze darted from one to the other and then she smiled. 'You are so right, Lady Hastings, and so very brave. Digby and I both think so.'

The conversation was interrupted by the sound of the gong and the company went into dinner. Vivien's dominant emotion was relief. After the trauma of reunion with Max she wasn't sure that she could have maintained a flow of casual conversation over dinner as well. This small hiatus would provide a breathing space, time to regain her composure. Then they could settle into their roles as polite, distant acquaintances.

She was seated between Major Andrew Dawlish and Sir Arthur Hurst, and good manners dictated that she confine her conversation to them. Fortunately they were both pleasant and interesting conversationalists. Once or twice she glanced across the table but Max was engaged in conversation with Cynthia Vayne who, it seemed, was hanging on his every word. He too appeared to be enjoying himself. Vivien looked away.

Eventually the ladies retired to the drawing room and she took the opportunity to speak to Annabel and Mary. They were easy company and their conversation was stimulating. As she hadn't seen them for some months there was plenty to talk about. It filled the time until the gentlemen rejoined them later.

Charles looked around. 'Shall we have some music? Perhaps one of the ladies would oblige me.'

Annabel made to rise but Cynthia was before her. 'I'd be glad to play but I shall need someone to turn the pages for me. Mr Calderwood, would you be so kind?'

Max acceded graciously and went to join her by the pianoforte.

Annabel exchanged glances with Mary and Vivien. Then, lowering her voice, she leaned closer. 'She's set her cap at him and no mistake.'

'I cannot entirely blame her,' replied Mary. 'He's fearfully attractive, isn't he?'

'Rather. Rich too, I hear.'

'Perhaps they'll make a match of it.'

Vivien sipped her tea and said nothing, caught unawares by a powerful sensation of sadness. She fought it, fixing her attention on the music. Although Cynthia lacked real flair she was a competent player and performed the piece creditably. Once or twice she looked up from the sheets in front of her and smiled at Max. However, his face gave no clue as to the thoughts behind. All the same they made a striking couple. Vivien's fingers tightened on the handle of the cup.

The piece ended to general applause. Cynthia played another and then people began to call for their favourites. Charles laughed.

'There's such a pile of music here, Mrs Vayne. Let me help you find the right sheets.'

Max smiled and ceded his place. Vivien saw the expression of annoyance that flitted across Cynthia's face. She recovered quickly and with an assumption of good grace turned her attention to Sir Charles. Under other circumstances it would have been amusing.

Out of the corner of her eye Vivien saw Max approach Sir

Arthur Hurst who was standing nearby. The two exchanged a few words. Meanwhile the conversation by the pianoforte continued. Mary put down her cup.

'I think I'd better lend them a hand. Excuse me.'

Vivien smiled. 'Of course.'

She feigned to watch Mary's progress across the room but all her awareness was on the man who now stood just feet away. The very air between them seemed charged. Would he take the empty seat beside her? It shocked her to discover how much she wanted him to. However, Max didn't move and presently the music started again. Vivien swallowed hard, forced to conclude now that he had no wish to resume their acquaintance beyond what was absolutely required by good manners. Probably he sought to save them both from embarrassment and so it behoved her to take her cue from him. It ought not to have hurt as much as it did.

Eventually the hour grew late and some of the ladies made their excuses and retired. Vivien was glad to follow suit and, having said goodnight, made her way to her room in company with Aunt Winifred. The older woman cast an anxious glance at her companion.

'I must confess I had no idea that Mr Calderwood was to be one of the guests,' she said. 'Did you?'

Vivien shook her head. 'It came as a surprise to me too.'

'It puts you in an awkward position.'

'Not in the least.'

'But, surely, given what went before…'

'That is over, Aunt Winifred. Max Calderwood and I are old acquaintances and that's all.'

'Even so, your situation is delicate, my dear. I did wonder if it might not be better to leave Oakhurst and return home.'

'Because of a romantic entanglement that is ten years in the past? I think you exaggerate the matter, Aunt. Besides, I would not offend Eleanor for the world and I certainly would not disappoint the children so. They have been looking forward to this for weeks.'

'Well, when you put it like that…'

Vivien stopped outside her door. 'I am not so poor a creature that I cannot make polite conversation with an old flame.'

'You kept your countenance well, I thought. All the same I did feel for you, my dear.' Aunt Winifred paused. 'You once cared for him very deeply, did you not?'

It was, thought Vivien, a masterly use of understatement. 'We were once close.'

'No one seeing you together could have doubted that. I have often thought that if your parents had not placed such importance on titles and wealth… Well, as you say, it was long ago.'

'It is kind of you to be concerned for me, Aunt, but there is not the least need, I assure you.' Vivien smiled and kissed her on the cheek. 'Goodnight, Aunt Winifred.'

'Goodnight, my dear. Sleep well.'

Vivien entered her room and closed the door behind her. Then she let out a long breath. For all her outward assurance she wasn't certain how easy it would be to maintain an air of unconcern around Max. They had barely spoken a dozen words together and already her mind was in turmoil. All the emotions she had thought dead and buried had risen up to mock her this evening.

After the ladies had retired Max joined his male companions in the billiard room. The game removed the need for conversation and afforded him leisure to try and order his thoughts. All his preconceived ideas about this visit had gone up in smoke as soon as he set eyes on Lady Vivien Hastings. It was more than just a shock: the encounter had given him a visceral jolt. She had always been beautiful but maturity had only enhanced that. Her figure, though a little fuller, was still superb, speaking of the woman now rather than the girl he remembered. The guinea gold hair was the same, the lovely bone structure of her face and that most kissable mouth. Only her eyes were different. Although still a vivid cornflower blue they lacked the sparkle he recalled. Of course, that was not to be wondered at when she had not long been widowed. He really hadn't known about that. Her sadness touched him deeply, and he felt a stab of envy for the departed husband. It was swiftly succeeded by guilt. He had no business feeling envious. After all, he'd had his chance and thrown it away. What mattered were Vivien's feelings, not his.

That was the reason he'd kept his distance all evening. It had been a lot harder than he'd anticipated. There were so many things he wanted to ask her, so much he would have liked to know, yet to enquire would have seemed like impertinence. Even though she was clearly as taken aback as he at their unforeseen meeting, she had been the model of courtesy. Considering his former behaviour that was magnanimous indeed. Taking his cue from her he had played his part, but the thought of having to maintain the role for the next fortnight filled him with dismay. He didn't think his acting ability was equal to it. The last thing he wanted was to create tension as a result of some unguarded word or action. For all sorts of reasons it would be better if he removed himself from her sphere as soon as possible. That meant leaving Oakhurst. It couldn't be done for a day or two until Christmas was over. Even then it was going to be awkward and he had no wish to offend his hosts, but somehow he was going to have to invent a credible excuse.

Vivien lay awake staring into the darkness. She guessed it was very late but sleep would not come because her mind was elsewhere, lost in a long-ago evening when she and Max last danced together…

She'd thought he seemed less cheerful than usual but had little guessed that the cotillion would be the prelude to heartbreak. When the dance ended they retired to the terrace but this time he didn't take her in his arms and his expression filled her with foreboding.

'Max, what is it? What's wrong?'

'There's no easy way for me to tell you this,' he replied, 'but I must, even though I feel like the greatest cur in England.'

'Tell me what?'

'That I must end this, Vivien. I wish with all my heart that I could offer you the hope of a future but I cannot. I have no title and no fortune, in short no means of supporting you in the manner to which you are accustomed and have every right to expect.'

She paled. 'I have never cared for those things. You know that.'

'Easy to say so now, my dear, because you have never experienced want.'

'I have a good dowry and in another two years I come into my majority.'

'Your parents have never approved my suit; they see me only as a fortune hunter.'

That was plain truth. Her parents looked far higher for their daughter's future husband and made no secret of the fact. Their attitude towards him was made clear by cold civility quite at variance with the warmth they showed to her rich and titled admirers.

'Your background is respectable, and you are not so very poor, Max.'

'My background may be respectable but it is hardly distinguished. My father was a merchant and not a particularly successful one. On his death he left me only a modest competence. It would never support a wife and family.' He took a deep breath. 'Until I have amended my financial situation I cannot think of marriage. That's why I'm going to accept my uncle's invitation to join his business in India.'

Her stomach lurched. 'India?'

'It's the best hope I have.'

'Then take me with you, Max. I could endure any hardship as long as we were together.'

'India is not the place for European women. The climate is harsh, to say nothing of the squalor and disease. I won't be responsible for subjecting you to that.'

'I…I wouldn't mind waiting.' Even as she said it she wondered at her own boldness.

'It could be years even if I am successful.'

'I understand that.'

'I couldn't ask it of you.'

Her heart sank. She had been so sure that her feelings were returned. Hurt mingled with bewilderment. 'Why could you not ask, Max? What is it you're not saying?'

'It's complicated.'

'Is it?'

'I can't allow you to sacrifice your life like that.'

'Sacrifice? Why should it be any such thing?'

'What I meant was that you would be left dangling for who knows how long, and without any certainty of a secure financial future. I care too much to let you do it.'

Pride began to reassert itself. 'No, Max, it's clear that I don't mean nearly enough.'

His cheeks were as pale as hers. 'Now I've hurt you and I'm sorry for it. I should never have allowed things to go so far, but I couldn't help myself. I allowed my feelings for you to overcome all common sense.'

She swallowed hard, forcing herself to meet his gaze. 'Well then, perhaps it's fortunate for both of us that you have recovered your common sense in time to prevent an imprudent marriage.'

'It's not what you think, Vivien. I care for you more than I've ever cared for anyone. You must believe that.'

'I think I've deceived myself quite enough.'

'No, never that. It's because I care that I must set you free.

The commitment that you want, that you deserve, is impossible. Please try to understand.'

'I understand very well and now have only to be ashamed that I didn't see it before.'

'I'm sorry, my dear, more sorry than I can say.'

'So am I, Max.'

They lapsed into tense silence for the space of several heartbeats. Then he said softly, 'I can only hope that in time you will forgive me, and forget.' With that he bowed and walked away...

Vivien closed her eyes. Memory still had the power to hurt. She'd heard it said that the first cut was the deepest. The details of that last conversation had never left her; at the time she'd felt sure there were things he hadn't said. That was just wishful thinking of course. The truth was that, being so young and so inexperienced, she'd failed to realise that his feelings were not as involved as her own, that he didn't want commitment. The humiliation of rejection stung for a long time afterwards, along with the shame of having thrown herself at his head. That part of it was her fault. She had been cautioned against boldness and broken the rules. He had been honest, albeit belatedly, and she had long since forgiven him the hurt. However, forgetting him was infinitely harder.

Chapter Two

The following morning was Christmas Day and the company walked to church. It was bitterly cold but dry at least and, ordinarily, Vivien would have enjoyed the fresh air and exercise. As it was her thoughts were elsewhere.

Aunt Winifred eyed the heavens doubtfully. 'I think we shall have snow ere long.'

Vivien nodded. 'You may well be right. I really don't mind as long as it doesn't start now.'

'Oh, no. We shall be safe for a little while yet, my dear.'

'You seem very certain.'

'My father taught me to recognise the signs…'

Vivien smiled and feigned interest but her gaze kept moving ahead to the tall figure walking beside Eleanor and Andrew. Beyond wishing each other the compliments of the season and exchanging a few polite commonplaces, she and Max had not spoken that morning. When everyone left the house for the walk to church he made no attempt to seek her out either. It was quite obvious that he found this close proximity as uncomfortable as she did.

The thought persisted when he seated himself as far away from her as possible in church. She tried to concentrate on the service, but it proved impossible and she had to fight the urge to glance in his direction. It was disconcerting to discover how unsettling a presence he was. After all these years it ought not to be. She began to wonder if Aunt Winifred had not been right about leaving Oakhurst.

Although she turned it over in her mind she already knew it wasn't a viable possibility for all the reasons she had given before. There was nothing for it but to put a calm face on the situation and ride it out. It was only for a couple of weeks. Then they'd go their separate ways and never meet again. The knowledge was like an icy chill around her heart.

Eventually the service ended and they filed out of the church again into the wintry air. Vivien darted a swift glance along the path but Max had his back to her and was currently engaged in conversation with Andrew and Peter. She swallowed hard and looked away again.

'What a rousing sermon that was,' said Aunt Winifred.

'Oh…yes.' In truth Vivien hadn't heard a word of it. 'Absolutely splendid.'

'I was sure you had enjoyed it. You looked rapt.'

They made their way back down the path towards the lych-gate and thence into the lane beyond. From the leafless copse nearby a flock of rooks rose cawing into a yellow-grey sky. Vivien shivered.

'Come, Aunt. This is no weather to linger out of doors.'

'I confess, my dear, I do feel rather chilly myself.'

'Then let us walk back. See, the others are coming now.'

'So they are.'

They began to make their way along the lane. Usually it would have been muddy at this season but frost had rendered it drier for walking. However, it had also solidified the ruts. They had barely gone a hundred yards when Aunt Winifred uttered a little cry and stumbled. Vivien grasped her arm.

'Good gracious! Are you all right, Aunt?'

'No harm done, dear. I turned my ankle a little, that is all.'

'You were lucky not to fall.'

A tall figure appeared beside them and they looked round to see Max. He regarded her aunt in concern.

'I hope you are not hurt, Miss Pritchard.'

'Oh.' Aunt Winifred reddened a little. 'Thank you, Mr Calderwood. I am quite well.'

'This frozen ground is treacherous,' he went on. 'Pray take my arm, ma'am.'

'That is most kind of you, sir, but I could not so impose.'

'It is no imposition, ma'am. However, a broken ankle certainly would be. It would ruin the festivities entirely.'

'Oh, dear. I had not thought of that. I believe I must accept your kind offer, sir.'

'That is a load off my mind, ma'am.' Max turned to Vivien, regarding her with a level gaze. 'May I offer you the other arm, Lady Hastings?'

Refusal was impossible without looking pointedly rude. Besides, she had no wish to let him think she attached any significance to the situation. So, thanking him politely, she slipped her arm through his and they set off again.

For a while no one spoke but then Aunt Winifred broke the silence.

'I suppose this weather must be a dramatic change from the Indian climate, sir.'

He inclined his head courteously. 'Indeed it is, ma'am.'

'Do you not regret the heat?'

He smiled at her. 'On balance I find the prospect of different seasons more attractive.'

'That is most interesting…'

As the conversation flowed on around her, Vivien slowly collected her wits. Then she upbraided herself for refining too much upon a simple act of kindness. This was not about her, it was about Aunt Winifred. Max had merely done the gentlemanly thing in the circumstances. And, of course, having offered to help her aunt he could hardly ignore her, however much he might have wanted to.

That realisation put the matter back in perspective. What wasn't so easy was being this close to him again; close enough to feel his warmth and his strength. His conversation with her aunt afforded leisure to study his profile and the curve of his lips as he smiled, the way his hair curved around his ear, to listen to every nuance in his tone. In these things at least he was unchanged.

'...would you not agree, Lady Hastings?'

Vivien looked up with a start. 'Oh, I beg your pardon. I didn't quite...'

The grey eyes held a gleam of amusement. 'We were discussing the relative merits of goose and roast beef at this season. It is our view that the goose wins. What say you?'

'Oh, er, the goose definitely.'

'That makes it unanimous then.'

She summoned a smile. 'I confess all this talk of food is making me hungry.'

'I am sure that a good dinner awaits us.'

'In truth, I hope so.'

They lapsed into silence again after this and Vivien could only feel relieved when they arrived back at the house. She was fairly sure that Max felt the same, although he was too polite to show it.

In this she was correct. Max had not missed her hesitation in accepting his arm or her reluctance to be drawn into the conversation. He hadn't intended to importune her in that way but when he saw her aunt stumble it had been an instinctive reaction to offer his help. Too late he realised he must offer the same to the niece and by so doing put them both in an awkward situation. More than awkward, since her nearness revived feelings he didn't care to explore. It was quite clear that she had no wish to spend any more time in his company than was necessary. Nor could he blame her. It only confirmed his decision to leave Oakhurst as soon as possible.

* * *

On reaching the house both ladies went off to change their clothes for the forthcoming dinner. When they were out of ear-shot Aunt Winifred confided that she thought Mr Calderwood a very gentlemanly sort of man.

'It was kind of him to help like that,' said Vivien.

'Most kind, and quite unexpected.'

'Yes.'

'I confess I did not imagine him to be so agreeable, but nothing could have been more polished than his manner.'

Vivien smiled wryly. 'Mr Calderwood always had a polished manner.'

Aunt Winifred shot her a quizzical glance but evidently decided not to seek further clarification of that remark. Nor did her niece make any attempt to explain.

Vivien retired to her room and changed out of her walking dress. Then she tidied her hair before donning a gown of soft mauve crepe. Glancing in the mirror she experienced a twinge of dissatisfaction. The demure style and colour were firm reminders of her status, a reminder she was coming to resent. She glanced at the clothes press across the room and hesitated. When she'd packed for this visit she'd included some of her other gowns on impulse, thinking that it might be time to wear them and announce to the world that she intended to be part of it again. For some reason it seemed more imperative to do so now. At the same time it would create a stir and at present she didn't feel equal to facing it. She sighed. Perhaps later...

The Christmas dinner was a veritable feast. There was beef and venison and goose accompanied by rich gravy and side dishes of seasonal vegetables, a mince pie and a great Christmas pudding followed by sugar plums, ginger nuts and short bread. Fresh air and exercise had sharpened Vivien's appetite and she ate with enjoyment. The convivial atmosphere lifted her spirits and, aided by several glasses of wine, she relaxed, joining in the conversation and laughter. Once she glanced across the table and, unexpectedly, met Max's eye for a moment. However, his expression was unreadable. She looked away quickly.

Eventually the ladies retired to take tea in the drawing room leaving the gentlemen to their cigars and port. Vivien helped herself to tea and then fell into a discussion of the latest London fashions with Annabel. It was a topic that Vivien was keen to pursue. Widowhood had left her out of touch with such things and she felt an increasing need to make up lost ground. It also provided a refuge from more disturbing thoughts.

'Oh, look! It's snowing!'

Mary's voice reached them from across the room. They looked round. It was dark now but the candlelight in the room reflected on the drifting flakes beyond.

'Why, so it is,' said Lady Hurst. 'We have a white Christmas after all.'

They went to stand by the windows, gazing out into the gathering night, watching the falling snow.

'You were right, Aunt Winifred,' said Vivien.

Her aunt nodded. 'It seems to be falling quite thickly. I wonder if it will settle.'

'The children will be so excited if it does.'

'I imagine they will. However, I confess that I prefer the fireside in such weather.'

'I quite agree, Miss Pritchard,' said Lady Hurst. 'The cold makes my bones ache…'

The conversation veered towards rheumatism and chilblains and the two older ladies returned to their chairs near the hearth leaving Vivien alone. She smiled to herself. In spite of the inevitable inconvenience associated with it, she loved to see the first snowfall. It had never entirely lost its magical appeal.

She was so absorbed that she failed to hear the door open and was only recalled by the sound of male voices. Somewhat reluctantly she turned from the window, mindful of her social obligations. Her heart sank as she saw Sir Digby approaching.

'I suppose you have been watching the snow, Lady Hastings. Ghastly stuff, what? Still with any luck it won't hang about for long.'

'Perhaps not,' she replied.

'If it does we'll just have to make the best of things, won't we?'

'As you say, sir.'

He eyed her appreciatively. 'If it comes to being shut up in the house for a while I cannot think of any company I'd rather have.'

Vivien summoned a polite smile. The thought of being shut up for any length of time with him was a distinctly unappealing prospect. Far more disturbing was being forced into closer proximity with Max Calderwood. Involuntarily her gaze sought him out. He was standing by a window at the end of the room, looking out into the darkness. To judge from his sombre expression he did not view the immediate future with any more equanimity than she did.

In that assumption she was correct, though not for the reasons she supposed. Max's emotions just then were complex and resisted close analysis. All through dinner he had tried to focus his attention on his immediate companions and not let it wander across the table towards Vivien. In spite of his best efforts he'd failed. It was like trying to keep iron filings away from a magnet. She had even caught him looking at one point. Of course she'd been quick to look away, no doubt thinking the attention impertinent which, given the circumstances, it probably was. He sighed. His best hope now was that this change in the weather would be of short duration. Otherwise his plans were going to be seriously disrupted. He shot another furtive glance across the room at Vivien. For both their sakes it would be better if the snow didn't linger.

Chapter Three

Max's hopes of leaving Oakhurst were completely dashed when he looked out of the window next morning and saw a landscape mantled in white. At any other time he might have enjoyed the pristine beauty of the scene, but just then all he could see were six inches of snow and the impossibility of travel for the present. A yellow-grey sky suggested more snow to come. Dismay vied with frustration and he sighed, turning over the remaining options in his mind. They were few. Now that his escape plan had been thwarted he was going to have to rely on ingenuity instead.

He went down to breakfast but, as he had hoped, none of the ladies had come down yet. Then, having eaten, he retired to the salon to read the papers. He had been there for an hour when the sound of voices reached him from outside. Glancing out of the window he saw a group of laughing children having a snowball fight. In spite of his frustration, Max grinned. They had the right idea. It was a matter of making the best of things. The thought of some fresh air was by no means displeasing. Besides, the solitude of the grounds would give him leisure to think.

Having lain awake until the wee small hours, Vivien was later than usual in rising next morning. By the time she went downstairs the men were gone so she breakfasted with Annabel and Mary. After that she checked to see that Aunt Winifred was all right. Having ascertained that all was well there, she went to find out what her children were up to. Although Miss Dawson was a kind and competent governess, Vivien was a regular visitor to the nursery. She had never subscribed to the view that children were only to be brought out for their parents' inspection for ten minutes once a day. Hugh had been rather surprised by her attitude. Although he was proud of his off-spring and treated them kindly, he felt no inclination to spend much time in their company, preferring to be in his library. As a result, their early years largely passed him by and, as they grew older, the habit of keeping to a respectful distance had become more ingrained. By then Vivien also avoided his company when possible. It hadn't been difficult.

On reaching the nursery she found it empty, save for a maid who was replenishing the coals for the fire. The girl bobbed a curtsy and volunteered the information that the children had gone out into the garden to play.

It wasn't entirely surprising news. Rachel and John loved to be out of doors and the fresh snowfall must have been too great a temptation to resist. After all the gloom of their father's death and their relative solitude during the period of mourning they deserved some enjoyment, and it would do them good to be in company with others of their own age. Besides, she could remember her own childish excitement when the first snow fell. She smiled to herself.

'If you can't beat 'em…'

She returned to her room to don coat, hat and gloves and, thus prepared, sallied out into the gardens. Then she paused and listened. As she had anticipated, it wasn't hard to find nine excited children. They were on the south lawn putting the finishing touches to a snowman, all of them laughing and chattering, their faces glowing from the cold. Seeing her approach, John and Rachel ran to meet her.

'Mama! See what we've been doing.'

'Yes, do look, Mama!'

'My goodness, you have been busy,' she replied.

'Lady Dawlish's cook gave us the coals and the carrot for the snowman's eyes and nose…'

'…and we found the twigs for his arms in the shrubbery…'

'…and his hat and muffler came from the dressing-up box in the nursery…'

Vivien smiled. 'I think you've done a wonderful job.'

Rachel nodded. 'The snowman's body was so big we couldn't reach to lift his head on. Mr Calderwood had to help us.'

Vivien blinked. 'Mr Calderwood helped you?'

'Yes. He's very strong.'

She cast a swift look around but finding no sign of him, relaxed a little. 'Well, it was very kind of him to do so.'

'Not at all.' A familiar figure stepped out from behind the snowman. 'I haven't made one of these in years.'

Vivien's heart leapt towards her throat. 'Mr Calderwood.'

He bowed. 'Lady Hastings, what a pleasant surprise.'

Under the steady scrutiny of that grey gaze unease crept in, and her innocuous outing took on a different significance. Surely he could not suppose that she had come out here on purpose to meet him? Yet it was quite possible that he did. After all, had she not thrown herself at him once before? The thought was mortifying. To her horror she felt warmth rising in her face.

'I confess I did not expect to see you either.' She hesitated. 'I came to see what the children were doing.'

Max studied her appreciatively. The rosy flush in her cheeks was really most becoming, though he suspected it wasn't entirely due to the cold air. Had he inadvertently made her feel uncomfortable?

'They are doing very well,' he said.

She glanced around. 'Is their governess not with them?'

'I sent the poor woman back indoors. It's far too cold to

stand around out here.' He gestured towards their creation. 'What do you think?'

The children stopped what they doing and looked round. Although they ranged in age from four to ten and would ordinarily have had different interests, the snow had created a common bond between them. Aware of all the anxious eyes turned her way Vivien gathered her wits.

'I think it's magnificent. Easily the finest snowman I've ever seen.'

They let out a collective cheer. In spite of herself she laughed, aware of a sudden lightening of spirit.

Max felt his heartbeat quicken. Laughter transformed her and suddenly the old Vivien was back with force. The result was deeply disturbing.

'Your judgement is faultless,' he said. 'It exactly coincides with my own.'

'You are clearly an expert in these matters, sir.'

'My skills had become a little rusty but I'm glad to have had the opportunity to hone them again.'

The children grinned. Then one of the older boys stepped forwards. 'Thank you for helping us, sir.'

The others chorused their thanks too.

'It was my pleasure,' said Max. 'However, I think that's enough for the present.' He bent down in front of the four-year-old and took her hand in his own. 'Your gloves are soaking wet, sweetheart. Your fingers must be very cold.'

She nodded solemnly. 'I can't feel them now.'

'It's time to go indoors and warm up.' Hearing a few murmurs of disappointment from the older ones he smiled. 'The snow will still be here later on, and by the look of things there will be plenty more.'

'Mr Calderwood is right,' said Vivien. 'Just look at the sky. We'll be up to our waists in snow very soon.'

The children giggled.

Max straightened. 'Off you go now.'

Obediently they began to troop off towards the house, he and Vivien bringing up the rear. She eyed him covertly. This was a side of him she had never seen and it intrigued her.

'I had no idea that you were so good with children.'

'I like them. They always keep things simple.'

'Yes, I suppose they do.'

'You have a fine son and daughter. Your husband must have been a proud father.'

The mention of Hugh stirred feelings compounded of sadness and guilt.

'I think he was in his way, but he saw relatively little of them all the same.' She smiled wryly. 'Enjoyment to him consisted of reading in his library.'

'Reading is a worthy pursuit.'

'Yes, but not when indulged to the exclusion of all else.'

He shot her a quizzical look. 'To do that would be to miss a great deal of fun.'

'Fun was an unfamiliar concept to Hugh.'

As soon as the words were spoken she realised that perhaps they revealed more than she had intended. It was hardly appropriate to be discussing her former marriage in this way. She had forgotten how disarmingly easy it could be to talk to Max.

'Was India fun?' she asked.

'Sometimes. Mostly it was hard work mingled with inconvenience.'

'You were engaged in business, I collect.'

'That's right. Spices mostly, but also silks and jewels.'

'It sounds very exotic.'

'It was a means to an end.'

They reached the house and entered through a rear door. As the children ran off to the nursery, Vivien paused in the hallway.

'Thank you for keeping an eye on them.'

'Not at all.'

'I'm sure they found your company far more agreeable than that of their respective governesses.'

'It was undoubtedly the novelty factor,' he replied, 'along with the fact that I can lift a greater weight of snow.'

'I think it was rather more than that. Children are generally good judges of character.'

'You speak knowledgeably.'

'Of course. I'm a mother.' She smiled. 'And now if you will excuse me, I must go and change.'

Max bowed and watched her walk away. The conversation had been most illuminating and it had, unexpectedly, exploded a few of the myths he had built around her. Some of the things she had let slip didn't tally with the idyllic marriage of his imagination. He hadn't found out about it until a year after the event in a letter from a mutual acquaintance. He had tried not to think about Vivien in the long months after they parted, and, by throwing himself into his work, had succeeded for a while. Eventually whole days passed without her image impinging on his consciousness. The news of her marriage shook him to the core. Night was the worst time, when he lay awake in the muggy darkness and remembered what he had lost. Or rather what he had allowed himself to lose. He hadn't let himself understand how much he wanted her; cared for her. The intensity of what he felt was unlike anything in his life before. It had frightened him and he'd backed off, uncertain about commitment. His jaw tightened. If it were all to do again... Unfortunately though, one couldn't turn back the clock.

Chapter Four

The advent of snow met with different responses from the adults in the household. Some of the male guests elected to go for a walk but the ladies preferred the fireside. They passed the time agreeably enough in conversation or reading and embroidery while the remaining gentlemen amused themselves with cards and chess. Major Dawlish challenged Max to a game and the two of them settled down to play.

Vivien ensconced herself in an armchair with the book she had borrowed from Charles's library. He was an avid reader and enjoyed a good novel as much as his wife did, so the selection was excellent. He owned all of Mrs Radcliffe's works and, much to Vivien's delight, a copy of *The Monk*. Matthew Lewis' novel had caused a sensation when it was published but, though hugely successful, it had not found favour everywhere. Hugh had refused to countenance the presence of such a scandalous book in his collection. It was, in his opinion, a highly dubious publication and quite unsuitable for a female readership. Vivien experienced a pang of guilty pleasure and eagerly opened the front cover.

She was so engrossed in the story that she lost all track of time. It was only when a discreet cough alerted her to Eleanor's presence that she looked up. With a sense of surprise she realised that they were alone.

'I hate to disturb you, dearest, but it is almost time for luncheon.'

'Good heavens! Is it? I had no idea.'

'You looked totally absorbed.'

'I confess I was.'

Eleanor glanced at the title. 'Ah, *The Monk*. It's riveting reading, isn't it?'

'Absolutely.'

'I vow that book gave me nightmares for a month after I read it. However, you may be made of sterner stuff.'

Vivien grinned. 'I'll let you know. In the meantime I'd better go and change my gown.'

She repaired to her room and made a hasty *toilette* before joining the others in the dining room. There she was disconcerted to find herself seated next to Max. However, she was also aware that other eyes were on them and had no wish to give rise to speculation of any kind.

Possibly the same thought had occurred to him. He turned her way with every indication of social ease. 'Did you enjoy your book?'

'*The Monk?* Very much.'

'It's an exciting yarn, isn't it?'

'Very much so. The stuff of nightmares too, I suspect.'

'Undoubtedly. Even so, I wouldn't have missed it.' He grinned. 'I've recommended it to several people, albeit those of a strong constitution.'

'It isn't for those of a nervous disposition,' she agreed.

'Well, you are not amongst them. You have far more spirit than that.'

For a moment she wondered if it was intended as flattery, but nothing in his expression suggested it. Besides, Max wasn't given to such devices. It was pleasing to think he held her in that much regard, but his comment touched on the personal. It was time for a change of direction.

'Did you win at chess?'

'Only just,' he replied. 'Major Dawlish is a dangerous opponent. He never takes prisoners.'

She smiled. 'The two of you have played before then.'

'Many times; I think the honours are about even.'

'You met in India, I collect.'

'Yes. Social circles tend to be smaller there.'

'What made you decide to leave?'

'My aim was to go and make my fortune, not to live there for ever. Having achieved what I set out to do, I decided to return.'

'Do you miss it?'

'In some ways. It's a vibrant and colourful land, but it's also a punishing environment.'

'The climate is harsh,' she replied, 'to say nothing of the poverty and squalor.'

For a moment his soup spoon paused in mid-air as an old conversation returned. Had it been an accidental echo or had she intended it? Her expression gave nothing away.

'Exactly so, my lady.'

'There is poverty and squalor in England too.'

'True. All the same, it is a more congenial place to live to my way of thinking.'

'I will take your word for that.'

Before he could reply Cynthia chipped in. 'Men are so fortunate in being able to travel to such exotic places. It must be so stimulating. Did you see tigers and elephants, Mr Calderwood?'

'Yes, I did.'

Her eyes widened, their gaze fixed on him with rapt attention. 'How exciting! What is it like to ride on an elephant?'

'Riding in a howdah is rather like being on a boat in a heavy swell. On the other hand the view is splendid.'

'Did you ever go on a tiger hunt?'

'Work took up much of my time, but I did once go on a hunt.'

The local rajah enlisted the help of all the able-bodied men he could find. We were after a man-eater. It had taken a woman and two children from one of the villages.'

'Good heavens, how terrifying!'

'The power of the tiger *is* terrifying,' he said. 'At the same time it is one of the most magnificent creatures on the planet.'

'Dangerous brutes,' said Sir Digby. 'If you ask me they should *all* be shot.'

Max threw him a swift look but made no reply.

'Did you succeed in killing it, sir?' asked Cynthia.

'Yes, we did.'

'Excellent. And did you keep the skin for a trophy?'

'That honour was given to the rajah.'

'What a shame. A tigerskin rug would be a real talking piece in one's drawing room. Do you not think so, Lady Hastings?'

'I imagine it would,' replied Vivien. 'All the same, I should prefer the conversation in my drawing room to arise from other topics.'

'What do you mean?'

'I mean that I am not in favour of killing things to provide trophies, though I concede that in this case the rajah had to protect his people.'

Several of the men surveyed her with genuine amusement. Sir Digby laughed.

'What else is game for but to shoot, pray?'

It drew a general murmur of agreement, although Max remained silent.

'I think the world would be a poorer place if such creatures disappeared as a consequence of hunting,' she said.

'I agree,' said Eleanor. 'Surely they were not put on this earth for us to persecute.'

'Why, there are many thousands of these animals. Bagging the odd tiger isn't going to make the least difference to their numbers.'

Vivien eyed him coolly. 'But you just said that they should *all* be shot, Sir Digby.' It drew a laugh from the others.

'*Touché!*' said Charles. 'Heist with your own petard there, Feversham.'

Sir Digby reddened a little, but quickly recovered his composure. 'First blood to Lady Hastings, what?'

The remark was greeted with more laughter. Max raised his glass to Vivien in quiet salute, although his expression was enigmatic. The gesture didn't pass unnoticed. Cynthia directed an arch look his way.

'I am persuaded that you do not hold such sentimental views, Mr Calderwood.'

'I don't know about sentimental,' he replied, 'but if that tiger hadn't been a man-eater nothing would have induced me to hunt it.'

Vivien regarded him in surprise. It was mingled with another emotion that eluded identification. Along with that was quiet enjoyment at the look on the other woman's face.

'Are you against all hunting then, Mr Calderwood?' demanded Cynthia.

'By no means, when the hunter intends to eat his prey and survival depends upon it.'

'I am relieved to hear it, sir. I thought for a while that you would have us all eat grass.'

Vivien heard another ripple of amusement from their companions but Max appeared unperturbed.

'I could not recommend it, ma'am. It is quite indigestible.'

'Do you speak from experience then?'

'Indeed I do. A boyhood experiment, much regretted afterwards.'

Guffaws of laughter greeted this and then the conversation moved to less contentious ground. Vivien sipped her wine, supremely conscious of the man beside her. Max continued to surprise in all kinds of ways and it only served to whet her curiosity. Not only hers it seemed. Cynthia Vayne had made her interest quite clear. Was she set to become the future Mrs Calderwood? It was an oddly unwelcome thought and Vivien tried to push it aside. After all, she had no claim on Max and he was an attractive single man. He had announced his intention to settle down, which implied that he would eventually marry when he found the right woman. It ought not to matter, but she knew it did.

After luncheon it began to snow again, thick and fast. Eleanor surveyed it rather anxiously.

'Oh, dear. I hope we shan't have to call off the supper dance at New Year.'

'It's a week off yet. With any luck things will improve by then,' replied Charles.

Cynthia beamed. 'I do love a dance. So does my brother, do you not, Digby?'

'Oh, rather,' he replied, 'especially when there are so many charming partners to choose from. What stronger inducement could there be?'

'Well said, brother.' Cynthia looked around the salon. 'If all the gentlemen are of the same mind we shall have a merry time.'

Charles smiled. 'I shall engage to do my part, Mrs Vayne. What say the rest of you gentlemen?'

The question elicited the expected affirmatives.

'Splendid!' he said. 'I expected no less.'

Vivien bent over her book and tried not to think about the last time she and Max had attended a dance together. A shadow fell across the page and she looked up quickly. Sir Digby smiled at her.

'I do hope that I may persuade you to dance, Lady Hastings.'

She assumed an expression of polite acquiescence. 'Of course.'

'I shall insist that one of them is a waltz.'

Vivien suppressed annoyance and gave him an enigmatic

smile. Then she returned her attention to her book, hoping he'd take the hint. He lingered a few seconds longer but, when she didn't look up again, he bowed and moved away. She let out a quiet sigh of relief. The man's attentions were becoming even more marked but he seemed impervious to rebuff. Short of downright rudeness she had no idea how to make him understand that she had no interest there. Since she was looking down at her book she failed to see the knowing smile that passed between him and his sister.

Across the room Max frowned, feigning to study the newspaper in front of him. Feverham's interest in Vivien was plain. Not that he could blame the man for that. Did Vivien return the sentiments? Her manner had been polite but hardly warm. On the other hand perhaps she felt reticent about too public a display of affection. Perhaps she was waiting for a more private moment to demonstrate her feelings. Max's frown deepened. She was young, attractive and now free to remarry. Why should she not? The answer was a flood of emotion in a deep shade of green. His jaw tightened. He had no right to think like that and yet he couldn't help it. The longer he was around Vivien the worse it got. He glanced out of the window at the falling snow and cursed mentally.

'Anyone for billiards?' asked Peter.

Jason nodded. 'Count me in. Mr Calderwood, can we persuade you?'

Max laid down the paper and summoned a smile. 'Why not?'

Vivien cast a covert glance across the room, her gaze following him to the door. When it closed behind him the sound only reinforced a sensation of finality and loss.

Chapter Five

She turned back to *The Monk* and read for another hour. Outside it was still snowing, though less heavily now, and the light was starting to fade. Putting the marker in the page she closed the book. Aunt Winifred looked up from her embroidery.

'Had enough reading for a while, my dear?'

'Yes. If you will excuse me I'll go and see if the children are behaving themselves.'

Cynthia regarded her in surprise. 'Surely their governess is with them. In fact, several governesses now.'

'I believe there are three in the house at present.'

'Three! In that case, Lady Hastings, I am sure you need not trouble yourself. They ought to be more than equal to the task.'

'I have no doubts about their competence, Mrs Vayne.'

'Well then, stay here and forget about them. After all, there is no point in keeping a dog and barking oneself.'

Vivien held on to her temper. 'All shepherds must check on the flock from time to time. Excuse me.'

With that she walked away, leaving Cynthia staring after her in open-mouthed astonishment.

The children were playing a game of skittles in the portrait gallery while their respective governesses watched from the sidelines and chatted amongst themselves. Vivien surveyed the scene from the doorway. It was evident from the laughter and occasional cheers that the participants were fully engaged with their task, and she had no desire to interrupt. Retreating quietly she left them to it.

At present she had no wish to return to the salon but the library offered a quiet alternative. It was a comfortable room with big armchairs and a large arched window at one end, which overlooked the gardens. She had been there many times, since Eleanor was generous about lending books. However, it wasn't reading that drew Vivien now. In any case, the fading light would have made it impractical. A swift glance around revealed that the room was empty so she slipped inside and shut the door behind her.

The remains of a fire burned in the hearth, giving off cheerful warmth. She added another log from the basket and watched it catch. Then she crossed to the window, looking out on the snow-covered garden and the park beyond. Light flakes were still falling, enveloping the earth in a great white silence. In the grey-blue twilight it had an unearthly beauty.

'Pretty, isn't it?' said a quiet voice behind her.

Vivien drew a sharp breath and spun round, heart pounding. Then she noticed the figure in the wing chair just feet away. As the chair was facing the window she had entirely failed to spot its occupant as she came in. Max got to his feet.

'Forgive me. I didn't mean to startle you.'

With an effort she found her voice. 'I thought you were playing billiards.'

'I was, but after the second game I opted for some peace and quiet instead.'

'Which I have now disturbed. I'm sorry.'

'Don't be.'

'I didn't know there was anyone here. The chair...I didn't notice...' She broke off in confusion. 'Please excuse me.'

She turned away but his hand stayed her. The touch was

light, almost tentative, but its effect was like a charge along her arm. He surveyed her steadily.

'Don't make yourself uneasy, Vivien.'

The familiar use of her name sounded easy and natural on his lips. It also stirred old memories and, with them, painful longing.

He let his hand fall from her arm and glanced towards the window. 'This is a restful place, isn't it?'

Restful wasn't the word she would have chosen just then when every nerve was resonating to his nearness. Striving for calm she followed the direction of his gaze. 'I've always thought so, although I haven't seen it in the snow like this.' She paused. 'But you're right: it is a pretty scene.'

'Better for having someone to share it with, I think.'

'Yes.'

'I had forgotten how compelling this season can be.'

She heard the ambiguity in that statement and kept her eyes resolutely on the window.

'Did you not miss it when you were abroad?'

'I missed a lot of things,' he replied.

'Did you?'

'So many things I took for granted before. I did not know their value until they were gone.'

Her throat tightened. 'But you had your work.'

'Yes, I had that.'

They lapsed into silence. She ought not to be here alone with him and yet she didn't want to leave either because being here made her feel more alive than at any time in the last ten years. And so she did nothing, content just to rest in the moment and watch the snow falling on the silent land.

Max watched too, aware of conflicting emotions. He should not have detained her but he couldn't have borne it if she had gone. When he'd heard the door open and the faint swish of a skirt across the floor he found himself fearing and hoping at the same time. Then he caught a faint elusive trace of her perfume and his heart leapt as the subject of his thought became reality. Her uneasiness was apparent and he spoke to quiet it but, after that first spontaneous gesture, he made no move to touch her again. Such a moment of privacy might never come again and he didn't want to do anything to jeopardise it.

'Did you tire of the company?' he asked.

'By no means. I went to look in on the children.' She threw him a sidelong glance. 'Does that make me seem like a fussy mother?'

'No, a concerned one.'

'I need not have been,' she admitted. 'They're having the time of their lives. It is so good for them to be with others of their own age.'

'They certainly seemed to be enjoying themselves when I saw them.'

'I'm glad of it. They've had little enough enjoyment since their father died.'

'It is hard to lose a father at any time,' he said, 'never mind at so tender an age.'

'They have coped remarkably well, although I worry that they may conceal their deepest feelings.'

He regarded her keenly. 'Why should they do so?'

'For fear of upsetting me, perhaps. John especially. Childhood is short enough. It ought to be a happy, carefree time.'

'We have no control over circumstances. At least your children are fortunate in having a mother who cares for them.'

'They give my life meaning.'

He analysed that with considerable interest. It tended to support his former thought that her marriage might not have been so happy after all.

'I can well imagine that children would add an entirely new dimension to life, although I have no experience in that respect. My own is skewed the other way.'

'I remember. Your own mother died when you were ten.' She paused. 'Your father sent you away to school soon afterwards.'

Max was very still. 'Your memory is good.'

'For some things,' she replied.

Hearing the echo of his former words he experienced a surge of confused emotions. He would have liked to pursue that remark, but he didn't dare. It was inevitable that she should remember things from the past. He just hadn't been expecting that particular detail. It was a painful time that he preferred not to dwell on; something he'd never discussed with anyone else. But then he'd found it easy to tell her such things. For some reason that one had stayed in her mind. It didn't mean anything.

Vivien turned away from the window. 'It's growing late. I must go and get ready for dinner.'

He wanted to stop her but knew he could not. 'Of course.'

His gaze followed her all the way to the door. When it closed behind her he turned back to the window and the darkening landscape beyond. This time, however, he saw nothing, conscious only of roiling emotion and deeper mental confusion. It was pointless to pretend that he wasn't still attracted to her. She drew him like a moth to flame. But it was more than that; it had always been more than that, only he didn't know his own heart until it was too late. *Take me with you, Max.* His stomach knotted. He'd been such a damned fool. Seeing her again had only reinforced that knowledge.

Yet, in spite of his best efforts to suppress it, their conversation had also kindled a tiny flicker of hope. He was too experienced not to realise that she wasn't entirely indifferent to him, but, quite understandably, she didn't trust him either. Could he ever change that? Could he somehow earn her forgiveness? After the way he'd behaved it was a desperately long shot. On the other hand they'd already lost ten years and if he didn't seize this chance he'd have to face another four decades without her. The thought was more chilling than the snowbound landscape.

Chapter Six

Vivien surveyed the gown in an agony of indecision. Since putting off deep mourning she had worn the various shades of lilac and mauve that society considered suitable for early widowhood. Her grief for Hugh had been of short duration but, perhaps for that very reason, she had allowed the muted colours to become a habit. Guilt manifested itself in strange ways. Now she recognised it for what it was; a habit she wanted to break. The invitation to Oakhurst had pointed that up very clearly. It made her realise that she wanted to put her former marriage behind her once and for all and move on with her life. It was why she had packed several of her other dresses for this occasion. Although she couldn't have said precisely why, Max's presence had only reinforced the original thought. Putting off muted colours was a clear signal of intent and, for all that she was ready to do it, the notion still filled her with trepidation. At the same time a small gathering like this provided the ideal opportunity. She needed to stop dithering.

'I'll wear the yellow gown this evening, Hewson.'

The maid was one of Eleanor's household and far too well trained to reveal the least surprise. She merely bobbed a curtsy and went to fetch the required garment. Vivien put it on and then surveyed herself in the mirror. The dress was one of her favourites and, despite being almost two years old, it didn't look too far out of fashion.

'What jewellery would you like, my lady?'

'The gold necklace and earrings, I think.'

As Vivien put them on the maid smiled. 'They look well with that gown, my lady.' She paused. 'Which shawl would you like?'

'The blue and gold.'

Within the space of a few minutes she was ready. She thanked the maid and then, summoning her courage, went to see if Aunt Winifred was ready. The older woman had evidently been coming to find her because they met in the corridor. She stopped in her tracks, surveying her niece in astonishment.

'Vivien, my goodness.'

'What do you think of the gown?'

'It's very pretty but…well, is it entirely appropriate, my dear? After all, your husband…'

'Has been dead these eighteen months. I have more than met my social obligations there.'

'I did not mean to criticise.'

'I know, and I don't mean to shock. However, I do mean to get on with my life.'

'I see.' Aunt Winifred swallowed nervously. 'It's your decision of course.'

'It's more than time, Aunt.'

'If you feel it to be so, my dear, then I expect you are right.'

She said no more and they went down together. For all her bold words Vivien began to feel distinctly nervous as they neared the drawing room. She knew her appearance was going to cause a stir, even if the reaction was never openly expressed. She also knew that there was only one person whose opinion really mattered now. However, as she entered the room there was no sign of Max. She wasn't sure whether to be relieved or disappointed.

Eleanor greeted her with an appraising smile. 'You look

lovely.' Then, bending a little closer so that only the two of them could hear, she added, 'Well done.'

Vivien gave her friend's arm a gentle squeeze in acknowledgement. Then Annabel appeared beside them.

'What a pretty colour, Lady Hastings. It suits you well.'

Vivien thanked her and felt some of her earlier tension fade. Their quiet support was a great morale booster. Sir Digby's look of warm approbation was unmistakable too, if not so welcome.

'You shine like the sun, my lady.'

She assumed a polite smile. 'You are too kind, sir.'

His eyes met hers. 'Not as kind as I should like to be.'

To her annoyance she felt herself blush. His smile widened. She was spared the necessity of a reply as his sister joined them. Her gaze swept Vivien from head to toe and was followed by a knowing smile.

'Why, Lady Hastings, how very charming you look this evening. You always do of course, but particularly so now.'

'That's well said,' replied her brother. 'It's exactly what I was thinking.'

'Naturally. Your taste has always been excellent.'

'Thank you, Cynthia. I flatter myself it is.'

The two exchanged brief knowing glances. Cynthia smiled. 'It's the reason Digby never married, Lady Hastings. He never found anyone who came up to his very exacting standards.'

'I'm sorry to hear it,' said Vivien.

'Never until now,' said Sir Digby.

Fortunately for Vivien's composure Eleanor returned.

'I'm so sorry to interrupt but I need to borrow Lady Hastings for a while. Would you excuse us?'

As they walked away Vivien regarded her friend gratefully. 'Thank you. That was becoming rather awkward.'

'A pincer movement?'

'It was beginning to feel like it.'

Eleanor grinned. 'I think that your choice of gown has provided your would-be suitor with encouragement.'

'It was never intended thus, but I fear you may be right.'

'You won't be able to hold him off for very much longer.' Eleanor glanced up and smiled. 'Ah, Mr Calderwood, good evening.'

Vivien's heart missed a beat. Evening dress might have been invented for Max, accentuating every line of his powerful frame to perfection. He always had a certain presence but the austere costume enhanced that dramatically. The man she had formerly considered handsome now seemed positively dangerous.

He made a polite bow and smiled. 'Good evening, Lady Dawlish. Lady Hastings.'

'I am hoping that we shall have some music later,' said Eleanor. 'Do you sing, Mr Calderwood?'

'I can hold a tune, ma'am.'

'Good, then perhaps I can prevail upon you to take part.'

'Certainly.'

'I'm much obliged to you, sir.'

As Eleanor left them Vivien regarded Max in surprise. 'I did not know you could sing.'

'I wouldn't wish to excite your anticipation.'

'Too late. You already have.'

'I'm flattered.'

'Not in the least,' she replied.

Max grinned. 'That's better.'

'What is that supposed to mean?'

'It means that I'm registering the rise of the phoenix, my lady.'

The accompanying expression was enigmatic, although it was impossible to miss the gleam in his eyes.

'The widow from the ashes?'

'Too doleful by far. Say rather, a golden goddess.'

'Pure hyperbole.'

'On the contrary.'

She regarded him askance. 'I never had you down as a flatterer, Max.'

His name had tripped off her tongue before she was even aware, and it could not be withdrawn. Her cheeks grew a little warmer, not least because she didn't want to withdraw it.

Max's gaze locked with hers. 'I was never more serious in my life.'

Vivien was trying to assimilate that when the gong sounded for dinner. Since they were not seated together it was impossible to continue the conversation just then, a circumstance that filled her with mixed emotions. Their light banter had been so much like old times that it was as if the intervening years had just rolled away. Her throat tightened. If only... She glanced across the table. Max was sitting next to Cynthia, apparently listening attentively to something she was saying. Then they both laughed softly.

'My sister and Mr Calderwood seem to get along famously, do they not?'

As Sir Digby's voice recalled her, Vivien forced a smile. 'Yes, indeed.'

'I wonder if we're looking at the beginning of a romance.' He lowered his voice. 'They make a handsome couple, do they not?'

'As you say.'

'Of course, it's early days yet but the signs are promising.'

'Are they?'

'Trust me. I have a good nose for such things.'

It was on the tip of her tongue to suggest he keep his nose out of other people's business, but she stopped the words there. With a sense of surprise she wondered at her own ill humour. It was uncharitable, and not at all in keeping with the jocular vein intended. All the same the thought that he might be right was an uncomfortable one.

Later, when the gentlemen rejoined the ladies in the drawing room, she caught herself watching for any indication of preference in Max's behaviour. However, she could not detect any; he spoke to all the ladies with the same quiet courtesy. Of course, it might be natural discretion. It was often hard to know what Max was thinking. Anyway, it was really none of her concern.

Across the room Annabel sat down at the pianoforte. She was joined there by Charles, Andrew and Max. Vivien listened intently as they began to sing. She soon realised that Max could do a lot more than merely hold a tune; his voice was a rich baritone, blending effortlessly with the others and filling the room with fluid sound. It was a revelation. When they'd been together in the past it was always at balls and parties and concerts. The occasion had never arisen then where he would be invited to sing. She began to wonder how many other things she didn't know about him and her curiosity was thoroughly roused.

When the song ended she joined in the general applause. The trio sang twice more and then Eleanor and Mary took their places. While they sorted through the music the gentlemen strolled away to mingle with the rest of the company. Max casually disposed himself in the chair beside Vivien's.

'Are you enjoying your evening, my lady?'

'Very much,' she replied. 'And I have to say that you have a fine voice.'

'Thank you.'

'Where did you learn to sing so well?'

'My mother was very fond of music. Hers was the earliest influence; then the choir master at school.'

'I could more easily imagine you playing cricket.'

'I did that too.'

'And did it just as well, I imagine.'

'Well enough to gain admittance to the sporting fraternity.'

'I'm sure you were a star in their firmament.'

He laughed. 'Hardly that; just convincing enough to stay on the team.'

'You were an academic genius perhaps?'

'Again, I'm sorry to disillusion you. I worked at those subjects that interested me and scraped by in the rest.'

'It sounds remarkably familiar.'

'Ah, your own children I take it.'

'John, anyway. Rachel is more diligent.'

'Do you have a school in mind for your son?'

'Hugh was set on Eton.'

'I see.'

'John is only eight. I'm reluctant to lose him just yet.'

'There's plenty of time.'

'So I think. Besides—' She broke off, suddenly aware that she had been about to mention the financial constraints involved. That was the trouble with talking to Max. It was easy to say too much.

'Besides?' he prompted.

'Nothing. As you said, there's plenty of time.'

He suspected it was something but he let it pass, unwilling to force her confidence. All the same, he was curious to know what she'd been about to say. There were a great many things he wanted to know. Moreover, he hadn't missed the fleeting expression of worry in her eyes as she spoke. It made her seem vulnerable and aroused his protective instincts. The world was a hard place, especially for a woman alone.

'Has your aunt always lived with you?'

'Not until after Hugh's death. My family are sticklers for propriety. In their eyes it is improper for a woman to live alone, even if she is a widow with two children. Besides, my sister-in-law had been looking for an excuse to get Aunt Winifred off her hands for a while.'

'And how did you feel about that?'

'It didn't matter how I felt.'

Max experienced both anger and indignation. He could well imagine such a degree of interference from her family, all done in the guise of helpfulness, of course.

'As it happens I am fond of Aunt Winifred,' Vivien went on. 'She is a kindly soul and her companionship has not been unwelcome.'

He glimpsed the loneliness behind that statement. He'd like to have pursued it, but, unwilling to pry, sought safer ground instead.

'How did you come to know Lady Dawlish?' he asked.

'Eleanor is a neighbour. We met shortly after Hugh and I married. We have been friends ever since.'

'You live quite close then?'

'Hastings House is only six miles from here.'

'I imagine you have a large circle of friends.'

'I know quite a lot of people, although we did not go out a great deal. Hugh preferred to be at home.'

'And yet I seem to recall that you enjoyed parties.'

'I did. I mean, I do, but after we married there were not so many. Hugh was a lot older than me and I suppose he had got such things out of his system.'

Max digested this with considerable interest, hearing the silences between the words. Her husband sounded like a very dull dog, though it would be impolitic to say so.

'I suppose marriage is always a big adjustment,' she went on.

'No doubt. However, I have no experience to compare with your own.'

'You were married to your work, I collect.'

'Yes, you could put it like that,' he said.

'And now you are back to stay. How will you pass your time?'

'I shall buy a small estate and work to improve it.'

'Of course. You mentioned a property before.'

'It's time to settle down. Travel has its advantages but I've had my fill of it. I intend to marry and raise a family.'

Her heart sank. 'Oh. Well, in that case I wish you good fortune.'

'Thank you. I was hoping you'd approve of my plans.'

'How could I not approve?'

'And yet I was not always good husband material, was I?'

She lowered her gaze. 'People change with time. We all learn from the past.'

'So we do, and avoid making the same mistakes again.'

'Yes.' Suddenly the magnitude of her mistakes was overwhelming. 'At least we can do that.'

Chapter Seven

The conversation remained with her afterwards and sleep was a long time coming that night. She might be able to act a part for the benefit of others but it was impossible to pretend to herself that she had no feelings for Max. If anything they had only strengthened with time. The knowledge that he intended to marry intensified the sensations of loneliness and loss. Along with it was an ache in the core of her being. Hugh had never made her feel like that; his nearness had never excited her, his touch never kindled desire. He had been considerate in the marriage bed, but his love-making was always lacking somehow, although she wasn't quite sure why. Was it the same with all married couples? For a moment her imagination substituted Max for Hugh, so that it was his body pressed to hers, his hands on her naked flesh. The result was sudden flaring warmth in the region of her pelvis. She shut her eyes and tried to banish the thought but it wasn't so easily commanded to leave. Nor was it any use to tell herself that it was foolish beyond permission. The illusion was too powerful. It seemed as though heartache hadn't finished with her yet.

The following day dawned clear and bright and the children clamoured to be allowed outside again, particularly as Eleanor's boys had mentioned the toboggans stored in the gardeners' shed and the possibility of going out on the hill. On learning of their request Charles consulted his wife at breakfast.

'I can see no reason why not, can you, my dear?'

'No, if they wrap up warmly then I am sure the fresh air will do them good,' said Eleanor. 'Nevertheless, it is hardly reasonable to expect their governess to traipse through all this snow, never mind to stand around in the cold as well.'

'One of the footmen can go out with them to keep an eye on things. Parfitt, I think.'

'Very well, my dear. I'll inform Miss Minching of the arrangement after breakfast.'

Sir Digby looked across the table. 'They're a lively bunch of youngsters, aren't they? Quite a handful, I imagine.'

'Children are usually little trouble if they are occupied in the right way,' said Eleanor.

'To be sure,' he replied. 'In any case, you'll soon be able to pack 'em off to school, won't you?'

Cynthia nodded. 'School is the best place for them.'

'Quite right,' said her brother. 'Out of sight, out of mind, eh?'

Vivien raised an eyebrow and exchanged glances with Eleanor. 'I never had the least wish to be rid of my offspring, did you?'

'No, never.'

Sir Digby reddened. 'I did not mean to offend. The words were only spoken in jest, I assure you.'

'No offence taken, sir,' said Eleanor. 'However, I have to tell you that I mean to make the most of my children while they *are* children.'

'And I,' said Vivien.

'Well, of course you do, dear ladies.' Sir Digby's flush deepened. 'One would expect no less.'

Across the table Max smiled quietly. That brief exchange only served to reinforce his opinion of Feversham. The man seemed to have little idea of what really mattered to Vivien, but then that was no bad thing either. Such sentiments could hardly endear her to him.

Cynthia's gaze flicked from her brother to Max. 'I am quite sure that the children will have great fun in the snow. However, the rest of us would doubtless prefer to remain in the warm. Would not you, Mr Calderwood?'

'Not in the least,' he replied. 'A good bracing walk will be just the thing.'

Vivien bit her lip to conceal a smile. Then, meeting Max's eye she said, 'You rather like the snow, don't you, Mr Calderwood?'

'It's because I saw so little of it for so many years,' he said.

'The novelty factor?'

'Just so.' He paused. 'Would you care to take a turn about the gardens after breakfast, Lady Hastings?'

Her heartbeat quickened a little. 'Thank you. I should like that.'

'I'll meet you by the rear door. Shall we say ten o'clock?'

'Certainly.'

'That's settled then.'

Sir Digby glared at him but Max seemed not to notice, having returned his attention to his coffee cup. However, Vivien had a suspicion that he not only knew but was enjoying the other man's chagrin. Quietly amused, she buttered another slice of toast. The thought of spending time in the company she would most have sought filled her with pleasant anticipation.

Although it was bitterly cold the sunshine was uplifting and she felt her spirits rise. For a little while she and Max walked in companionable silence, enjoying the beauty of a landscape transformed.

'It still appeals to the inner child, doesn't it?' he said at length.

'You're right, it does. Even now I can recall the excitement I felt when I woke to see new-fallen snow.'

'Going out of doors to play in it was a compulsion.' Max grinned. 'My friends and I used to lie in wait for other children to pass by and then pelt them with snowballs.'

'I hope they replied in kind.'

'They did. We had some splendid battles.'

'I have no trouble in visualising you in the thick of the action.'

'I confess I usually was.'

The path led through a shrubbery towards the gate that separated the garden from the parkland beyond. From the sloping field they could hear the excited shrilling of children's voices. Max nodded his head in that direction.

'Do you want to go and watch for a while?'

'Yes, let's.'

He stood aside to let her pass through the gateway. Then he offered his arm. 'The snow is deeper here.'

For a second she hesitated, then slipped her arm through his and they set off in the tracks left by the tobogganing party. In fact Max was correct: the snow was deeper on the open land than in the relative shelter of the garden. Vivien was concentrating on walking rather than looking at her companion, but every nerve was attuned to his presence. At the same time it felt natural and right to be with him. Just then it was as though a dark cloud had lifted to admit the light once more.

After a hundred yards or so the field sloped away and they found the children there, along with the attendant footman. The air rang with shrieks and laughter as the toboggans hurtled down the slope. It levelled out at the bottom allowing the speeding vehicles to come to a safe and gradual stop. As the passengers toiled back to the top again John caught sight of Vivien and waved enthusiastically.

'Mama!'

The others looked up then and waved too. Vivien laughed and waved back. Presently the children reached the top again and John hurried to meet her.

'You look as though you're enjoying yourselves,' she observed.

'It's the greatest lark, Mama!' He looked at her companion and smiled. 'Good morning, Mr Calderwood.'

Max returned the greeting. 'How many times have you been down the slope so far?'

'Four, sir.'

'Splendid! Perhaps next time you should take your mama with you.'

A chorus of delighted approval greeted this. Vivien stared at him in appalled disbelief but before she could protest John leapt in.

'Oh, yes, Mama. Do say you will.'

Rachel nodded. 'Do, Mama.'

Her cheeks, already pink with the cold, went several shades deeper. 'I couldn't possibly.'

'Why not?' asked Max.

'Well, I…it's…I mean…' She broke off floundering.

His expression evinced polite interest but the glint in his eyes was decidedly mischievous. 'Yes, Lady Hastings?'

John regarded her earnestly. 'Please, Mama. You'll love it. I know you will.'

'There, you see. Straight from the horse's mouth,' said Max.

She returned an eloquent look but if she hoped to shame him the attempt failed dismally. His expression revealed keen enjoyment. Moreover, the grey eyes held a distinct challenge now. The children looked on in expectant silence.

Vivien sighed and gave in. 'Oh, very well.'

The words were greeted by a rousing cheer. She smiled at them for a moment, then turned to Max and lowered her voice. 'I shan't forget this, you villain.'

'Indeed I hope not,' he replied.

Before she could ponder that obscure utterance John seized her hand and led her to the waiting toboggan.

'Climb on behind me, Mama.'

Vivien sat down gingerly and put her arms around her son's waist. Then they were away, hurtling down the slope at eye-watering speed. She gasped, feeling the cold air rushing past her face, but the sensation was not about fear, only pure exhil-aration. By the time they reached the bottom she was breath-less and laughing. A second toboggan drew up just a few yards away. As she wiped the water from her eyes she recognised Max with Rachel and little Eliza, all of them laughing too.

Rather shakily Vivien got to her feet and waited for him to join her. He grinned.

'Did you enjoy that?'

'I confess I did.'

'Good. So did I.' He gestured to the top of the slope. 'Shall we have another go?'

In fact they had several more turns, much to the delight of the younger contingent who took it in turns to ride with them. As Max set off again, accompanied by two of the other boys, John stood with Vivien looking on in approbation.

'This is just the best Christmas ever, Mama.'

Vivien put an arm around his shoulders. 'I'm glad you're enjoying it, darling.'

'I thought it might be fun, but not as much fun as this. Mr Calderwood is a complete hand, isn't he?'

She smiled. 'Yes, he is.'

'He used to live in India, you know. Lady Dawlish told James and Michael that he was there with their uncle.'

'So he was.'

'I wonder if he ever saw a tiger.'

'I believe Mr Calderwood once went on a tiger hunt.'

'Really? Do you think he would tell us about it sometime?'

'He might, if you ask him nicely.'

'I will, Mama.'

With that he went off to rejoin the others. Vivien smiled to herself. She couldn't remember the last time her children had looked so happy or so animated. It truly was as though a cloud of gloom had been lifted. Her gaze found Max and rested there. He was instrumental in helping to bring the change about. For the life of her she could not imagine Hugh engaging in such activities; the very idea would have outraged his sensibilities. Max on the other hand had a zest for life that was infectious, a pointed contrast to all that had gone before.

'Beg pardon, my lady.'

She looked round to see the footman at her shoulder. 'What is it, Parfitt?'

'Sir Charles told me as I was to have the children back at the house in time for luncheon. It's nigh on that now.'

'All right. We'd better start to round them up.'

When Max returned she enlisted his help and between the three of them they gathered the little party together. Then they set off back to the house. Vivien smiled to herself, letting the children's chatter wash over her. All trace of cold had gone now to be replaced with a deep glow that suffused her with a sense of well-being and banished care. At that moment she felt truly happy, at ease with herself and the world in general.

When they reached the house the children were dispatched to the nursery for their lunch. As they clattered off up the stairs Max paused in the hallway with Vivien.

'I hope you enjoyed yourself this morning.'

'I cannot remember the last time I had such fun.'

He surveyed her critically. She glowed with fresh air and exercise but, more important, the old sparkle was back in her eyes. He thought she had never seemed more desirable than now.

'You should have fun more often,' he said. 'It suits you.'

It appeared that he was not the only person to think so. When she appeared in the dining room later on Aunt Winifred surveyed her in surprise.

'How well you look, Vivien. The fresh air has done you good.'

'Thank you, Aunt. I really think it has.'

Sir Digby pursed his lips. 'You were out so long I feared you might take a chill.'

'There's no danger of that, as long as one keeps moving,' replied Vivien.

'I had no idea that the gardens were so extensive.'

'We went out into the park,' said Max.

Sir Digby's fork paused in mid-air. 'The park, sir? In this weather?'

'Yes, the children were tobogganing there.'

'Indeed.' Sir Digby smiled stiffly. 'Well, I do hope the little dears enjoyed themselves.'

'I believe they did, sir.'

'I'm glad to hear it.'

'And not only the little ones,' Max went on. 'I enjoyed myself too. Uncommonly so.'

Sir Digby eyed him coolly. 'It must have been a pleasant sight.'

'Oh, it was. Don't you agree, Lady Hastings?'

Vivien fought the urge to laugh. 'Indeed, sir.'

'Your presence must have been an unexpected treat for the children, my lady,' said Sir Digby.

Max nodded solemnly. 'You never said a truer word, sir. I only wish you could have seen their faces.'

Vivien shot a warning glance across the table. It was met with a disarming smile.

Chapter Eight

For the remainder of the afternoon and evening they mingled with the other guests and Max made no attempt to monopolise her time. Although she made every effort to join in Vivien found her thoughts wandering. It occurred to her now that the earlier romp with the children might just have been Max being kind. He knew what her situation was, or most of it at least, and perhaps sought to alleviate some of the strain. If so, he had succeeded very well. All the same, it would be a mistake to refine upon it.

A burst of laughter from across the room drew her attention to where Max was engaged in a rubber of whist with Charles, Annabel and Cynthia. His expression just then gave every indication of enjoyment and when Cynthia said something to him he smiled at her. Vivien looked away. Now more than ever her feelings seemed foolish. Circumstances had thrown them together again and he was endeavouring to make the best of things for both their sakes.

'May I join you, dear?'

She looked up to see Aunt Winifred. 'Yes, of course.'

Her aunt took the vacant seat beside her. 'This is a pleasant gathering, is it not?'

'Very pleasant.'

'I am so glad that you are enjoying yourself, my dear.' Her

aunt paused. 'All the same I cannot help but feel a little concerned.'

'Concerned? How so?'

'I think that perhaps you are not indifferent to Mr Calderwood.' Seeing Vivien's look of surprise, Aunt Winifred hurried on. 'I do not mean to interfere, but I do not wish you to be hurt either.'

'Do you think I might be?'

'My dear, I would be the first to admit that he is a very attractive man with the most courteous and agreeable manners, but his station is life is still far below your own. Your family—'

'Rate a man's worth by his rank and by how much he owns,' replied Vivien. 'It is a faulty yardstick as I have discovered.'

'I'm not sure I follow, my dear.'

'I once married to please my relations and had nine years to repent the mistake. I shall not repeat it.'

Aunt Winifred's expression registered shock. 'I had no idea…I thought… Oh, my dear, I'm so sorry.'

'So was I, every day.' Vivien sighed. 'The fault was not Hugh's; it was mine for failing to appreciate how ill suited we were; for thinking respect would be enough. You may believe me when I say that I shall be very cautious about taking such a step again, if indeed I ever do.'

'Yes, after what you have said I imagine you will.'

'I have shocked you and I'm sorry for it, but I can't pretend any longer.'

Her aunt surveyed her sadly but made no reply.

That night there was a hard frost which, combined with fog, contrived to keep everyone within doors the following day. Several of the gentlemen opted for billiards or cards. Seeing Cynthia sit down with Max to a game of piquet, Vivien's heart sank. Since their walk he had made no attempt to single her out and, although he was unfailingly courteous, gave no sign that the episode meant anything to him other than being part of the festive fun. Like a fool she had placed too much construction on the event. Thus, when Sir Digby asked if she would like to join him for backgammon she agreed. It would pass the time and occupy her thoughts.

The next hour passed uneventfully enough. Vivien deliberately kept her attention on the board and from time to time made an appropriate response when her companion ventured a comment. Across the room she heard Cynthia laugh. Sir Digby smiled.

'Those two certainly do seem to be getting on famously.'

Vivien schooled her expression to polite neutrality. 'Do they?'

'Oh, yes. I thought so from the first and my instinct is infallible.'

'That must be very useful.'

He beamed at her. 'Very useful indeed.'

When the piquet game ended Max collected the cards and then laid the pack down. He had no particular desire to play another hand but good manners required that he ask. Cynthia shook her head, eyeing him speculatively.

'I think I'd like to stretch my legs a little. Perhaps you would care to take a turn with me, Mr Calderwood.'

'I fear it is too cold to go out, ma'am. I should not wish to be responsible for your taking a chill.'

'How very thoughtful.' She smiled up at him. 'You are quite right in saying that it is too cold to venture out of doors, but I believe we might safely walk to the gallery and back.'

He resigned himself. 'As you wish.'

Vivien glanced up from the board and saw the pair leave the room together. Her spirits sank as she realised that her earlier assumption had been right. Max was nothing more than an old acquaintance. His interests lay elsewhere.

Sir Digby followed her glance and smiled triumphantly. 'You see, I told you my instinct was good.'

His smug expression made her want to slap him. She controlled the urge. 'So you did.'

'I foresee a match there.'

'Well, your instinct is infallible.'

He laughed softly. 'That is not the only match I foresee.'

'Goodness. At this rate you'll have the whole population paired off.'

'My interest is in one lady only.'

Vivien's heart sank further.

Max and Cynthia strolled along the gallery, pausing occasionally to examine the portraits. He wished now that he had not agreed to this; good manners were one thing but this had all the potential for turning into something rather different and quite possibly awkward. He needed to bring it to a conclusion as soon as possible.

'It is quite cold in here, Mrs Vayne. It might be better if we returned to the salon.'

'It is a little chilly.' She turned to face him. 'Although I am in no hurry to leave.'

Max pretended to misunderstand. 'Your love of art does you credit, ma'am.'

She laughed and took a step closer. 'That is not what I meant.'

'I can think of no other reason for you to linger here.'

'Oh, come now, Max. You don't have to pretend to me.'

'It was never my intention to do so.'

'I'm glad. I do so abhor pretence. Besides, it wastes so much time.' She smiled and laid a hand on his breast. 'If you put your arms around me we would both be a lot warmer.'

'If you wish to be warm, ma'am, you will return to the salon as I suggested.'

'I don't understand…'

Max's gaze locked with hers. 'Mrs Vayne, when I see

something I want, then I'll go after it. I don't want it to chase after me.'

With that he bowed and strode away leaving her staring after him in speechless fury.

Max didn't follow his own advice and return to the salon. Instead he headed for the library, needing time and space to cool his annoyance. Most of it was directed at himself for having allowed the situation to happen in the first place. It hadn't occurred to him that Cynthia's flirtatiousness was anything more than her natural manner. Now he knew better. He had no intention of making any further reference to it and could only hope that the woman had enough sense to follow suit.

Fortunately the library was empty and he shut the door behind him with a grateful sigh. It was also warmer than the gallery thanks to the fire in the hearth. He sat down in front of the arched window at the far end, surveying the scene beyond. As he did so Vivien's image returned with force. He tried to imagine her making advances, inviting him to put his arms around her. It was a tantalising prospect. He smiled ruefully. It was also wishful thinking—at present. He'd been doing a lot of that lately. All the same, he'd been careful not to overplay his hand; it wasn't enough that she should be relaxed in his company. He wanted her to actively desire it. By limiting the time he spent with her at first he hoped to bring that about, but it was a tricky proposition, especially since he knew that he had a rival for her affections. He hadn't seen any indication of special fondness there, but it wouldn't do to be complacent. It was time to step up his campaign.

When the backgammon game ended Vivien declined another and rose from the table. Sir Digby rose with her.

'You are quite right,' he said. 'We have sat down long enough. Let us take a stroll instead.' Seeing her doubtful look he smiled. 'Not too far though. I know you will not wish to be too far from the fireside on such a day.'

Seeing that there was nothing for it she reluctantly complied.

'Have you finished reading that book yet?' he asked as they walked slowly along the corridor.

Relieved by the choice of topic she relaxed a little. '*The Monk?* No, I'm about halfway through it.'

'And what do you make of it?'

'It's an exciting read if rather a frightening one at times.'

'You enjoy Gothic, I collect.'

'Very much. Do not you, sir?'

'I hate to admit it, ma'am, but I haven't read any. My sister tells me I should. Am I missing something?'

'Indeed you are.'

'I wonder if Sir Charles has any Gothic novels in his library.'

'He has quite a few,' said Vivien.

'How very fortunate. What do you think I should start with?'

'Well, what about one of Mrs Radcliffe's stories?'

'All right.' He paused. 'Perhaps we could go and find one now.'

Vivien hesitated but nothing could have been more respectful than his expression. She upbraided herself for being uncharitable.

'Very well, sir.'

They walked together to the library. Sir Digby opened the door and stood back to let her enter, then shut the door behind them. Vivien fought down a sudden feeling of apprehension and moved away from him, turning her attention towards one of the bookcases nearby.

'The Gothic novels are here, sir.'

He came to join her. 'So they are to be sure. However, I think you must know that I did not bring you here just to talk about books.'

Vivien's stomach lurched. 'Forgive me, but it *is* a library, sir.'

He smiled. 'You are naturally modest, my lady, but you cannot have failed to notice my attentions towards you.'

'I confess I did but I must tell you...'

He stepped a little closer. 'I did not declare myself before out of consideration for your circumstances.'

'Sir Digby, I am flattered but...'

'Come, my lady, don't be coy.'

Annoyance began to replace apprehension. 'Coy? I can assure you, sir, you are mistaken.'

'You've held me at arm's length for long enough. Now I intend to admire you at closer quarters.' He seized hold of her waist. 'You and I are going to be married.'

'Let go of me!'

'No, my lady, I shall not.'

A wet, loose-lipped mouth descended on hers. Vivien struggled in revulsion and turned her head aside.

'Stop this at once!'

'You're doing it too brown, my dear. Don't pretend that you don't prefer my embraces to any that dried-up old stick of a husband gave you.'

He planted another slobbery kiss on her neck. She got a hand free and slapped him hard.

'How dare you?'

He let go of her, clutching his cheek incredulously. Vivien glared at him.

'I have no idea why you should imagine your suit agreeable to me. I have never given you the least encouragement and neither will I. Under other circumstances I might have tried for greater civility but this boorish treatment obviates any such need. I find you quite obnoxious, sir, and your addresses disgusting.'

He stared at her in scarlet-faced disbelief. 'You can't mean it.'

'I can assure you that I do mean it, sir.'

As it dawned on him that she was serious his expression

altered and the last vestiges of amiability vanished. 'You will live to regret this day's work, my lady.'

'I doubt that.'

He returned a sneering smile. 'We'll see, won't we? I know all about your late husband's investments. When you and your children are in the poorhouse you'll think back on this conversation and rue the day you rejected Digby Feversham.'

With that he turned on heel and left her, banging the door behind him. Vivien's fury erupted and she began to pace the floor.

'Of all the loathsome, detestable, slimy little reptiles...'

A muffled choking sound from the far side of the room stopped her in her tracks. She listened intently but the sound was not repeated. However, the silence had a different quality now as though the very air had been stretched taut, and she knew with certainty that she wasn't alone. A swift look around contradicted the thought until her gaze fell on the arched window and the wing chair in front of it. A dreadful suspicion took root in her mind.

Chapter Nine

Taking a deep breath she marched across the room. Her heart leapt towards her throat to see the familiar figure ensconced in the chair.

'You!'

Max came to his feet. 'I'm afraid so.'

'You should have made your presence known, sir.'

Far from expressing contrition his eyes were alight with amusement. 'And missed that? I wouldn't have done so for the world.'

'Why, I believe you are utterly shameless.'

'I confess it.'

'What are you doing here anyway, apart from eavesdropping on other people's private conversation?'

'I came in search of some peace and quiet. A library is usually a good choice.'

'Don't be flippant, Max.'

'I beg your pardon. It's the residual effect of hearing you send that posturing fool to the right about.'

'I imagine you enjoyed it immensely.'

'You're quite right.' He paused, regarding her appreciatively. 'That was a magnificent slap, by the way. Richly deserved too, in my opinion.'

'Do you not deserve the same?'

He held up his hands in mock surrender. 'Probably, but I beg you will be lenient since my offence was unintended.'

'Only you could find entertainment in that sordid little scene.'

'Entertainment at his expense, not yours.'

'Really?' Her chin tilted to a militant angle. 'I have another theory. I think the whole charade has just been part of the Christmas festivities as far as you're concerned.'

His amusement faded. 'No, never that.'

'Perhaps I should be flattered to know that I can still amuse you.'

With that she turned on heel and headed for the door.

'That isn't what I meant. Vivien, wait!'

She flung the door wide and kept going. Half-walking half-running she reached the side door to the garden, so angry that even the icy air had no power to deter. She was fifty yards along the path before Max eventually caught her up.

'Vivien, please stop!'

She swung round to face him. 'What now?'

'I apologise if I hurt your feelings. That was not my intention, I swear it.'

'You may not have intended it, Max, but you did all the same.' The blue gaze locked with his. 'You're good at it.'

He stared at her, appalled. 'Vivien, I…'

'You've had your fun. Now go away.' To her horror her eyes began to fill with water.

'I'm not going anywhere until we've straightened this out.'

'There's nothing to straighten out.'

'I think there is.' He took a deep breath. 'I should not have eavesdropped on your conversation with Feversham, but I had no idea what he was about until he declared himself. After that I thought it would be more embarrassing for everyone concerned if I did make my presence known.'

Vivien surveyed him in glowering silence although privately she could see the dilemma.

'It was my intention to remain where I was until you'd both gone,' he went on. 'Unfortunately I gave myself away.'

'By laughing.'

'Wrong of me, I know, but you will allow that there can scarcely have been a less gentlemanly proposal of marriage in the whole history of the world.'

That was certainly true, though she wasn't going to admit it to him.

'Even had his addresses had been more polished I would not have accepted him. I will never again marry a man whom I do not love.'

'Never again?'

She hesitated but, as some of her anger began to ebb, it was replaced with sadness and a sense of futility. 'I did not love Hugh. I married him to oblige my family.'

'I see.' As he assimilated her words all his former assumptions were blown out of the water and his mind reeled at the implications. At the same time the flicker of hope grew stronger.

'It was a mistake I had plenty of time to regret. I shall not repeat the error. Only the very deepest love would ever induce me to remarry.'

'We all learn from our mistakes. Those who are really lucky do so while there is still time to reshape their lives.'

She shivered and drew her shawl closer. 'Yes, they are fortunate indeed.'

Max saw the gesture and his hand closed over hers, a warm clasp that sent a very different kind of shiver along her skin. He frowned. 'My dearest girl, you're icy cold and no wonder. Let's get back indoors before you catch your death.'

Vivien blinked. What had he just called her? Before she had time to ponder that, his hand was under her elbow and she was steered gently but firmly back to the house. They retraced their steps to the library. Max sat her down in a chair by the hearth and threw a couple more logs on the fire. Then he reached for the decanter on the side table and poured two measures of brandy.

'Here.' He handed her a glass. 'Drink this. It'll warm you.'

As she took it his fingers brushed hers, a light and possibly accidental touch that was nevertheless disturbing. She lowered her gaze and swallowed a mouthful of brandy. The fiery liquor carved a path to her stomach. It was strong and dangerously heady but she could already feel its seductive warmth.

'Better?' he asked.

She nodded. 'Yes, I thank you.'

Presently the logs caught and began to throw out comforting heat, but the tingling in her blood was more to do with the present company than with cold.

Max remained by the hearth, one booted foot resting casually on the fender. For a little while he surveyed her in silence. Then another part of the overheard conversation returned.

'Vivien, what did Feversham mean by his parting shot?'

She looked up quickly. 'His parting shot?'

'When he spoke of the poorhouse?'

'Oh, that.' She sighed. 'Sheer spite. My husband made some bad investments in the year before his death. As a result my financial situation is not as good as it could be.'

'Are things as bad as Feversham implied?' Max caught himself there. 'Forgive me, I didn't mean to pry.'

She shook her head. 'No matter. Feversham exaggerated a little, but I cannot pretend that I'm not anxious about the future, especially for the children.'

Although it was said matter-of-factly the words only reinforced the impression of her vulnerability. He also heard what she wasn't saying and his concern increased.

'Have your husband's solicitors spoken to you?'

'Yes, but to be honest I hardly took it in at the time. I was still too disorientated by Hugh's death. It was only afterwards that the extent of the damage became apparent.' She smiled ruefully. 'Marriage to Feversham would have gone a long way towards solving the problem.'

'And created far worse ones.'

'As you say.'

The warmth began to penetrate and combined with the brandy. Vivien relaxed a little. Being able to voice her fears like this made her feel better, and Max had always been a ready listener. She also knew he wouldn't divulge the details of their conversation to anyone else.

'Besides,' he said, 'you have vowed not to follow that route.'

'So I have, in spite of all my family's urging.'

'Are they pressing you to remarry?'

'Yes, but I shall not yield to it.'

'I'm pleased to hear it.' He thought she would never know how pleased, or how much this conversation gave him hope.

'You are fortunate in not having a set of pushing relations.'

'I am not easily pushed into doing anything I don't want to do.'

'I only wish I'd had that kind of resolution,' she replied. 'It might have saved me a deal of heartache.'

'Heartache?'

'I should never have married Hugh. I knew I didn't love him, but I thought respect would be enough. It didn't take me long to realise that I'd made a terrible mistake.'

'Oh, my dear girl.'

'He was a good man, a kindly man, but we had nothing in common except the children. As time went on we just grew further apart.'

'I'm sorry.'

'My being unhappy made him so. It was never my intention to do that.'

'We all do things that have unintended consequences,' he said.

'His death came as a relief in the end—for both of us.'

'You were only half of the relationship. The fault lies as

much with your husband for failing to ascertain your true feelings before he married you.'

'Would that he had, or that I'd had better sense. I deserve to feel guilty.'

Max shook his head. '"Use every man after his desert, and who shall 'scape whipping?" It does no good to repine over what cannot be changed.'

'I cannot dodge my share of the blame. After all, we are the decisions we make.'

Max felt his heart constrict as he acknowledged the truth of that observation.

'It wouldn't have happened if I'd possessed a grain of common sense.' He met her gaze and held it. 'Letting you go was the biggest mistake of my life and there has not been a day since when I have not regretted it.'

It was as though all the breath had left her body and she could only stare at him. Misinterpreting that expression of astonishment he nodded.

'After the way I behaved I know I do not deserve that you should listen to me now, but I beg that you will nevertheless.' He paused. 'Ten years is a long time to repent of youthful folly, but if there is one thing I have learned it is not to throw away the chances that life brings. Seeing you again has reinforced that lesson.'

Somehow she found her voice. 'What are you saying, Max?'

'That I did not know my own heart until it was too late. I was a damned fool, but I have never stopped loving you and I never will.' He took a deep breath. 'You are too open-hearted to sport with my feelings. I do not know if you can ever forgive my behaviour towards you but if I thought you might, if I thought there was a chance for us, I'd gladly wait another ten years.'

Vivien clasped her hands in her lap to keep them from trembling. 'You have no need to speak of forgiveness. You had that long ago.'

'Then…is there a chance?'

How tempting it was to say yes, tempting and dangerous. She'd given him her heart once before and been hurt. If she made the same mistake it would only lead to even greater pain, the kind that she wouldn't get over.

'It's too late, Max. You must see that.'

His heart sank. 'You no longer feel the same.'

She came out of the chair to face him. 'It's not that simple. We're not the people we once were.'

'No, we're older and wiser.'

She swallowed hard, almost overpowered by his nearness; by the intensity of his gaze. The brandy had gone to her head as well making it harder to think. But she had to think. It wasn't just about the fear of being hurt again. It was about possibly hurting him too. To say yes now would be to offload a huge burden. It would be very easy to agree to that; easy and wrong. No matter what had gone before she couldn't take advantage in that way. The thought was unbearable. She understood then how much she did care.

'You're not wise at all, Max. If you were you'd know I have nothing but encumbrances to offer you.'

She would have turned away but he caught hold of her hand. 'Nothing?'

The touch seemed to burn her skin and gave rise to dangerous and forbidden thoughts. If he took her in his arms now… With an effort she controlled herself. For both their sakes she had to stop this.

'Nothing.'

'You're lying, Vivien, and we both know it.'

'You're mistaken.'

'No. You were never a good liar.'

She tried ineffectually to disengage her hand. 'Let go of me, Max.'

'What are you so afraid of?'

'I'm not afraid.'

'Then why are you trembling?'

'Damn you, Max. What do you want from me?'

His gaze locked with hers. 'The truth.'

'I've told you. I have nothing to offer you. The house and the estate may have to be sold. I've already had to dispose of some of my jewellery…'

'I don't care if you're down to your last farthing. Forget about what's in the bank and tell me what's in your heart.'

'I cannot forget about the bank, that's the trouble.'

'I have more than I could ever spend.'

'Marry you for your money?'

'That isn't what I meant.'

'You'd always wonder, wouldn't you?'

'You're the last woman I'd suspect of such a thing.' He paused. 'You're evading the question. Tell me what's in your heart.'

Her throat tightened. 'I've already told you, Max. There can be no future for us.'

He relinquished his hold on her hand. 'This isn't just about money, is it? It's about trust.'

The observation was painfully accurate and he saw it in her eyes. It hurt more than anything else. He sighed.

'I cannot blame you for that. All I'm asking for is another chance.'

'I couldn't go through it all again, Max. My heart wouldn't survive another experience like that.'

'Give me a chance to earn your trust. You won't regret it.'

It was as near to a plea as she had ever heard him utter; the temptation stronger than any she had ever known. She didn't trust herself to speak and so vouchsafed no reply, knowing only that she had to leave the room now before her resolution failed. Turning away from him, she headed for the door.

'Vivien, please don't leave.'

Somehow she kept moving. His gaze followed her until she was gone.

* * *

Unable to rejoin the rest of the company in her present over-wrought frame of mind, Vivien took refuge in her room. Unfortunately, the solitude was no more conducive to a state of calm. For some time she paced the floor, reliving every moment of her interview with Max. He was right; money wasn't at the root of her refusal of his suit. It *was* about trust, or rather her lack of it. Yet past experience wasn't so easily forgotten.

Tears pricked behind her eyelids. It would have been so easy to say yes. She'd wanted to. Why had she not trusted him then? He'd admitted his mistake, confessed his feelings. In declaring himself thus he had taken a risk. He'd also offered her a glimpse of a future very different from the one she'd envisaged for herself after Hugh died. A future she'd just rejected. The implications began to sink in. Dejectedly she sank down on the window seat and stared out at the snow-covered garden, a scene that was every bit as bleak as her own thoughts.

Chapter Ten

Over the next few days the bitter weather gradually gave way to milder air so that, although there was still plenty of snow on open ground, the roads again became passable with care. Max assimilated the fact with detached interest. His original plan to leave Oakhurst had long since been abandoned. With just a few days left until the end of the festive period he could bide his time.

A polite cough drew him away from the library window. He turned in surprise to see a small boy standing a few feet away. Max recognised him at once.

'John, whatever are you doing here? Shouldn't you be with the others?'

'They've sent me to speak to you, sir.'

Max stared at him, torn between curiosity and amusement. 'What do you wish to speak to me about?'

'There's something that I…we…particularly wanted to ask you…'

Eleanor heard the news about the roads with relief since the proposed supper dance could go ahead as planned.

'It would have been such a disappointment if we had been forced to forgo it.'

'Yes, it would,' replied Vivien. 'I have been looking forward to it very much.' It was no longer true but it would have been discourteous to say anything else.

'Unfortunately Sir Digby will not be able to attend,' Eleanor continued. 'He is feeling indisposed and regrets that he must return home. I must say he has seemed rather out of sorts these last few days. Do you not think so?'

Vivien had a fairly shrewd idea as to what ailed him. Ever since his failed proposal he had only spoken to her when he had to and then with cold politeness. Neither of them had made any reference to what had passed and she certainly had no intention of telling anyone else. She wanted only to forget the whole sordid episode.

'I thought he looked out of humour,' she said. 'Perhaps it was a consequence of his feeling unwell.'

'I think you must be right. It's a shame but there it is.'

'Will Mrs Vayne be accompanying him?'

'Yes, although she didn't look very pleased about it.'

'I don't suppose she was.'

'It's understandable. She will be sorry to miss the dance,' said Mary. 'I know I'm looking forward to it…'

Vivien left them to talk and slipped away with the intention of looking in on her offspring and having a few words with their governess to ensure that everything was as it should be. Not that she was unduly worried. All the youngsters had behaved exceptionally well thus far and had evidently enjoyed themselves. From that point of view the holiday season had been a great success. It had gone so quickly though. In a little while the company would go their separate ways. After this she would never see Max again. It was her own stupid fault; the result of inner turmoil and muddled thinking. Clarity had come too late. He *knew* what he wanted. After all, he'd had ten years to think about it. That was why he had taken a chance and laid bare his heart. It was she who had lacked the courage to do the same. The knowledge was like a cold shadow over her soul.

As she approached the nursery she was surprised not to hear the sound of children's voices and, for a moment, wondered if they had all gone outside to play. Then she heard a man's voice.

'…and the tiger snarled, baring its great white fangs…'

Vivien's heart lurched. Surely it couldn't be. Tiptoeing to the door she peered round the edge and then stared in astonishment. Max was ensconced in a chair by the hearth with nine children sitting at his feet in rapt silence. They were so engrossed that none of them even noticed her presence. Only Miss Dawson saw her and made to rise but she motioned the governess back again and slipped quietly into an unoccupied chair.

'…and the hunters closed in…'

Watching the little scene Vivien was both amused and touched. His being here at all was an unlooked-for kindness and yet he seemed quite at home. Hugh had never possessed such ease with children, even his own.

'…and the tiger sprang at the foremost hunter, huge claws unsheathed for the kill…'

It occurred to her that Max would have made a wonderful father. The thought was poignant, underlining what had been lost. Not lost this time, she amended, thrown away.

'…the hunter stood his ground and fired. The deadly beast gave a fearsome roar as the shot pierced its heart and, carried by its own momentum, crashed to the earth only a yard from where the man stood. Then it lay quite still, eyes staring, its lips drawn back in a last defiant snarl. The man-eater of Mulgore was dead.'

For a few seconds after the tale ended silence endured and the children continued to stare at the storyteller. Then they burst into spontaneous applause. Heart full, Vivien joined in. Max glanced round and, seeing her there, got to his feet at once.

'Lady Hastings. I had no idea.'

'I didn't want to disturb you.' She managed a smile. 'I only heard the end, but it sounded like a wonderful story.'

John came to join her. 'It was, Mama. It's a great pity you missed most of it.'

'Never mind, we can tell you the rest, Mama,' said Rachel.

'I'll look forward to that.'

John looked up at Max. 'Will you tell us some more stories about India, Mr Calderwood? If you have the time, of course.'

The request was endorsed by eight other voices. Max surveyed the hopeful faces and then smiled.

'If you like.'

'Will you tell us one tomorrow, sir?'

Vivien caught the governess's eye. Miss Dawson stepped in to chivvy her charges away with the injunction not to be a nuisance if they hoped to have a story ever again.

As she and Max left the room and began to retrace their steps, Vivien regarded him apologetically.

'I'm sorry about that. My son can be a perfect little pest at times.'

'He's not a pest. He just has an enquiring mind, that's all.'

'That's one way of putting it. I'm afraid you'll be plagued half to death now.'

'I've enjoyed the company,' he said. 'Who could object to such an uncritical and attentive audience?'

'You certainly had them in the palm of your hand. You have a gift.'

'I merely recounted what I saw.'

'You brought it to life for them.'

'India is a colourful land. That helps.'

'If the children have their way you may run out of stories.'

'Never fear. There's plenty more where that came from.' He paused. 'Enough to last the holidays—and beyond.'

She looked up quickly but his face gave nothing away. It must have been a chance remark. After what had passed between them there could not have been a deeper implication. All the same, the vision it created was dangerously seductive. If only reality were as uncomplicated. If only she hadn't been such a confounded fool. He had asked for her trust and she hadn't given it, hadn't listened to her heart. As the silence stretched out she cast around desperately for a change of subject.

'The supper dance is going ahead after all. Eleanor is greatly relieved.'

'I'm sure she is.'

'It will end the festivities on a high note.'

'Let's hope so,' he replied.

She swallowed hard. 'The Christmas season has gone so quickly. It's hard to think of it being almost over.'

'But it's not over yet.'

'No, not yet.' She hesitated. 'What will you do afterwards? Will you begin your search for a property?'

'If everything goes according to plan.'

'I hope it will.'

'So do I,' he replied.

They reached the door of the salon and paused there. Vivien summoned a smile.

'Thank you for your time with the children. I know how much it meant to them.'

'It was a pleasure.'

She glanced towards the door. 'Are you coming in?'

'No, I'll join you presently. I want to take a walk first; the orchard this time, I think.'

'The orchard?'

'That's right.'

Astonishment vied with curiosity for a moment, but she recollected herself quickly. 'Until later then.'

He bowed and walked away. For a moment or two she watched him go, feeling utterly bereft, knowing that very soon he would walk away for the last time. Water welled in her eyes. Determinedly she blinked it back. Then, taking a deep breath, she opened the door and rejoined the company.

* * *

She had just changed for dinner that evening when Aunt Winifred put her head round the door.

'May I come in, my dear?'

Vivien summoned a smile. 'Of course.'

'I just wanted to ask if you're all right? You haven't seemed quite yourself these past few days.'

'I am perfectly well, I thank you.'

'I'm glad to hear it. I was afraid that you might have contracted the same ailment as poor Sir Digby.'

'Oh, er...no. I am not indisposed, truly.'

'And yet something is amiss, is it not?'

Vivien sighed and sank down on the edge of the bed. 'It's complicated, Aunt. I thought it wasn't but it is, far more than I ever imagined.'

'Forgive me, but does this concern Mr Calderwood?'

She nodded, no longer able or willing to prevaricate. 'He asked me to marry him.'

'I was sure he still had a *tendre* for you.'

'He says he loves me.'

'I think you are not indifferent to him.'

'No, but that is not the only consideration now.'

'Then what is, my dear?'

'Circumstances are different now. I have so many responsibilities and so little money. I am a positive liability, Aunt. I told him as much.'

'Did that weigh with him?'

'No.'

'Then why should it trouble you? After all, he's a mature man and presumably knows his own mind.'

'You think I should have accepted him?'

'What I think is not the point at issue here. What does your own heart tell you?'

'My heart is unchanged. It was always his.'

'But...'

'He once hurt me very badly.'

'It sounds as if he deeply regretted that,' said her aunt. 'Is it rather that you do not trust him?'

It hit the nail on the head, as Vivien recognised all too well.

'His declaration took me so much by surprise…I didn't know what to think.'

'And now?'

'I *do* trust him, Aunt. It has just taken me a while to realise it.'

'Well then, you have a second chance. It is not given to many.'

'I know. Yet the possibility of such happiness almost frightens me.'

Aunt Winifred surveyed her steadily. 'If you find that frightening, my dear, perhaps you should try to imagine a future where he is not.'

Vivien could imagine it very well, every cold bleak detail. Suddenly she wanted to weep. 'It's too late now. I've refused him.'

'Tell him you've changed your mind.'

'Throw myself at his head?'

'You could be a little more subtle than that, my dear.'

'I've been such a fool.'

'You're not a fool; you've been confused, that's all. It's hardly to be wondered at, in the circumstances.' Aunt Winifred squeezed her hand. 'But things are never as lost as we think.'

Vivien wished she could believe it.

Chapter Eleven

As the supper dance approached the atmosphere at Oakhurst became charged with excitement. Vivien did her best to look enthusiastic, but in the back of her mind was the knowledge that it marked the end, and not only of the holiday. Would Max dance with her? Perhaps good manners would dictate that he ask for one at least; one dance that would have to last her a lifetime.

She had settled on a gown of white silk overlaid with span-gled gauze. It was pretty and exquisitely feminine and, with its plunging neckline, seemed excitingly daring after the demure gowns she had worn in recent months. It was accompanied by white satin slippers and long white gloves. A few match-ing silk flowers nestled in her hair. She limited her jewellery to a single strand of pearls. For a minute or two she surveyed herself critically in the glass and decided that her appearance would pass muster, although there was only one opinion that mattered. Not that he would care what she wore. He would likely be glad when this was all over.

Max was in the anteroom talking to some of the other gen-tlemen when she appeared. Then he glanced up and saw her and everything he had been about to say went out of his head. For a moment or two he just stared. She might have been the snow queen from a fairy tale, a fabulous being, beautiful, remote and unattainable. With that last thought a knot of tension formed in his stomach. Nevertheless, he took a deep breath and then went to greet her.

She saw him across the room and suddenly every other man faded to insignificance. Not only was he dangerously attractive, he carried himself with his usual quiet self-assurance. She, on the other hand, felt more like a green girl at her first ball. As he approached her heartbeat quickened.

He bowed, his gaze appraising every detail of her costume. 'You look stunning.'

Vivien felt warmth creep into her cheeks. 'Thank you.'

Max did not miss that sudden tinge of colour or the way it enhanced the blue of her eyes. It also helped dispel the notion of the snow queen.

'That is a wonderful gown.' It was more than that, he thought, and was glad she couldn't read his mind just then.

'It is good to have the opportunity to wear it again,' she replied.

'Let's hope there will plenty more, now that you are out in the world again.'

'It feels a little strange to be at a function like this after so long a time.'

He raised an eyebrow. 'Never tell me you're nervous, Lady Hastings.'

She was about to deny it but Max was too astute for that. 'Just a little.'

'A peerless beauty cannot feel nervous. That's ridiculous.'

It drew an unwilling laugh. 'Be serious, I beg you.'

'I was never more serious in my life,' he said. 'While we're speaking of serious matters, may I have the pleasure of the first two dances?'

'You may.'

'I thought I'd better ask before you're besieged by admirers.'

She smiled ruefully. 'I'm flattered, but I think you would have been quite safe.'

'I regret I am not so sanguine.'

'This is very good for my self-esteem.'

'I meant it. Had I not possessed the presence of mind to speak now, I should have been reduced to fuming silence on the sidelines.'

She laughed, unreservedly this time. It lit her whole face and caused his heart to perform a wildly erratic manoeuvre. As usual she seemed quite unaware of the effect she was having. When she'd admitted to feeling nervous she could have had no idea that the boot was on the other foot.

As the other guests began to arrive they drifted apart for a while to mingle with the company. As Vivien had anticipated, her choice of gown did not pass unremarked to judge from the covert glances and swiftly concealed expressions of surprise. However, she was officially out of mourning now and didn't care who knew it. Their opinions didn't matter.

A short time later the musicians began to tune up and people gravitated slowly towards the ballroom. Max appeared at her side again.

'Shall we?'

Almost shyly she placed her hand in his and they went in with the other couples. Her attention was so entirely focused on the man beside her that she failed to notice the glances that followed their progress or the looks of envy from other quarters.

The first dance was a cotillion. Vivien came back to earth abruptly. She had been so absorbed in the excitement and novelty of the situation that she hadn't taken that in when Max asked her to partner him. Had he realised its significance when he spoke? His expression was hard to read. He led her on to the floor and the set formed up around them. And then the music began and it was as though ten years rolled away and they were back at the Harlstons' ball on that long-ago summer evening. The last time they had danced together. Her throat tightened.

Max had not missed the fleeting expression of sadness in her face before she schooled it back to neutrality. He understood it very well and the reason for it.

'You remember,' he said.

'How could I not? Was this a deliberate choice?'

'Very much so.'

A movement separated them briefly and then brought them back together. She regarded him quizzically.

'May I ask why?'

'This was where we left off before,' he replied, 'but I hope with all my heart that it might be where we pick up the thread again.'

Her heart leapt towards her throat and it became impossible to speak. He still wanted a future with her; trusted her with his inmost feelings.

When she made no further reply Max felt a sudden chill around his heart. Was history about to repeat itself? Had he really lost her? The thought of all the empty years ahead filled him with terror. He understood then that if he could not marry her he would never marry anyone. Such a compromise was unthinkable now.

The dance parted them again and he watched her move away down the room, briefly smiling at other partners who smiled at her. His jaw tightened. For all that she denigrated her appeal as a marital prize he knew enough about the male sex to realise that there would be suitors for her hand. Not idiots like Feversham either, but mature men of good character with polished manners and kind natures who wanted to make her happy.

The next steps brought her back to him and then her hand was in his again where it belonged. She smiled at him and negative thought receded. It wasn't over yet. He took a deep breath, glad now that he'd had the wit to ask for the first two dances. Perhaps the second might banish the spectres of the past.

* * *

It was a waltz, and that too was no coincidence, she realised. They'd never waltzed together because the dance had only taken the fashionable world by storm after she and Max had parted. Intimate and shocking, it had caused a stir at its inception. Vivien had only danced it on a few occasions and, while it had been enjoyable, the experience had been nothing like this. Of course then she had been partnered by men for whom she cared nothing and who were long forgotten. This close proximity was quite different; intimate and heart-stoppingly exciting.

'A good choice?' he asked.

She smiled tremulously. 'A very good choice.'

'I hoped you would think so.' He paused. 'After all, we never got a chance to do this before.'

'Making up for lost time?'

'No, moving on to something better.'

'Symbolism again, Max?'

'If you like.'

She did like. Now there were no sad associations; this time there was only exhilaration and the rightness of being in his arms. As they whirled around the room she let go of conscious thought and surrendered to the music and the moment. It was as though everything else had drawn away and there were only the two of them, flying. She didn't want it to end.

Eventually it did and they withdrew together into the anteroom and then, by tacit consent, across the corridor into a small parlour beyond. For the space of a few heartbeats they watched each other in silence. Then he was suddenly much closer, his eyes searching hers.

'I love you, Vivien. There will never be anyone else.' He hesitated. 'Could you ever feel the same for me?'

She found her voice. 'I do feel the same, Max. I always have.'

'Then…will you trust me with your heart?'

'Yes, if you're quite sure you want a mature widow with no money and two—'

The sentence ended abruptly as she was crushed against him for a passionate kiss. Unable to help herself she surrendered to it, relaxing against him, her mouth opening to his, every nerve alight with the taste and scent of him, her entire being filled with desire and longing.

He drew back a little, looking into her face. 'I didn't know how much you meant until I'd lost you. We've both paid a heavy price for that.'

Her arms slid around his neck. 'Let's not dwell on the past, Max. Let's just seize the chance we've been given. We've wasted enough time already.'

'Why so I think.' He kissed her again, gently this time and lingering. 'I mean to give you a thousand more of these.'

She raised an eyebrow. 'It might be regarded askance in such a public place.'

'No, it won't.' He glanced toward the ceiling. 'It has been sanctioned for the purpose.'

She followed his gaze and saw an enormous bunch of mistletoe overhead. Her eyes widened in amused disbelief. 'Why, that looks like an entire plant.'

'It is.'

'Where on earth did it come from?'

'The orchard.'

Slowly, the details of an earlier conversation returned. 'You mean you…'

'Yes.'

'Then you hadn't given up at all, in spite of the foolish things I said.'

'I told you it wasn't over.'

'You had it all planned, even then. Right down to the mistletoe.'

'A desperate man needs all the help he can get. I couldn't put my faith in a small sprig.'

Vivien laughed. 'I didn't know you possessed such a romantic streak.'

'Ah, but I do, as I intend to prove, my love.' He bent closer, his lips brushing hers. 'Starting now.'

* * * * *

COMING NEXT MONTH from Harlequin® Historical
AVAILABLE NOVEMBER 13, 2012

OKLAHOMA WEDDING BELLS
Carol Finch
Independent Josephine Malloy is determined to stake her own claim during the latest Oklahoma land run. But to fend off the countless suitors seeking a wife and a homestead she needs a fake fiancé for cover. Enter horse trader Solomon Tremain...
(Western)

SOME LIKE IT WICKED
Daring Duchesses
Carole Mortimer
Risqué behavior is beyond Pandora Maybury, widowed Duchess of Wyndwood. If only the Ton knew just how innocent she really was... including Rupert, Duke of Stratton, who, after rescuing her from a compromising situation, seems intent on wickedly compromising her himself!
(Regency)

BORN TO SCANDAL
Diane Gaston
Scandalous Lord Brentmore is in need of a reputable governess. Anna Hill is too passionate, too *alluring*, but she fills Brentmore Hall with light and laughter again—and its master with feelings he'd forgotten.... But a lord marrying a governess would be the biggest scandal of all!
(Regency)

WARRIORS IN WINTER
The MacEgan Brothers
Michelle Willingham
Spend Christmas with your favorite warriors—the MacEgans! Three tales of warriors, Vikings and passion!
(Medieval)

REQUEST YOUR FREE BOOKS!

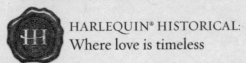

HARLEQUIN® HISTORICAL:
Where love is timeless

2 FREE NOVELS PLUS 2 **FREE GIFTS!**

YES! Please send me 2 FREE Harlequin® Historical novels and my 2 FREE gifts (gifts are worth about $10). After receiving them, if I don't wish to receive any more books, I can return the shipping statement marked "cancel." If I don't cancel, I will receive 6 brand-new novels every month and be billed just $5.19 per book in the U.S. or $5.74 per book in Canada. That's a savings of at least 17% off the cover price! It's quite a bargain! Shipping and handling is just 50¢ per book in the U.S. and 75¢ per book in Canada.* I understand that accepting the 2 free books and gifts places me under no obligation to buy anything. I can always return a shipment and cancel at any time. Even if I never buy another book, the two free books and gifts are mine to keep forever.

246/349 HDN FEQQ

Name _____ (PLEASE PRINT) _____

Address _____ Apt. # _____

City _____ State/Prov. _____ Zip/Postal Code _____

Signature (if under 18, a parent or guardian must sign) _____

Mail to the **Reader Service:**
IN U.S.A.: P.O. Box 1867, Buffalo, NY 14240-1867
IN CANADA: P.O. Box 609, Fort Erie, Ontario L2A 5X3

Not valid for current subscribers to Harlequin Historical books.

Want to try two free books from another line?
Call 1-800-873-8635 or visit www.ReaderService.com.

* Terms and prices subject to change without notice. Prices do not include applicable taxes. Sales tax applicable in N.Y. Canadian residents will be charged applicable taxes. Offer not valid in Quebec. This offer is limited to one order per household. All orders subject to credit approval. Credit or debit balances in a customer's account(s) may be offset by any other outstanding balance owed by or to the customer. Please allow 4 to 6 weeks for delivery. Offer available while quantities last.

Your Privacy—The Reader Service is committed to protecting your privacy. Our Privacy Policy is available online at www.ReaderService.com or upon request from the Reader Service.

We make a portion of our mailing list available to reputable third parties that offer products we believe may interest you. If you prefer that we not exchange your name with third parties, or if you wish to clarify or modify your communication preferences, please visit us at www.ReaderService.com/consumerschoice or write to us at Reader Service Preference Service, P.O. Box 9062, Buffalo, NY 14269. Include your complete name and address.

HH11B

HARLEQUIN® HISTORICAL:
Where love is timeless

Fill your Christmas with three tales of warriors,
Vikings and passion with author

MICHELLE WILLINGHAM

IN THE BLEAK MIDWINTER

It's a year since Brianna MacEgan's husband was killed, and she
remains coldly obsessed with avenging his death. But Arturo de
Manzano is intent on distracting her with his muscled fighter's body.

THE HOLLY AND THE VIKING

Lost in a snowstorm, Rhiannon MacEgan is rescued by a fierce
Viking. Her lonely soul instantly finds its mate in Kaall,
but can they ever be together?

A SEASON TO FORGIVE

Adriana de Manzano is betrothed to Liam MacEgan, a man she
absolutely adores. But she's hiding a terrible secret.

Look for

Warriors in Winter

available November 13 wherever books are sold.

Looking for a scandal?

Don't miss Carole Mortimer's fabulous new duet,
DARING DUCHESSES, *where the men are wickedly
devilish and the women just can't help but be tempted....*

Enjoy a sneak peek of

SOME LIKE IT WICKED

"OH..." PANDORA HAD NEVER FELT SO HUMILIATED.
"I apologize if I have caused you insult, Your Grace—er—
Rupert," she amended as those furious silver eyes narrowed
in dire warning. "It was not my intention to do so. I merely
wished to—"

"Refuse the *dubious honor* of becoming my mistress
before I felt compelled to voice it."

She had said that, Pandora acknowledged with an inward
wince. A remark he'd obviously taken exception to. "Well.
That is… Of course, I'm sure that many women would be
deeply flattered to so much as be considered—"

"Oh, give it up, Pandora." He bit out the words harshly.
"And accept that there's no going back from your insult to
me."

Her wince was outward this time. "I was angry when I
made that remark—"

"Because you had assumed *I* meant to insult *you* by
making such an offer!" A nerve pulsed in his tightly
clenched jaw.

"Well…yes."

Rupert felt some of his initial anger begin to fade as he
considered the amusement of their present situation instead.
Pandora Maybury, with her unusual beauty, golden curls
and mesmerizing violet eyes, had minutes ago insulted him,

and his honor, more roundly, more completely, than any other living person. Perhaps because any gentleman who had ever dared to speak to him like that would have very quickly found himself at the other end of Rupert's dueling pistols.

His amusement faded somewhat as he recalled that to have indeed been the fate of Pandora's husband *and* her lover....

He moved away from her until he stood with his back to the room, looking out the window into the street below. His carriage and four still stood on the cobbles below, waiting to take him back to Stratton House, an option he would perhaps be wise to take.

If not for the presence of the woman who awaited him there…

His shoulders stiffened with renewed resolve as he turned back to face the now cautiously watchful Pandora. "Contrary to general belief, the offer I intend making to you is not of becoming my mistress—but my wife!"

Read more of Carole Mortimer's
SOME LIKE IT WICKED, available from
Harlequin® Historical November 13, 2012.

And catch the next installment
SOME LIKE TO SHOCK
in January 2013.

When legacy commands, these Greek royals must obey!

Discover a page-turning new Harlequin Presents®
duet from *USA TODAY* bestselling author

Maisey Yates

A ROYAL WORLD APART

Desperate to escape an arranged marriage, Princess
Evangelina has tried every trick in her little black book
to dodge her security guards. But where everyone else
has failed, will her new bodyguard bend her to his
will…and steal her heart?

Available November 13, 2012.

AT HIS MAJESTY'S REQUEST

Prince Stavros Drakos rules his country like his
business—with a will of iron! And when duty demands
an heir, this resolute bachelor will turn his sole
focus to the task….

But will he finally have met his match in a world-
renowned matchmaker?

**Coming December 18, 2012,
wherever books are sold.**